Rock Me, Gently

by

M.J. Schiller

Published By Kissmet Publishing

DEDICATION

To the ladies and gent of my RWA local chapter- Heart and Scroll- I have brought this book in, five pages at a time, over the last several years. Your wisdom and support have improved it immensely. Thank you for listening and offering your insight so freely.

To my editors, Laurie Larsen and Katherine Tate- thanks for teaching me and making my writing stronger one word at a time, and for doing it with such grace. There's a fine line between critiquing and criticizing, and you recognize that. I am blessed by your thoroughness and professionalism, and thankful for your encouraging words.

CHAPTER ONE

It was seven-thirty, and he wasn't even halfway trashed yet. Knowing he needed to make up for a late start, Josh serpentined his way through the press of suntanned gamblers to the bar.

The muscular, dark-haired bartender appeared to be stuffed into the tux he was wearing. "What can I get you, Mr. Dunningham?"

Stardom had its perks, such as prompt service at the bars.

"I'll have a shot of tequila."

While the bartender turned to prepare the shot, Josh let his eyes roam over the crowd. He loved the ding of the bells and the calls of the craps table and roulette wheel, along with the smell of hot bodies squashed together in a greedy, hedonistic bunch. Yes, this was his kind of place. When he surrounded himself with lights flashing, buzzers going off, shouting, groaning, and cheering, it provided him with a lot of distractions. A sort of artificial life to make him forget about his lack of a real one.

Life after his meteoric rise hadn't changed much for him. He was still drinking every night like he had in his little hometown in Iowa and trying to make it with the girls. The only difference was now it wasn't Falstaff or Pabst, it was Crowne Royal or Dom Perignon; that, and the fact that now the girls didn't need any persuading.

"Here you go, sir."

The golden liquid key to oblivion lay on the bar in front of him, with a slice of lime and a saltshaker. Without a moment's hesitation, he downed the fiery fluid, ignoring the lime and salt, and then brought the shot glass down on the bar with a satisfying sharp rap. He grimaced. "Smoooooth!" His voice sounded hoarse. "Another, please. I'm behind."

"Yes, sir," the bartender replied with a grin. While his quick hands poured a second dose of the lethal liquor, another bartender sidled up and slammed a shot glass down next to his.

"Pour me one, would ya?"

Josh kept the amber stream under his surveillance as it flowed into the newly offered glass, a liquid lifeline for some other poor slob. He watched with idle curiosity, the voyage of the little glass as it headed to the other end of the bar, accompanied by the standard accoutrements of salt and lime. A short blonde stood with her back to the bar, resting her elbows casually on its top, apparently interested in some action elsewhere. As the bartender approached, she turned around.

And his heart about catapulted out of his chest to do a belly flop on the bar. She was breathtaking. She wore her hair in a practiced tousled style, a stunning contrast of light and dark shades of spun sunshine. It was the kind of rumpled approach which made him think she must look good when she rolled out of bed, and more about what she would look like when she rolled into it. Her makeup was perfect; her look fresh, not done up. And her lips, man...her lips were so full and lush he could almost feel the drool pooling behind his own. She ran a fingertip up and down the side of the glass where it was sweating and glanced around self-consciously.

Seeming assured that no one was looking in her direction, she licked the side of her thumb and poured the salt on.

Watching as her tongue ran the short gamut along her glowing skin, a single thought ran through his head, *I think I'm in love.* If the alcohol didn't soothe him, he was certain she would.

She knocked the shot back like a pro and sucked on the lime. The expression of sweet pain on her pixie-like face was classic. Though he couldn't hear it, he was almost sure she muttered, "Smoooth!" with a little shiver and a smile. She lifted her gaze, catching him watching. Her eyes were a pair of blue thunderbolts, electric, in a shade the contact lens companies had yet to capture. With a line of black around the edges of the iris and thick, curling lashes fanning out gracefully along the perimeter of her lid, his eyes were drawn to hers like a target.

Her eyes grew wide when she saw him, and she scrambled to remove the spent piece of lime, dropping it into her glass as her cheeks flushed red. Her gorgeous mouth hung open a second and he could see the glint of recognition in her eyes. BINGO!

A second benefit of his fame, and the best, in his opinion, was the way it moved the ladies. The money meant nothing to him. He hadn't even bought himself any expensive toys, except for one red Lamborghini. It was about the sex. The sex fed his lust for something beyond himself. It was the rush of power it gave him. The power he felt now as he strode confidently around the bar toward the girl.

THE SHOT BURNED ALL the way down her throat. Cassie McCallister snatched up the lime; it killed a little of the numbing sensation in her mouth, while still allowing her to feel the strangely comforting heat as it slid deep down inside her. She grimaced, as always, at the acidic taste and the little shudder it sent through her system. "Smoooth!" she said under her breath, as was her custom when her friends bought her the shot. They often ordered it just so they could watch the effect it had on her. Always open to being the comic relief, she rarely turned down tequila.

Setting the glass down in front of her, she glanced up, having the odd sensation someone was watching her. She saw him across the room, tall, and beautiful, and...oh, my gosh...it was Josh Dunningham. She quickly spit her lime out. *I must look quite the picture with the dark green rind wedged against my teeth.* He flashed her a smile which had her knees shaking even more than the tequila, and she realized he must have watched her throughout the whole stupid ritual—salt, tequila, lime. He started ambling in her direction, and she dropped her gaze, feeling foolish.

AS JOSH WALKED TOWARD her, the blonde glanced down, seeming certain he was headed somewhere else. In fact, she appeared genuinely surprised when he stopped by her side. He spread his long legs out in front of him, resting on the stool next to hers, and propped one elbow on the bar, sure of himself, as he leaned in to talk to her.

But when she peered up into his face with a nervous smile, that power he felt when he first began his trip around the bar, deserted him completely. His heart started beating so loudly it replaced the sound of the amplifiers still ringing in his ears from practice. Unaccustomed to such a physical reaction to someone, he almost couldn't find the words to speak.

"Hello," he managed after a beat, his deep voice coming out awkward in his own ears.

"Oh..." she stuttered, obviously mortified. "You saw me staring at you. I'm sorry. I-I'm not a stalker, I swear."

His amusement flushed away his momentary apprehension. "No. I figured that out. Stalkers generally, well...stalk people. I approached you."

"Yeah." She continued to peer down and fiddle with her glass, an action he found absolutely adorable. "But I *was* looking at you."

"Yeah," he said, feeling his old charm coming back to him. "Why is that?" He pitched his voice, so it was as smooth and sweet as hot fudge and flashed a cocky grin.

"Why wouldn't I?" she breathed, almost involuntarily, her head still down.

He chortled.

"Oh my gosh, I'm acting like a fool." She reached for her clutch on the bar, knocking her shot glass over and then diving to straighten it. "I'll go now."

"Hey...hey, hey," he said, grabbing her elbows as she turned to go. "Slow down. We're just having a conversation here."

"Yes, one in which I am making a complete ass out of myself." He slid his hands down to her wrists as she pulled away, restraining her. She turned back to say, "I'm sorry."

He didn't understand why he did it, maybe because he just had to have a look at those fascinating blue eyes again, but he reached to curl a finger under her chin, lifting her face. "I'm not."

Although she seemed determined to hide it, he could feel her pulse race underneath his fingertips as she gazed up at him helplessly. She was at least a foot shorter than him, even with the sexy little boots she was wearing. The boots told him she was hot, but not easy, like stilettos would have portrayed her. He prided himself in being able to pin down a girl in less than fifty seconds and knowing whether he would be spending the night with her or not. The sleek black jeans hugging her hips gave him the same information the boots had. They made her look extremely appealing, but not outright advertising it, like leather would have. Her silky camisole, a confusion of browns and purples, revealed a hint of full breasts, sending his own pulse racing. She was not what he would call a hard body but was deliciously toned and feminine; her breasts were large but not sloppy, with inviting curves which dove mysteriously into the shadow of her top.

She shifted her feet, and he was overwhelmed by the sweet scent of honeysuckle. He found himself swamped by a memory.

He was walking to school, dragging his feet as he went, as was his general custom, when he came across the white and yellow honeysuckle vines covering his neighbors' fence. He set his books down and plucked one of the white blossoms. He pulled at the base of the flower like he had seen the owners' son do, and watched, in wonder, as the delicate green and white stamen slid out, peppered with yellow dust. He slid his tongue along it, tasting the sugary, honeyed flavor of the pollen. Delighted, he quickly pulled off a yellow flower to see if it tasted the same.

The innocent memory seemed, at the moment, highly erotic and he let himself imagine his tongue trailing down the girl, tasting her in a similar way.

She blushed, as if reading his thoughts, or perhaps having a few similar thoughts of her own.

"Let me at least—" He wracked his brain. She was nervous, he was moving too fast. What did normal guys do with girls? "—take you out for a cup of coffee."

"That sounds nice, but I don't drink coffee."

"Come to think of it, neither do I." He laughed. "Pepsi is my choice of caffeine."

She nodded, a smile replacing her anxious look. "Diet Pepsi."

"A new generation, I guess." He shrugged, releasing her hands. He peered into her eyes, and knew he couldn't leave it at that. The blue of her eyes was like the sky on a crystal-clear night after sunset, just before the stars came out, layer upon layer of unequalled blue. He tentatively brought one finger up to one of the velvety brown spaghetti straps at her shoulders, letting it glide underneath the fabric and wrap around it.

The move was bold, risky, even; but he hadn't gotten as far as he had in life by taking the easy way out. After all, he didn't even know the girl, and she seemed the type to run like a rabbit. And yet, it was as if he couldn't help himself. He let his eyes follow his finger as he fantasized about pulling the straps down, allowing the satiny fabric to disappear, so he could gaze upon those spectacular breasts. A ripple of desire ran through her as he cruised up and down the strap, the back of his finger against her silky skin. But when he gazed into her eyes, he saw a flash of fear. *I'll have to work for this one.* He hated to have to work, it made him feel somewhat vulnerable, but on the flip side, he also relished the challenge.

"What if I just buy you another drink?" he asked, a hint of huskiness slipping into his voice. Before she could respond one way or another, he raised two fingers to the bartender. Then, he turned his attention back to her.

Another shot or two, and she'll be mine.

JOSH DUNNINGHAM WAS talking to her. It was like a dream come true. How many nights had she fantasized about just that?

And, unbelievably, he was even more gorgeous in person, every little bit of his six-foot-five-inch frame. As he stretched his legs out in front of him, her eyes fought to take in all of his luscious length. He smelled fantastic, too, a spicy scent which screamed rock and roll. *They should bottle it and name it something like, 'Totally Josh,' and I could run the ad copy for it...*

She shook her head. *Get a grip. You're acting like some silly schoolgirl.*

But then again, a second voice reasoned, *it is Josh Dunningham.* If a person could squeal in her head, she was pretty sure she just had. And then, she opened her mouth, and the stupidest things flew out. She felt like ramming her head against the bar, but he grabbed her elbows with his big, skilled hands, and all logical thought—that was, whatever semblance of logical thought she had remaining—abandoned her in a whoosh. He curled his finger under her chin and lifted her face, and Cassie found herself staring into his incredible green eyes, the kind of green which had her thinking of making love with him in the deep grass of some meadow...and the gold specks she saw in his irises were the sun, filtering in through the blades of grass as they rolled around...

She realized he was observing her, and her face grew warm, as she wondered if he could read her thoughts. Those smoky green eyes traveled to one of the straps of her top and he slid a finger along its length. The touch of his skin on hers in such an intimate way, made her just about come unglued, and then she was scared. She hardly even knew the man. What the hell was she doing? What the hell was he doing? And why was he doing it to her?

CHAPTER TWO

"What's your name?" Josh asked, shaking his jet-black hair out of his face. It was thick and flipped out at the ends, as unruly as the stubble growing along his jaw, emphasizing the lines of his strong face.

I know this one. I do, she thought in a panic. "Cassie. Cassie McCallister."

Shooo. Dodged a bullet there. Again, she had the overwhelming desire to crash her head into something.

"I'm Josh Dunningham," he said with an easy smile, clasping her hand.

"I know."

Again, he laughed, and she realized she liked the sound of it.

"Well, *Cassie*, where do you hail from?"

"Chicago."

"Ahh, the Windy City. What do you do there?"

"I work in advertising at Orenstein and Cruthers."

"I see."

Their shots arrived and the bartender gave Josh a wink which had her wondering.

"Ladies first."

"Oh. Okay." Aware he was watching her this time, she uneasily licked the side of her thumb and poured the salt on it. Picking the glass up with her other hand, she licked the salt, downed the drink, and sucked the lime with only a small shiver.

"Impressive. My turn." Surprising her, he grabbed her wrist, turning it to expose the inside of her arm, and brought it up to his mouth. She fought him, weakly at first, then, curious, she complied. He ran his tongue along her wrist and lifted his head again. He smiled at her and reached for the salt, shaking the tiny white crystals all along the path he created with his tongue. Slowly, his eyes on hers, he brought her arm up again, and this time lingered as he licked the salt off her.

She felt the blood leave her head and travel to other parts of her body as she watched him. His gaze was so intense, heat emanated from it like some Saturday morning cartoon superhero. She wanted to glance around, to see if anyone was watching them, but she couldn't remove her eyes, riveted by his every movement. He threw back his shot expertly, although this was highly anticlimactic after what he had just done.

Once his tongue left her skin, the fire in her changed from desire to anger. How dare he? Just because he was a famous rock star, he thinks he can just walk up and, and...lick any girl he liked? What balls. An undercurrent of fear swam in the pool of her emotions, but she didn't explore it, choosing instead to hang on to the anger which strengthened her against him.

AS JOSH WATCHED, CASSIE'S face changed as quickly as an image in a fun house mirror. She seemed surprised, scared, angered, turned on, and embarrassed in succession. He released her arm, and she jerked it back, taking a half-step away from him, nearly knocking over her stool as she sat back down. Her elbow remained bent, her arm up in the air, but her opposite hand flew to it to circle her small wrist, rubbing it, although he was sure he hadn't harmed her. She dropped both of her arms into her lap, and looked down at them, seeming stunned as she tried to formulate her next sentence.

He instantly regretted what he did but seemed compelled to fall back on his habitual routine in a desperate need to stabilize himself, as every nerve in his body seemed to be firing. He stepped forward, sliding his hands around her waist and drawing her off the stool to him before she had time to resist. He tilted his head to nuzzle her ear and whisper, more urgently than he intended to, "Come to bed with me."

THE WORDS SLID INTO her ear and slithered down inside her seductively. His rough stubble brushed her face, sending a tingle to follow his voice along the path it created through her body. For one crazy instant, she wanted to surrender, to give in to him and melt against his long, hot body; but, instead, she brought her arms up to push him back.

"No, no. You have the wrong girl. I'm sorry. *Believe me,*" she added with a sigh. "I'm sorry. I just can't do it."

"Why not? You're an adult."

"Yeah? Well, sometimes I don't feel like one," she muttered.

"Me neither. Although I don't usually admit that."

Cassie continued to stare at him pointedly.

"Okay, okay." He sighed, loosening his grip on her.

He was making her feel foolish and nervous, and that made her angry. "I suppose it's easy for you. Hell, this is a nightly thing for you, sleeping with someone new."

"Oh, yeah, sure. Gosh, I've had so many women, maybe I've slept with you before and I just don't remember," he returned sarcastically.

"If you'd slept with me before, you'd remember," she shot back.

"Oh, yeah?"

"Yeah."

A long pause ticked by before he spoke again. "Somehow, I don't doubt that." He chuckled.

Cassie started to giggle along with him, relieved he wasn't going to force the issue. She gazed into his eyes, studying him for a second, and then gave another exasperated snort, swatting him on the chest as she did so. "Like I would just leave with the guy who wrote 'I'll Always Be There.'"

"OH, YES, MY STALKER song." He had to admit, she was right. Brains, as well as beauty. While that combination was usually a turn-off for him, it wasn't this time; she seemed to contradict everything he knew about himself. He felt a need to defend his sullied reputation. "Everyone has one, you know. The Police, 'Every Breath You Take'..."

"'Watching You' by Melissa Etheridge."

He nodded, pleased she had a sense of humor. "That's a classic. Or how about 'Always Something There to Remind Me' by Naked Eyes?"

"Oh, no. That's a love song."

"He says he's walking the same streets they used to walk together."

"But he's not stalking her. He's stalking her memory, so to speak."

"True, true. Well, how about The Gin Blossoms' 'Found Out About You?'"

She nodded with a smile. "Yeah. He's always driving past her house."

"Watching the lights go out when her boyfriend's over," he added.

"Yeah, definitely creepy. Kind of like your 'I'll Always Be There.' I mean, you were like...smelling the girl's clothes."

"Hey. That wasn't me. It's about something that happened to a friend of mine's girlfriend."

"Yeah. Sure it is." A teasing grin lit her face.

He chuckled. "I'll give you one thing," he stated, toying with the earring dangling from her right ear, and noting the way she tensed when he did so, "you sure know your music." He pulled back. "Come to think of it, if I was a girl, I don't think I'd go anywhere with me either. I *am* the guy who wrote 'I'll breathe the air you breathe, fogging up the window as I press against your house.' But," he ended thoughtfully, "no one's ever said that to me before."

"I don't doubt it. But I say some pretty weird things when I'm nervous and had a shot or two of tequila to boot."

"I make you nervous?" He reached over again to play with her hair.

She cleared her throat, searching the casino floor. "I should introduce you to my girlfriend, Heather. You'd like her. I've told her all about you, so she's a fan."

"Sounds like you're more the fan."

She grinned up at him. "Maybe."

"How many of our albums do you have?"

"Counting the one you did before you made it big? All of them. But I'm not a stalker or anything."

"No. We've already established that."

"There she is." Cassie pointed to a bodacious redhead who was jumping around at a craps table, wearing sardine-tight leather pants and six-inch heels. He had to admit, she was more his type; but tonight, for some inexplicable reason, he had eyes only for the girl sitting next to him. He slid a look in her direction. She was studying her friend, a fond smile lighting up her eyes. "I think she might be winning," she added with deliberate understatement, noting her friend's antics.

"How about me, Cassie?" he said, suddenly serious. "I get the sense I'm losing."

"Listen, Mr. Dunningham, it's not that I—"

Josh laughed. He realized he had done a lot of that this evening. "Seeing as I've already licked you and all, I think it's okay if you call me Josh."

She smiled slowly. "Josh. I'm sorry...it's just...things move a lot slower in my world."

"Dance with me."

"Huh?" she mumbled, looking confused. "There's no place to—"

He grabbed her hand and started threading his way through the crowd, guiding her behind him. "There's a lounge on the other side of the casino."

JOSH DRAGGED CASSIE through the doorway of a low-lit lounge and onto a nearly empty dance floor. Before she even had time to get her bearings, he turned to her, sliding his hands around her waist and pulling her close. The music was slow and sultry, and his movements matched the mood it created. Their eyes met, performing a dance of their own, locked on each other unalterably.

As though weakened by her, he bent in, resting his forehead on hers, eyes closed. "Cassie..." His voice was thick with desire.

He began to caress her back and she was unable to do anything other than follow his lead. "I...," she said breathlessly, unsure of what she even wanted to say.

And then, without warning or forethought, those tantalizing lips were on hers, soft, almost tender at first, but pulling her deeper with each kiss. His longing filled her, blocking out all other thought. With a barely perceptible moan she slid into a tighter embrace, giving in to her desire, seeking him as he sought her. His tongue wreaked havoc with her, tempting her, taunting her, breaking her with its demands. Her hands explored the sides of his face, playing with the textures, the smooth skin, the coarse hair, the tip of her thumb slipping between their mouths, feeling the heat and the moisture there as lips frantically met again and again, tasting more, wanting more. His hands moved up her sides nearly to the curve of her breasts, the fingers strong, possessive.

My God, she thought frantically, *what is he doing to me?* And then it was like a ray of light broke through the fog of pure desire. *We're in a public place.* She pushed back. "Josh. Josh. Wait."

He pulled her in, kissing her neck. "Come on, Cassie," he whispered in her ear. "You know you want me."

Yes. Yes, I do, her body screamed. "There are other things to consider..." His tongue ran down her neck, his teeth nipping at her shoulder. Her moan shook them both. "Oh, God, Josh...*please.*"

Josh registered the pleading note in her voice and drank it in, finally letting it ring within him like a gong. He let her go, perplexed as much by his own actions as by hers. He saw the hazy desire he produced in her eyes before she completely surfaced from within. Her eyes were even more intense in the darkness. He longed to see them looking down on him in bed and the thought nearly killed him.

She stared into his face, both panting, wide-eyed with their hunger. She seemed to force the words from her mouth. "I need a drink."

Minutes later, the bartender set the shots on the counter with lime slices and a saltshaker. "No salt." Cassie said emphatically and pushed it away. They put their drinks back in unison, staring at each other without saying a word. Before a syllable could be spoken, a fast dance came on and Cassie's eyes lit up. "I love this song!" She grabbed his arm. "Come on. Let's dance."

He tried to keep up, but she shifted emotional gears so fast, she stripped them, leaving him baffled. But before long, he found he was relaxing and enjoying just dancing with her. As the tequila started to affect her, her hips began to move more fluidly. She turned her back to him and reached behind to grab his neck. He bent in, unable to resist nibbling on her ear, but it soon disappeared as she bent her knees, swinging her hips and getting lower and lower to the ground. The hand behind his neck moved to his back, pulling herself closer as she shimmied against him. He groaned, closing his eyes as she vanished between his knees, her hand straying to his butt.

"Cassandra Jo McCallister! What the hell are you doing?"

He opened his eyes with a jolt and saw the redhead, standing in front of him, looking pissed as hell.

"Heather," Cassie shouted joyfully in a high-pitched voice. She reached out and her friend pulled her away from him.

Heather frowned at him. "You'll excuse us." It was a statement, not a request.

"Sure." He moved to the bar to get another drink, watching the pair warily. It was not hard to overhear their conversation as Cassie had lost control of her volume dial.

"Hey."

"Hey, yourself. What are you doing?"

"Dancing," she said happily. "With Josh Dunningham." She turned and waved at him and he raised a finger or two tentatively.

"Josh Dunningham...of Money Back Guaranteed?" Heather whispered, loud enough for him to hear. She suddenly seemed excited.

"Yeah."

"You're kidding?" She skimmed her eyes over him, then shook her head. "Wait just a second here. You're coming with me." She grabbed Cassie's arm and tried to pull her out of the lounge.

"No, Heather. Ouch. Let go of me. What are you doing?"

Josh hopped off his stool and took a few steps toward them, unsure of the friend's intent.

"Getting you out of here," she hissed.

"Hey, I'm a big girl, I can handle myself."

"Yes, but—"

A dark-haired guy called to Heather from the doorway. "Hey, babe." He smiled and jingled a key on a large ring, holding it up so they could read the "High-Roller Suite" spelled out in rhinestones.

"*You* found somebody," Cassie pointed out accusingly.

"Yeah, but that's different."

She stuck her hands on her hips. "How?"

"I know how to handle myself. You'll get all hung up on this guy and end up with a broken heart."

"Are you coming?" Heather's date interrupted.

"Hold your horses." Her brow creased. She glanced at Josh, biting her lip. "Mr. Rock and Roll Bad Boy. You couldn't have picked anybody worse if you had tried. You're coming with me."

Cassie jerked her hand away. "No, I'm not. I'm staying here with Josh." She ran the short distance between them and latched onto his arm, stretching up to give him a peck on the cheek.

Josh tried to appear innocent, but Heather would have none of it. She sashayed over and then leaned in, saying through gritted teeth, "If you're thinking of taking advantage of her—"

"I'm not. I swear," he lied. She looked utterly unconvinced.

"Cassie," she warned.

Cassie just smiled at her and hugged his arm tighter.

"Ugh." She gave up and walked out with a huff.

He breathed a sigh of relief.

As her friend disappeared, Cassie announced blithely, "I've got to find the bathroom," and trotted off in the opposite direction.

He shook his head, bewildered by the way she darted from one thing to the next like a hummingbird, without any apparent transition. He turned back to have a seat on a stool, ordered a scotch on the rocks, and wondered what the hell was wrong with him. He should just ditch this girl. With a snap of his fingers, he could pull any girl from the casino floor and take them upstairs. What was it about this girl that made him so crazy? Sure, she was hot, *definitely* hot. But the casino was full of dozens of other attractive women; he could pick and choose from a dozen in any size, shape, and color. Okay, it's true this girl had him turned on without even touching him. But, if it took a little work for any other girl to get his pulse racing, he'd end up in the same place eventually; he could be patient. But there was something else about her, her innocence, wrapped as it was in hidden depths of desire, her sense of humor, her forthrightness...

He glanced up and saw Heather marching toward him in the mirror behind the bar. He turned, but before he could say a word, she blurted out, "She is the sweetest person I know and my best friend. Please don't take advantage of that." Her voice was pleading, then she shifted gears as fast as her friend had. "If you do, you'll have to answer to me."

He didn't doubt for a second, she meant it. With one last long, meaningful look, she turned and left.

CHAPTER THREE

Josh sat, sipping his drink and wondering what the hell he was going to do, when arms wrapped around his waist, getting dangerously close to other areas. She laid her head briefly on his back but lifted it as he spun around to face her. Before he could utter a word, she was kissing him. The kind of kisses that rocked his world as she slipped between his legs and her hands found their way underneath his shirt.

As she caressed the skin of his back, he thought, *Dear God, I better stop this now, or I won't be able to stop it.*

"Cassie," he said, pulling back and holding her shoulders at a distance. "Let's go for a walk."

"I thought you wanted to take me up to your room," she whispered loudly, twisting a strand of his hair around her finger. Looking into those baby blues, he found himself on the teetering edge of his resolve. He swallowed, shutting his eyes for a minute, and saying weakly, "I think we should take a quick walk first."

JOSH STEERED CASSIE toward an exit, hoping fresh air would help to sober her up. They ended up at the outdoor pool, a monstrosity complete with overhanging palm trees.

Away from the casino hubbub, it was easier to talk. She eyed him. "Tell me about the band."

"What do you want to know?"

"Well, as an advertising person, I'm interested in the gimmick, Money Back Guaranteed. Did you ever have to back up that promise?"

Josh took a couple of seconds to think about that. "Yeah. A few times. Once, when an elderly couple came with their granddaughter. They didn't like the show at all." Remembering their reaction, he grimaced. "And once, when a girl caught her fiancé in the hall with another girl. Hardly our fault, but she didn't enjoy the concert, and that's our promise, so..." He shrugged.

"Interesting. Interesting." She lifted a leg, grabbing his shoulder for balance, and tugged on the heel of her boot.

"Uhh...what are you doing?"

"My feet are killing me. You're so lucky you are a guy and don't have to wear heels."

"Yes. I was just mentioning that to my friend, Ryan, the other day."

She didn't look up. Having successfully removed one boot, she switched legs to work on the other. "Really?"

He smiled. "No. Go on."

Yanking the other boot off, she nearly toppled over, though still holding on to him. She squeezed his arm. "You're built."

He nearly laughed at her frank statement. "Thank you."

Holding her boots in one hand, her brow furrowed as she concentrated on her next question. She began to balance on the edge of the pool, which was deserted, and scoop stepped, trailing one leg in the water, not seeming to mind at all that her jeans were getting wet.

"I don't think that's such a good idea," he warned, taking her arm to steady her.

"I'm fine," she assured him, breaking away for an instant to do a pirouette in the pool's gutter to demonstrate.

"Okay, okay," he muttered, grabbing her arm again. "No need to show off. So why are you in the advertising game?"

"I like the creative aspect of it. And, I can be *very* persuasive," she said, smiling at him. As if he somehow silently challenged her, she stopped with a jerk and turned toward him, lifting onto her toes to kiss him. The taste of her was just as intoxicating as the booze had been and left him equally dizzy. The flavor of sweet lime and midnight rolled across his tongue and sank into him unbidden. Someone in the hotel rooms surrounding the pool above them slammed a door, startling Cassie, the sharp sound almost like gunfire. She jumped away from him like she had been shot herself and started to lose her balance. He reached to save her, but too late, she fell into the pool, dragging him in after her.

She surfaced, spitting water and laughing. The water was cold, or perhaps it was just the unexpectedness of the plunge that made it feel that way. He felt a flash of anger, but, seeing the amusement on Cassie's face, he couldn't help but chuckle.

She put a hand to her mouth to stem her own giggles. "Oh," she managed between chuckles. "I'm sorry. You're mad, aren't you?" She treaded water in front of him, although he could stand.

"Damn right, I'm mad, Little Missie." He reached over and dunked her head under the water again.

She came up, gasping for air. "Hey. That wasn't very nice." Her hair shimmered in the lights from above and the reflection of the pool water, which was lit from beneath.

"Well, how about this, then?" He spun her to press her against the cement wall with his body, his hands grasping the edge of the pool on either side of her. Her eyes went wide and then she blinked the water away with those long lashes of hers, her mouth still open when he covered it with his own. The water weighed her blousy camisole down and he could see more of her cleavage, and he liked what he saw. With one hand he began to search for her in the water. He cupped her breast even as strong legs wrapped around him and she was buoyed up by his bent legs, exposing more of her to view. The water made the line between them blur, their shirts sticking together as much as their bodies were.

He wondered briefly if they would get caught by the press. *They'd have a field day with this,* he thought, even as he slipped his hand under her shirt to feel her better.

Her hands rested on either side of his face at first, then bunched in his hair. She pulled away. "Take me to your room," she begged.

For several seconds all he could hear was his heavy breathing in the still night air, and the water lapping against the sides of the pool, rushing into the filter. He struggled with an inner debate. "You're sober?"

She nodded her head. "As sober as a court hearing. The walk and the water did it. Take me upstairs and make love to me, Josh," she ended, her voice becoming quiet.

He didn't need to be asked twice. He scooped her up into his arms, her hands clasped tightly around his neck, and walked to the shallow end, a pair of dripping creatures rising from the depths of the lagoon.

"Oh, my boots!" They turned to spot them where they now lay, on the bottom of the pool.

He set her down, "I'll get them." He dove back into the deep end and returned with the sopping pair of boots, handing them to her.

She circled her arms around his neck and gave him a quick kiss for a reward. She moved one hand up to play with his hair. "Mmm," she smiled. "You look like some sexy merman." She gave him one last deep kiss and then they climbed up the steps at the end of the pool, side-by-side.

"We can't go through the lobby like this." Cassie wrung her shirt out, while he shook his head to fling drops from his hair.

"I know where there's an outside entrance. We use it sometimes to avoid fans."

He had them to it in minutes. They were lucky enough to pass only one other couple. They smiled at Josh and Cassie conspiratorially.

"Sudden cloudburst," Josh explained with a shrug.

"Uh-huh," the guy returned with a *you dog* look. His girlfriend just giggled. Josh and Cassie continued on their way, leaving a telltale trail of wet footprints on the concrete, until they reached an elevator.

When the elevator doors closed, leaving them in their own private cocoon, they looked at each other. "You're sure?" he asked softly.

She nodded, but her lip twitched, and she glanced away. Was she nervous?

He stood in front of her, and she trembled. "Are you cold?"

"A little." The air-conditioning in the elevator was going full blast to counteract the Las Vegas heat.

Josh glided his hands up and down the smooth skin of her arms. He watched as they traveled over her small, tight biceps and around the tantalizing curve of her shoulders. One hand slid over her throat, as she tipped her head back against the wall, her hands clasping the rail behind her. He brought his lips down over hers and began bringing her to him kiss by kiss. He had never wanted a woman like this before, with more than just a physical need. He didn't know what it was she had done to him, only that this was different from anything he'd ever experienced before. His heart not only hammered inside him, it clutched at him, making him desperate for her. Although he'd experienced the tug of lust in his gut before, this time it gripped him, taking control in a way he found unnerving.

By the time the little bell rang, releasing them from the confines of the elevator, they were wrapped around each other. They stumbled out, her hands clawing at the buttons of his shirt, his hands on her backside, pulling her into the room with him. He was barely aware of the beautiful penthouse—the mahogany bar, the grand piano in the corner, the spectacular view of Vegas—all he knew was her, her taste, her touch, her urgency equal to his own.

Cassie ripped the shirt off his back just before he pulled the top off over her head, dumping it with a wet *plop* onto the hardwood several feet into the room. She had on a lacy, red, strapless bra. His hands skimmed up her sides, his thumbs against her rib cage, and then he brought them back down to tug at her jeans button. As he fumbled, her hands superseded his, tearing at the button. When the denim released, she wriggled out of the black mess, continuing to kiss him and back up until her heels hit the side of the bed.

Matching red, lace underwear. Of course she did. God, don't women know what that does to a man? He laid her back on the bed. His thumb hooked under the elastic waistband of her panties and traced a line across her abdomen. Desperate for her, he pressed his palm between her legs, pushing up, cupping her as she moaned and writhed. She scooted farther on the bed, inviting him to join her.

He laid over her. As her hands wandered over his chest, he stilled, smoothing the wet hair from her face. He bent to kiss her throat, working his way down while she pitched with desire for him. He pushed her back firmly onto the bed. The message was unambiguous; he was in command here. One hand slid into her panties, one into her bra simultaneously. He slipped a finger inside her, at the same time pressing on a nipple. She moaned, her body responding as he had wanted it to.

"Wait. Wait."

He started to withdraw his hands, but she stopped him. "No," she begged. She kissed him. "I was just...I need to know...do you have...protection?"

"Mmm." He kissed her as he withdrew his hands this time, sitting up to reach into a side-table drawer. He moved things around. "Wait, they're in the bathroom." He got up, looking back at her sprawled across the bed, the vibrant red of her bra and panties standing out against the cream-colored comforter. "I'll be right back," he called, darting off, but then hurrying back seconds later to plant one more kiss on the inside of her knee. She laughed at his rushing around.

It took him several frantic minutes to dig through his suitcase for his shaving kit, and then again to dig through his shaving kit for a condom. When he triumphantly discovered it, he glanced up at the mirror above the sink, catching his reflection. What was he doing, scrambling around so he could return to this woman's side? That wasn't how he worked. He was always cool, calm, and collected in the bedroom. It was the lady of the day who was supposed to feel out of control with passion, begging him for just a little more. As he looked at himself in the mirror, he smiled, realizing he really didn't care. Tonight, he didn't need an explanation; he needed her. He smoothed out his hair before returning to the bedroom.

His heart sank when he saw the hotel stationery on the empty bed. He read the one word—

Sorry.

CASSIE ZIPPED UP HER wet jeans as the elevator descended. Tears rolled down her face but she ignored them, angry with herself. She alternated between being mad about starting something with Josh and being mad about not finishing things with him. She was not the one-night stand type; she had tried to tell him that.

I'm never drinking tequila again, she lamented.

But she realized it hadn't been the alcohol driving her to his bed.

It was just an overwhelming attraction to a member of the opposite sex, she reasoned. But, no matter how hard she tried to rationalize it, she knew it was more than that. *I was taken in by his stardom, that's all. He's got sex appeal. Lord knows thousands of women have fallen for it.*

And that was really what bothered her. She didn't want to be only one in a pack of a thousand; that would hurt her too much.

Damn, Heather. She was right. She let a small sob escape. She had allowed herself to fall for him, and now it felt like someone had stuck a knife into her belly and twisted.

CHAPTER FOUR

"Could you tell me Cassie McCallister's room number?" Josh asked the hotel clerk the next morning, with his most charming smile.

"Of course, Mr. Dunningham." She typed the name into her computer. "Oh, now I know why that name sounded familiar. She just checked out."

He scanned the lobby and saw Cassie as she opened the big front door, an overnight bag slung across her shoulder. "Cassie." He rushed across the room, dodging bellhops and guests alike. The glass door was closing behind her. "Cassie." She turned, and saw him approaching, frozen on the sidewalk as if he shot a ray gun at her. "Cassie," he jogged the last several steps, taking her arms. "You're leaving?" he asked, breathing hard.

She nodded. "I have to get back to Chicago."

"You look like hell," he noted, taking in her bloodshot and puffy eyes.

She smiled. "You're quite the charmer."

He shrugged with a grin, relieved he caught her. "I do my best."

"You sure do," she mumbled, not seeming to be addressing him. She hung her head, fiddling with the tag hanging from her bag. "I'm sorry...about last night. I didn't mean to tease you...although I guess that's exactly what I did. I just..."

"I want to see you again."

She looked up, eyes wide. "You do?"

He nodded.

"Why?"

He searched for an answer. "I don't know." It was the most honest reply he could give. All he knew was that he'd been thinking of her all night, reliving each sentence she'd uttered, each electrifying look, each touch she gave him that left him rattled.

"Josh...," she said, regret heavy in her voice. She looked over his shoulder, avoiding eye contact. "We got caught up in the bright lights and the magic and—" A car pulled up behind her and honked. She stepped off the curb, meeting Josh's gaze. Tears threatened to spill out. Had he put them there?

Heather stepped out of the rental car, staring at him with resentment. "Cassie, we're going to be late."

"I know," she replied, a little sharply. Heather rolled her eyes and got back behind the wheel.

He took a step toward her, but Cassie spun to open the passenger door, hurling her bag in the back seat and slamming it shut. She opened the front door but hesitated. Her hand shook on the door frame. She appeared to have something more to say, but she swallowed her final words and before he knew what was happening, she was gone.

JOSH WAS IN A FOUL mood. His head ached like a worse-than-usual hangover, made more painful by the drone of the tour bus's tires against the unending road in front of them. Only thing was, he hadn't imbibed in days.

His best friend and bassist, Ryan Sandoval, sat across from him, legs stretched along the seat, eyes closed as the sun pressed against his face. Between the leather seats they occupied, facing each other, was a small, rectangular table. The light from the window on the left alternately lit Ryan's face then bathed it in shadow as they went under the huge highway signs spanning the road. He sat up suddenly, startling Josh. "What's eating you?"

Josh stared at him a minute, taken off guard, then simply got up, saying darkly, "Nothing a couple of fifths of booze won't cure." He began searching the cabinets for any alcohol they would offer up. Spotting a bottle of scotch behind a roll of paper towels, he took it out to pour himself a drink. He and Ryan told each other everything, but he wasn't ready to share with his friend yet. Wasn't ready because he couldn't even figure out what was wrong himself.

The good thing about Ryan, though, was he knew when to call it quits. He frowned but resumed his position, closing his eyes and threading his fingers together behind his head. Josh slid back in his seat, taking a drink of his scotch before setting it on the table between them. He appreciated that they could sit together like this in silence. Even in his funk, he had to smile and shake his head at his friend, though the gesture went unseen. The armrest hit Ryan in the middle of the back, so after a minute or two, he shifted to take a nap.

Josh turned to stare out the window as place names and mileage signs ticked past. As fatigue took over, he found himself traveling back in his mind to another time, another place.

It was fifth grade, and he was attending Pierce Elementary School in Cedar Rapids, Iowa. He was going through the motions, much like he was now, putting in his time at school, then going home to a house that was empty, whether his parents were there or not. He didn't have many friends, didn't care to have any at the time, content to meander through life without purpose.

In his memory he turned the corner in one of the long hallways that made up his elementary school and saw Ryan pressed up against the lockers by a kid three times his size. The kid had the sides of his jacket bunched up in both of his meaty fists, his knuckles pressing into Ryan's chest. Books lay scattered at their feet. Ryan's books, Josh surmised, as the brute picking on him didn't look intelligent enough to read.

"Listen, *Sandy*—"

He forgot they called Ryan that, because of his last name, Sandoval, and his hair color, which was a lot lighter then. At least he thought he forgot it. Yet he could hear it now, as the boy's voice rang out loud and clear in his head.

"—you think you're all that because you live in your big house, with your white picket fence—"

"We don't have a fence."

The kid slammed Ryan's head into the locker for that, the noise ricocheting down the hallway like a stray bullet. Josh thought the sound would summon a teacher, but the doors along the hall stayed inexplicably closed.

"Oww!"

"—and your Daddy don't work at the factory, and your sisters are pretty enough to fuck—"

Ryan's jaw tightened. "Shut up about my sisters, man."

"Oh," the bully taunted, "you don't like me talking about your pretty sisters?"

"No, I don't. And you better stop or..."

"Or what, Sandoval? You gonna cry all over my new sneakers?"

Josh turned his head to get a better look at Ryan now. Tears shimmered in his eyes, probably from his smarting head, but his face was determined, fists clenched. As far as he was concerned, Ryan Sandoval was an okay kid. He'd never acted uppity around him, even though Josh lived in a trailer on the wrong side of town. He even gave Josh money once, when Ryan saw he didn't have anything to eat at lunch. When Josh tried to pay him back the next day, Ryan waved him off, saying it was an early Christmas present, though it was barely even October.

"Leave him alone." He couldn't believe the words came out of his mouth. He never got involved with anyone else, their problems, or their everyday lives.

The bigger kid turned his head in Josh's direction, his round, freckled face tight, the flaming red hair that surrounded it ghoulishly haloed in the half-powered florescent lights overhead. He released Ryan's coat, a grin splitting his face. His name was Jimmy Swartz, he remembered. His brother had committed suicide when they were younger. But that didn't give Jimmy permission to be an asshole.

"Well, if it ain't Josh D., trailer trash." Jimmy took a few steps forward. "Why don't you just run along to your remedial reading class, Joshie?"

Josh was in honors English, but he wasn't sure anyone knew it, even the kids in his class. He slid his eyes to Ryan for a second. He was staring at Josh with his mouth hanging open. He returned his gaze to his tormentor's face.

"I think you need to move on and leave Ryan, here, alone."

Out of the corner of his eye, he saw Ryan blink, as if surprised Josh even knew his name.

Jimmy Swartz stepped forward. He had a couple of inches on Jimmy, but that's where the advantage ended. Jimmy was chunky and mean where Josh was rail thin and generally indifferent. "You really think you can take me, Dunningham?" His upper lip curled into a sneer.

Josh spun around as if to walk off.

"Yeah. That's what I thought—" Jimmy's words caught in his throat as he watched Josh carefully put his books and spirals down.

He turned back, his demeanor serene. Then he stepped up so that his face was within a few inches of his challenger, his expression unchanging. "Yeah. I think I can take you," he returned evenly.

Jimmy's mouth hung open a second before he snapped it shut, his brows coming together as his fists came up. "This is gonna be fun." He swung with all his might, but Josh was quick. He ducked, Jimmy's fist sailing harmlessly over his head, and stuck one of his long legs out, sweeping it in an arc and taking Jimmy out at the base like felling a big, redheaded tree. He went down as if in slow motion and his head bounced, actually bounced, off the indestructible surface of the school's floor. Josh, Ryan, and Jimmy all froze for several seconds before Jimmy released a wail the likes of which had never been heard at Pierce Elementary before.

"I'm telling, Dunningham. You'll get suspended for this."

Ryan, who seemed to have regained his cool, began to pick up his books one by one. "I don't think I'd do that, if I was you, Swartz. Since you started the fight, you'll probably end up with an even longer suspension."

A door opened to their right.

"What's going on here?" Coach Ridenhower stepped out into the hall. With a whistle perpetually slung around his neck, the teacher was built like a linebacker and had the sense of humor of a broomstick.

"Josh and I were just walking down the hall when Swartz ran into us. He must have tripped or something, huh, Swartz?" Ryan bent to offer his free hand to Jimmy. Jimmy stared at it for a beat, incredulous. After a tense few seconds, he slapped his hand into Ryan's, perhaps a bit harder than necessary, but he let Ryan help him up.

Josh loaded his voice with concern. "You okay, Swartz?"

Jimmy touched his head and came back with a bloody palm. "I'm bleeding."

"You need to get down to the nurse's office, then." The teacher turned to Josh and Ryan. "You boys get along to class."

"Yes, sir," Ryan answered for them both. He nudged Josh, who picked up his stuff.

"And next time be more careful, Mr. Swartz."

Josh and Ryan spun their heads, catching Jimmy's eye just before he turned away. Josh winked. The pair continued down the hallway together in silence, letting their heartbeats return to normal and catching their breath.

After a few seconds, Ryan slid him a sideways glance. "The way you took Swartz down, that was a slick move."

Josh felt a surge of pride. "Thanks."

For several seconds more, all they heard were their footsteps and the whine of a water fountain down the hall as some kid bent over it. "I didn't even know you knew my name," Ryan commented.

He stared straight ahead, feeling the corners of his lips quiver slightly as he tried to suppress a smile. "Well, you do have some pretty good-looking sisters."

Ryan chuckled. They had reached the door to his classroom. "See ya around."

"Yeah." Josh grinned and continued on down the hall.

After that incident, Ryan came to idolize Josh like a big brother. But as months passed, he must have come to realize through trips to Josh's house that he was really a pretty messed up big brother, one who needed Ryan as much as Ryan needed him. A strange, unbreakable bond formed between the two. Josh guessed it was born from the obligation Ryan felt to take care of the boy he once revered. That only made the friendship stronger, more real, as they both stood on equal ground.

As the tour bus slogged ahead, Josh glanced back in his bass player's direction, but Ryan's eyes remained closed. Though he hadn't yet unloaded his thoughts on Ryan, the two were still tight, he reflected.

Reminiscing about his hometown only reminded him of the Midwest, and the girl who probably had returned to Chicago by now. For the life of him, he couldn't understand why he couldn't get Cassie McCallister out of his mind. It was a brief encounter, *too brief, as far as I'm concerned,* he thought with a wry grin. Yet he still smiled as he remembered her dancing and singing in the lounge, shook his head when he thought about how he had the guts to lick the salt from her skin, got turned on when he thought of her in his bed. He flashed back to the seconds before their two bodies hit the pool, to her dripping in the elevator, to her climbing into the car and driving away, leaving him standing, helpless, on the sidewalk. He didn't know what it was about her; he just wished he would have had the time to figure it out.

What seemed like minutes later, but was actually hours, they arrived in L.A. The band and crew set up the equipment and ran sound-check. Still, they had several hours before the show. Josh sat moodily staring out of the window of the bus again, even though there was nothing to look at, since they were no longer moving. Ryan plopped a glove down on the table in front of him, startling him for the second time that day.

"Let's throw the ball around."

THE GLOVE FELT GOOD on his hand and smelled good, like boyhood laughter and good-natured taunts. He went loosely through his motion, letting his muscles warm up. Getting the feel for things, he let go and zinged one in there. Ryan's glove closed solidly on the ball, but Josh bet he was beginning to wish he brought his more heavily padded catcher's mitt instead. Ryan smiled that easy, slow smile of his, and for Josh it was like they were back in the ball field of Pierce Elementary, instead of in an empty parking lot outside a stadium in L.A. The school's field was horrible, a mixture of grass and scattered weeds which never gave the ball a true hop. But it was their field, home of The Panthers.

He was the pitcher, and Ry was the catcher. Dunningham and Sandoval, quite the battery. He could throw a curve when most kids their age couldn't. He doubted coaches these days would allow a kid to use their arm like that, while it was still developing, but watching the ball curve as it came in over the plate was a thing of beauty. He could still remember the sound the ball made as it hummed through the air, followed by the resounding smack of leather, a little cloud of dust bursting out of Ryan's glove like an exploding supernova.

No one else could catch Josh like he could. It was as if they shared a brain. Ryan said he could tell just by the look on Josh's face what pitch he would throw, and where it would come in over the plate, and at what speed. And he was no slouch as a catcher, that was for sure. There was no such thing as a pass ball when he was behind home plate, and he could throw a line to second if anyone dared try to steal. Kids thought twice about coming home when he caught, knowing anyone who tried to get past him could leave on a stretcher. He was shorter but stockier than Josh, who had always been tall and lanky, with short, straight, dark-brown hair to Josh's black. Complete opposites, except under the skin where it was most important. There, they were soul brothers.

Ryan tossed the ball back and Josh took a deep breath, feeling his shoulders relax. He could still smell the hot dogs, blowing dirt, and Bazooka bubble gum. He could still feel Ryan's hand over his shoulder at the end of the game and see his thousand-watt grin when they swapped stories in the dugout. He remembered the championship game when he struck out six batters in a row to end the last two innings. He could hear the wonderful sound of "S-T-E-E-E-R-I-K-E," as the ump punched the last batter out. Ryan dumped the ball in the dirt and raced toward the pitching mound, only making it halfway before Josh grabbed him up in a bear hug and they jumped around like a pair of morons before the others reached them and knocked them off their feet.

Mr. Sandoval rushed to them as soon as the pair left the field. A tremor laced Ryan's dad's voice. "What a game, boys! You played one hell of a game." He clapped his son on the back and pulled the bill of Josh's hat down.

Josh recalled scanning the crowd for his parents. He should have known better. They never came to his games. When Josh turned back with his head down, Ryan's dad asked him to join them in a celebratory ice cream cone. That was so cool. He shook off the memory.

He rubbed the ball around his palm thoughtfully, enjoying the feel of the soft, smooth leather juxtaposed with the texture of the somewhat scratchy, red stitches. Ryan still crouched several yards away, waiting, as patient as ever. He brought his hands together, staring into the center of Ryan's glove, then reared back and let it fly. Ryan caught it and sent it back, shaking the blood back into his hand a little, but returning to his crouch without a word. The two played without speaking for twenty-five minutes. Sweat dripped down his back and his face, but his frustrations had worked their way out of him as the perspiration had. He tossed the baseball up and down as he walked over to Ryan, setting it into his glove with a smile.

"Thanks, buddy. Geez," he added, mopping his forehead. "I need a shower." They walked toward the bus together. "Where'd you find this stuff, anyway?" He indicated the gloves and ball.

Ryan shrugged. "I've had them for a while, I guess." He looked up at his friend. "You've still got it, ya know."

"Yeah, sure." He grinned and rubbed Ryan's head hard. He took a playful shot at Josh's exposed ribs, and they climbed back onto the bus.

CHAPTER FIVE

Josh stood framed in the doorway of his dressing room, arms stretched above his head, grasping the edge of the door. A girl stood in front of him. She was pretty, with long, wavy black hair, petite, but shapely, and from the way she was tossing her hair and batting her eyelashes, *way* into him. He reached down and ran a thumb softly over the girl's cheek, then shook his head, "I'm sorry. Not tonight."

The girl stood for a moment, dumbfounded. Then, as if on cue, a door farther down the hallway creaked open and light scissored out from Lanny's dressing room.

"Hey, babe. Come here," the drummer called to her, his voice scratchy from years of smoking and drug abuse. The girl gave Josh one more look of longing, then slowly walked in Lanny's direction. When she got close enough, he pulled her in the room by her hips. The pair giggled, the door closed behind them, and Josh turned, closing his own door with an almost inaudible click.

He sighed. Why had he turned her away? He pulled off his shirt, but before he could explore the question further a rap on the door interrupted his thoughts.

He rolled his eyes. "Go away."

After a slight hesitation, a voice called out tentatively, "Josh, it's me, Ryan."

He scrambled and jerked the door open. "Sorry, man. I thought you were someone who got past security." He mopped his face with the T-shirt in his hand and tossed it near a duffle bag on the floor. The dressing room was mostly a wide-open area, with dressing tables along one wall, a couch, a few chairs, and a low coffee table. The couch had seen better days, perhaps trashed by a band or two.

"Come on in. There's beer in the fridge. I need to take a quick shower, and then I'll join you."

"That's cool." Ryan headed for the mini fridge.

"I thought the show went well tonight," Josh called over his shoulder as he entered the bathroom.

"Yeah," Ryan yelled after him. "You sounded fantastic."

"Only as good as you guys make me sound, partner," he replied, sticking his head back out the door for a minute with a wink and a grin. He ducked back in the bathroom.

The hot water felt so good, Josh took a little longer than he anticipated. Still, when he came out, he was surprised to see that Ryan was well into his second beer, the first dead soldier on the table in front of him. Wearing a towel around his waist, he rubbed his hair with another one. "Hey. Sorry I took so long."

"I met a girl," Ryan blurted out.

Josh, wiping his face, froze for a minute. Slowly he peered up over the edge of the towel, his eyes studying his longtime friend. "You met a girl?" he repeated.

"Yes. Her name is Paige, and she's—" he sighed "—she's something, Josh."

His tone, his expression, everything clearly said that he was seriously into this girl. How was he supposed to respond to this kind of news? Josh moved around the couch and was going to sit, when he remembered he was still only in a towel.

"I'll be right back," he mumbled, snatched the duffle bag from the floor and took it into the bathroom with him. A few minutes later he returned, wearing fresh jeans and a T-shirt, along with a serious expression.

He flopped on the couch next to Ryan, accepting the beer he was handed, and stretching his feet out on the coffee table in front of him. He lounged a second before asking, a little uncertainly, "So...what is she like?"

A spontaneous smile split Ryan's face. "She's great. We stayed up all night talking—"

"In Vegas?"

"No, in Atlanta."

"Atlanta? That was weeks ago."

"Yeah...I was a little nervous about telling you."

"Why?"

"Because..." Ryan sat up with a jerk, leaning forward to rest his arms on his knees and pick at the label on the bottle which now swung between his legs. "I'm serious about her, man. I can't stop thinking about her. And...I think it might be time for me to leave the band."

"Leave the band?" Josh exclaimed. Was he really hearing this?

"I can't build a relationship with somebody from two thousand miles across the country, Josh."

"I know, but—"

"This is something I want. Something I need."

Josh was stymied by the sudden announcement. He swallowed, letting it sink in even as he sank back into the couch. "You'll stay for the rest of the tour?"

"Of course. You know I wouldn't leave you high and dry."

He took another long pull on his beer. "Maybe you could go see her next week. We have two travel days before the show in Cincinnati..."

"You're not mad?"

"Are you kidding? It is kind of a shock. But Ry, I knew you wouldn't tag along with me forever. You're from the whole backyard-trampoline-Kool-Aid-on-the-counter kind of home. I've always known someday you'd go back."

Ryan grinned, his shoulders relaxing. "As I recall, you did pretty well on that trampoline with Mary Jo McFeeney," he joked.

"Yeah, until I chipped my tooth on the springs."

Ryan snickered. "Oh, yeah. I forgot about that."

"H-mmm." He took another drink before slapping a hand on his friend's knee and pushing off it to rise. "Seriously, Ry. I'm happy for you. I hope things work out the way you want them to."

"Thanks, man." He was getting a little choked up, so Josh decided to call it a night before he did anything to embarrass them both. He walked Ryan to the door and then watched him stroll down the hall. He looked like the yoke had been lifted from his shoulders. Josh felt like one had been dropped on his.

LANCASTER MOON GAZED at the girl lying on his dressing room floor. He ran an unsteady hand through his stringy hair as he surveyed what he'd done. She was face-up, totally naked and passed out. Her long hair, once a sheen of black, now matted and tangled, splayed across her so all he could see was a vague impression of her face. When she'd entered the room, he had locked the door behind her. He convinced her to let him shoot her up with some "good drugs," but purposefully gave her a heavy dose, to make her more compliant.

Then, his mood turned dark, as it always did. He made her strip down while he watched from a chair, his arms folded across his chest. At first, she seemed to be into it, smiling at him seductively. But then she hesitated. He barked at her to continue, and she went along with him, though now she seemed a little wary, not looking him in the eyes fully, her hands shaking. When she finished, he made her stand there for several minutes in the middle of the room. She shifted her weight, the corner of her upper lip trembling a little. She put on a forced smile and cooed as she strutted toward him.

"Come on, baby—"

"Be still, dammit!"

The girl jerked to a halt, staring at him.

He lit a cigarette. Through the haze of smoke he blew at her, he let his eyes rove over her body.

She crossed her arms over her chest. "I'm out of here," she huffed, reaching for her clothes.

He snapped at her, his voice like a whip. "Where the hell do you think you're going?"

He threw his cigarette to the floor and stood to grind it under the heel of his boot. He crossed to the girl in two long strides, grabbed her violently by the shoulders and spun her around, pushing her so she was bent awkwardly over the side of the couch. Before she even started to struggle, he had his pants unzipped, letting them slide down to his ankles so he could enter her with force. He reached around to dig his nails into her breasts as he plunged into her brutally, over and over and over again.

It went on for what seemed like hours. When the girl finally passed out, he was sweaty and breathing hard, still giving her vicious thrusts, but infrequently. As usual, he hadn't been able to complete the act; he was never able to complete the act. Finally, disgusted with himself, as much as with the girl, he backed away from her, letting her slide to the ground, discarded. He sat back in the chair, exhausted, lighting a cigarette with shaking hands and smoking it with his pants still around his ankles.

When he was finished, he planned on leaving her there. She would most likely wake up in the dark empty stadium dressing room hours after everyone had gone. She would probably be scared. He liked the idea. *Dumb bitch.* He finished the cigarette, pulled his pants up, and stood over her for a minute. With his foot, he pushed back some of her hair. She was pretty, he noticed somewhat indifferently. She would wake up confused, like the others, unsure of herself enough not to press any charges.

Yes, being part of the band had its advantages. The girls would come to him, young, innocent, trusting. Of course, Josh, being the lead singer and all, had an easier time of it. Good God, one girl had literally thrown herself at his feet, launching herself from her boyfriend's shoulders and breaking her collarbone when she crashed onto the stage. Even then, she was so wasted she still wanted to do him. Some guys had all the luck.

He began to throw his stuff into an open suitcase on the dressing room table. Not that Josh was all that bad, really. And he had certainly been his meal ticket, that was for damn sure. But the fact that Josh and Ryan thought he was really their friend cracked him up. The jerks had no idea. They had befriended him in junior high, when he and his parents moved into the trailer park across the river so his dad could work at the cereal factory, or at least collect a check from them. As his dad was fond of saying on payday, "I act like I'm working, and they act like they're paying me."

The thought of his old man turned his stomach. *Sick, old bastard.* He spat on the scarred wooden floor in contempt. *Yeah, good, ol' Joshie thought he had it bad 'cause his parents ignored him*, he sniggered. *I wished my old man would have ignored me.*

He zipped the suitcase, jerking it to the floor with a loud thud. He glanced over, but the girl hadn't moved a muscle. A pair of drumsticks he'd overlooked behind the suitcase rolled forward, but he snatched them up before they could fall off the dressing table. As nicked and abused as they were, they still felt good in his hands.

Because if there was one thing he could do, it was drum. It began when he picked up rhythms while thumping on the door to his bedroom whenever his father decided to lock him in, sometimes for days at a time. Occasionally his father would let him out, just so he could beat him. But, in time, Lanny built up. He was never anything but thin, but he had steel-like arms. And after a while, the old man didn't beat him anymore. He sneered, remembering the last time his dad tried.

Bolstered by the memory, he turned to leave, snapped off the light, and closed the door behind him. He ignored the low moans which were now issuing from the girl's throat.

CHAPTER SIX

Cassie stared blankly at the portfolio on her desk. It contained storyboards for a new ad campaign for a major food retailer. She wished TV's Darren Stevens and his persnickety boss, Larry Tate, would show up, and with a little twitching of noses the company would be sold on her work. She got up abruptly and paced behind her desk. She had fifteen minutes before she was due in the boardroom, and she was all ready to go. She hated that. Fifteen minutes for her to stew before facing the firing squad. She crossed her arms and stilled herself deliberately, looking out her large office windows at the view of the city. That was what she liked about advertising agencies. So much depended on presentation, thus they were willing to shell out the bucks to make the offices stylish and technologically innovative.

Staring back at her from the opposite building was a ten-foot-tall Josh Dunningham. She couldn't believe it when he showed up *the day after* they returned from Vegas, an ad banner for a new radio station in town. She must have somehow angered the advertising gods, and her punishment was to have "Josh" perpetually watching over her shoulder at work.

Some days the irony of it all made her laugh. Some days, like today, it gave her a queasy feeling in her stomach. What in the world was wrong with her that she couldn't sleep with such a gorgeous hunk of a man? The shot on the oversized poster was taken from below, the camera traveling up his long, lean legs in worn blue jeans impossibly tight in the crotch. He wore another band's black concert T-shirt, and had his arms crossed, accenting his bulging biceps, as he gave the camera a hard stare with a near snarl on his lips. His hair was splayed out from his face, seeming careless, although she knew some stylist had fussed for hours with it. The Rock and Roll Tough Guy, hot, with his mysterious edge. It was enough to make even an eighty-year-old woman salivate. So, what was wrong with her? She was single, twenty-four, with no ties. Lord knew she was drawn to him, like a spark to dry kindling. So, why did she hesitate? And then, after deciding to make love with him, why did she just leave, like a coward?

She kept remembering his face outside the lobby the morning they left Sin City. He wasn't angry, as she had expected. He actually said he wanted to see her again. Josh Dunningham, mega rock star, wanted to see *her*. It had to be a mistake. It had to be.

Had Troy messed her up that badly? If she couldn't make it with someone as wonderful as Josh, was there any hope for her future at all?

"McCallister. You're late!"

Cassie hated that her boss always called her by her last name like a high school gym teacher. His voice was nearly as shrill as the coach's whistle. Jumping, she scurried after him, feeling much more the peon than she was.

Ten minutes later she returned to her office, exasperated, to snatch a portfolio from the desk and return to her presentation, considering herself an even bigger fool than before.

LANCASTER MOON COULD smell the winds of change, and he liked the stench about as much as he did the smell of burnt oats which had issued from the cereal factory when he was a kid. Josh had talked to him last night about Ryan. It seemed he'd found himself a little tart in Atlanta. Josh asked him not to give Ryan a hard time about it. Said he would be going to Atlanta next week to visit with her, and after the tour, he might give up the band. Give up the band for some chick. The thought had Lanny's insides churning.

On top of that, Josh now seemed to have something stuck in his craw, and *that* worried him. Oh, sure, Ryan was a good guitarist and all, and his background vocals were top notch, but they could get by without him. They wouldn't be as good maybe, but they wouldn't fold. If something happened to Josh, now that was a different story. It was his voice and music that had launched them to stardom, and without him, the band was history. Lanny was not going to let that happen.

He edged over to Ryan at the kitchen sink in the tour bus. "What's up with Josh?" he whispered, jerking his head in the singer's direction. Josh had taken up a familiar position as of late, sitting at the table and staring out the windows at the world going by. Lanny sensed it wasn't all about Ryan's leaving either.

Ryan leaned his head in conspiratorially. "You've noticed too, huh? I don't know. I can't get anything out of him."

"You just let ol' Hot Sticks Lanny Moon take care of him." He winked, pulling a bottle out of the freezer and reaching into a cabinet for a couple of shot glasses.

Ryan dried his hands on a dish towel, and turned to watch the proceedings, crossing his arms.

"Hey, Buddy," Lanny said with forced cheer. "How about some of the hair?" He set two glasses down on the table with a loud clink and began to take the cap off the bottle.

"Geez, Lan, it's only two-thirty." He pushed the glass away.

"Aww..." Lanny chuckled. "That's never stopped ya before." He slid the glass toward Josh again and downed his own drink. Alcohol was Josh and Ryan's drug of choice, so he'd use it to find out what the hell was going on.

Josh spun the glass on the table thoughtfully, then turned to peer at Ryan, who shrugged and looked away, wiping at something on the counter with his towel. Josh sighed and drained the clear but deadly liquor from the glass, breathing out loudly, "Whooo!" He coughed. "That stuff is potent!"

"Aww, nothin' the ol' Joshmeister can't handle," Lanny wheedled. "Have another." He filled their two glasses again, raising his to clink against Josh's. His sharp eyes watched him. "Come on over here, Ry-boy, and have a drink with Joshie and me." He patted the seat next to him.

Ryan eyed the pair skeptically but ambled in their direction.

"Now, git yo'self a glass, pardner," Lanny instructed. "There ya are. Good boy." Lanny filled the little glasses and handed them out, the three emptied theirs in unison without a word.

Ryan gasped. "Good God, Lanny. What's in this stuff?"

"Yeah," Josh agreed. "My gums are numb." He chuckled.

All three laughed as Lanny poured again. "This here is like the good ol' days. We haven't tied one on in a while."

"Yeah, well, Lan," Josh commented, reaching for the bottle himself this time, "you're not usually much of a drinker."

"Well, I figgered this was a sort of special occasion, with Ryan here goin' off to meet his lil' filly soon."

"Yeah," Josh said with a lopsided grin. "To...what's her name again?" he slurred.

"Paige," Ryan replied with a burp. "I think." He giggled.

Freakin' pair of lightweights. Lanny filled again. "So, we know what Ryan here has his mind on," he sniggered lustily, "but what's got your goat?"

Josh tried to wave them off.

"Naww, come on, now. We can tell somethin's bothering you."

"You mean besides my head feeling like a bowling ball?" He laughed, then shrugged. "Well...I sort of met a girl, too."

"A-a-a-ah," Ryan and Lanny declared simultaneously. Lanny fought not to roll his eyes and kept his face as expressionless as a woman who'd had too much Botox; but inside, alarm bells were screaming.

"You dog!" Ryan made a move to punch his friend in the shoulder but fell off balance a little and only landed a glancing blow. "All this time I've been tellin' you about Paige, and you've kept quiet. So? What's she like? Where'd you meet her?"

"Awww. Never mind. It's no big deal." Josh tried to rise, but seemed to think better of it, sinking back down and grabbing the bottle to pour himself another draught of forgetfulness.

"Uh-uh-uh. I told you about Paige, now you tell me."

"But it's not like you and Paige. I haven't talked to her since that night, and—"

"Why not?"

"'Cause I didn't get her number," Josh growled, appearing angry now. "And...I'm not all that sure she would want to hear from me anyway. She...sort of...ran out on me."

Lanny chortled and Ryan elbowed him hard in the ribs. He looked up to catch Josh's fierce green eyes glaring at him. He looked like he was ready to tear his head off and throw it under the wheels of the bus.

"So..." Ryan began tentatively, "you're obviously still thinking about her. The question is, why?"

Josh shifted his eyes to his best friend; then peered down at the drink in his glass, spinning it on the table. The liquid sloshed all over his fingers. "I'm not sure," he answered quietly. He took the glass, and sipped half of it. Giving a loud sigh, he leaned back and laced his fingers behind his head, staring up at the ceiling. "She's just so damn...I don't know." He let his breath out in a huff.

Lanny and Ryan exchanged glances.

"Well," Lanny began, "how did you meet?"

A smile flickered over Josh's face briefly. "At the bar in the casino. She was doing a shot of tequila."

"Just your type," Lanny said with a suggestive chuckle.

"No," Josh snarled. "She was...funny...gorgeous...I mean, absolutely drop-dead, pick-your-chin-up-off-the-floor gorgeous. She had a sort of...shyness, I guess. But the way she kissed..." His smile returned.

"So, you kissed her?"

Josh nodded, adding in a rush, "And we ended up in my room, but when I went to the bathroom for a condom, she left."

"Why do you think she did that?"

"She was scared, I guess."

"What?" Lanny interrupted. "You get a little rough with her?"

"No. Of course not!" Josh spit out, his eyebrows raised in shock. "I think I was just...moving a little too fast for her."

"Ahh. One of those." Lanny rolled his eyes.

"Listen, Lanny—" Josh leaned across the table, his hands clenching.

"Just ignore him," Ryan ordered, shooting Lanny a withering glance. "What did she look like?"

"Short, blond, with these killer blue eyes, and lips that don't quit...built..." He sighed. "And she had good taste in music. Had all of our albums." He smiled.

Ryan grinned. "Ah, yes. Excellent taste in music."

"Helps when they're already hot for you before they even meet you," Lanny cackled. Ryan and Josh ignored him.

"What does she do?"

"Ad exec in Chicago. Some firm like, Orstein and Crutcher, or something."

"So, she's smart. Sexy."

"Yeah." Josh blew out a breath. "And you should see how good she looks wet."

Ryan sat up eagerly. "Explain, please."

"We were walking by the pool. I was trying to sober her up—"

"How come?" Lanny asked, truly confused.

Josh frowned at him but continued. "She lost her balance, and we both ended up in the pool." He laughed.

"No shit?"

"Yeah."

And as he thought about it, snapshots of their night together appeared in his head like a haphazard slide show: Cassie lying dripping in his arms as they made their way out of the pool, her arched throat as his hands glided over it in the elevator, her lying in his bed as he turned from the bathroom door. Irritated with himself, he got up clumsily and walked over to the sink, leaning his arms on the edge of the counter. "But I don't know why it matters. I'll never see her again anyway. But the thing is, I can't seem to stop thinking about her."

"You know what it is, don't ya?" Lanny inquired, matter-of-factly.

"No, Lancaster. Please illuminate me," he muttered wryly, turning toward him.

"Have you ever had a girl turn you down before?"

"Not since high school. And then, only once," he said, unable to keep the pride out of his voice.

"Then, that's it!" he shouted triumphantly. "The only reason you keep thinking about her is because she didn't put out. If she had done you, you wouldn't have wasted another thought on her."

Josh didn't comment, because he'd tried that line of reasoning on himself earlier, and it simply didn't ring true. There was more to it than that, but damned if he knew what it was. "Yeah...well...," he muttered, shuffling his feet. "I'm going to lie down. I'm beat." And it was true, he hadn't slept well, and he knew the alcohol was going to give him one nasty headache, at any rate.

"See ya, buddy," Ryan called.

Josh entered his bedroom at the back of the bus. He tore off the T-shirt he wore, pulling it over his head, and dumping it on the floor. He rubbed his hands over his chest absently, remembering how it felt when her hands searched him, trembling with desire. She *had* wanted him. It showed in her eyes, in the heat of her kisses, in the racing of her pulse.

He stumbled to switch on the lamp, falling and flipping around at the last second to land on his backside on the mattress in the middle of the room. He stared up at the ceiling fan as it whirred lazily above him, hands folded behind his head on the pillow. In his mind's eye she danced with him, saying over and over again, "I love this song!" Her antics had made the laughter bubble out of him in a completely unexpected way. He closed his eyes but could still hear Cassie's chuckles, her whispers, the sound of her impatient breathing as her mouth sought his.

Why then, did she leave his bed and return to Chicago the next morning? Suddenly he sat up, causing his head to roll precariously on his shoulders. *Ornstein and Cruthers! That's the name of the firm she works at. That's where I can find her.* He laid back down, moving more slowly this time, and began to formulate a plan.

CHAPTER SEVEN

Cassie stared out the window at the larger-than-life Josh. She had had the worst week of her life. Her original concept for a product launch got shot down by the higher-ups, her car was in the shop, needing over five hundred dollars' worth of repairs, and now the air-conditioning was out on the entire floor. It was stifling. Although illogical, she blamed her misfortunes on that mocking image across the street. She vowed she would never listen to the radio station responsible for the awful billboard and fought a strong urge to stick her tongue out at it. Then she reminded herself that some level of maturity was required for a woman in her position.

But unable to totally resist some sort of retaliation, she shouted at it, "You're making my life a living hell!"

"Excuse me?" came a voice from the hallway. A delivery man stood outside her door.

"Oh, I'm sorry. Not you. I was just...never mind." She labored with the cords to pull the blinds shut on the abhorrent face outside her window. "Can I help you?"

"Are you Cassie McCallister?"

She nodded.

"I have a package you've been requested to sign for." He stuck his electronic clipboard into her hands, and she signed. She gave it back to him and he handed her a flat package.

Interested in the unusual box's contents, she immediately zipped the little tab along the top of the box to open it, pulling out a simple white envelope. She shook the box over her desk to see if it contained anything else, but it was empty. An envelope inside of a box, what was this all about? The outside of the envelope said only "Cassie." She took her yellow suit jacket off and slung it over a chair, revealing a cream-colored, sleeveless blouse with thick straps. The material was rather flimsy, and she never wore it by itself, but desperate times called for desperate measures, and since she could feel a bead of sweat trickling uncomfortably between her breasts, she definitely considered it desperate times.

She sat at the desk and returned her attention to the envelope. She ran her fingers over the written name, studying the handwriting, but not recognizing it. She flipped the envelope over, but the back was blank. She frowned uncertainly and ran a nail under a bubble near the right corner of the flap, breaking the seal. She reached in to pull out a plane ticket and a small note, written on a neatly torn piece of sheet music.

Please come see me.

was all it said. She glanced at the ticket. San Diego. Turning the envelope over, Cassie gave it a little shake, feeling something else in it. Out fluttered an event ticket of some sort. She stared at it a minute, not comprehending. She turned the sheet music over, looking for a further explanation, but found none. With shaking hands, she reached for the ticket on her desk, her fingers hesitating before picking it up, as if she was lifting a live cobra. "San Diego's Petco Park," she read, "presents Money Back Guaranteed, Saturday June 1st." She glanced at her desk calendar to verify; yes, June first was this Saturday.

She dropped the ticket on the middle of the desk and pushed an arm length away from it. *What the hell? Doesn't he get it? I'm not interested in a one-night stand with him. Okay, I'm interested, but I'm not going to follow up on that interest.* She just couldn't do it, couldn't throw her heart out there again, even casually. Why was he toying with her like this? Like he didn't have enough groupies throwing themselves at him on a regular basis? But that was it, wasn't it? *She* turned him down; it was a blow to his overinflated rock star ego.

The more she thought about it, the more belligerent she became. *I guess he thinks I can take off whenever I want to and traipse around the country after him. Okay, so it's on a Saturday and I could make it without missing work, but I've got other things to take care of...like...like...* Okay, so she couldn't think of anything pressing that needed to be done, but still.

Why, I ought to just go out there and give him a piece of my mind. That would teach him. That's just what I should do. He'd never expect it. She stood up abruptly and pulled the shade open with a hint of violence.

She stared at her nemesis on the building across the street. "Okay, Mr. Josh Dunningham. I'll play your little game," she said aloud, her voice snide. She tried to ignore the fact that her heartbeat was racing at the thought of seeing him again. A warmth had spread over her that had nothing to do with the failed air conditioning.

SATURDAY CAME AND JOSH was incredibly nervous. During practice, he missed chords while glancing up at any noise to see if she had entered the empty auditorium. He wished he had just called and talked to her, instead of leaving things so up in the air. He didn't even know for sure if she was coming. But he hated to talk on the phone, was afraid he'd say something wrong, and she'd hang up and he wouldn't have an opportunity to fix it. He was better in person, he could read her, and she could read him. If only he knew for sure whether or not she was coming.

For all he knew, she may not have even received the tickets. But no. That was something he had done right; he asked to have her sign for it. The tickets had gotten there; it was just a question of whether she decided to use them or not. As he looked up for the hundredth time to see a janitor sweeping the aisles, Ryan piped up.

"Josh, who are you expecting to see come walking through those doors?"

"Cassie."

"Cassie? Cassie who? ...Oh. The girl. You called her?"

"I sent her a plane ticket and a ticket for the show tonight."

"Smoooth." Ryan smiled and nodded his approval. "What time is she supposed to get here?"

"I'm not sure. I didn't actually talk to her."

"Okay. Well, what does she look like again? I'll keep my eye out for her, too."

"Five-two, five-three, maybe, short blond hair, great figure—"

"And, I know, I know, 'killer eyes.' Blue, right?"

Josh nodded. "Killer blue. Knock-your-socks-off blue. The kind of blue that makes you dizzy just looking at it."

"Oh, that kind of blue." Ryan leaned over to Lanny, but said loud enough for Josh to hear, "He's got it ba-a-ad."

Josh threw a guitar pick at him.

A FEW HOURS LATER, they stood behind a tarp with Money Back Guaranteed's emblem on it. The crowd had spotted their silhouettes and was already raising the decibel intensity to an unhealthy level. Josh adjusted his guitar strap, looked over at Ryan and smiled. Though he had done this a hundred times, his heart still beat a little faster in anticipation. With a pop of pyrotechnics, the curtain before them dropped and they launched into their latest hit.

He scanned the auditorium. A full house. That would mean big money. But that didn't matter to him. People didn't understand it. They thought coming from such a poor background he'd be wild to spend his money. However, having done without, he didn't feel the need for a lot. It was this—the surge of the crowd, the shared pulse of the music in their veins—that made him come alive.

The song wrapped up with another wave of flames burning on the stage. He barely registered the searing heat. "Hey! You all sounded good on that! We are so glad to be back in San Diego tonight." He paused while the crowd cheered for their home city. "We actually got to sing the national anthem at the Padres game last night. Anybody catch that?" They were hanging on his every word. A girl waved frantically from the front row. "You did? And the Padres won, too." Another pause as people hooted over the victory. "I'm not saying we had anything to do with that," he looked at Ryan. "Did we, buddy?"

Ryan smiled. "It was pretty much us." They laughed.

"Are you sure? Because I was thinking it might have been their bullpen."

Ryan looked at the crowd and shrugged. "They might have helped some."

Josh laughed again. "Well, I'm thinking these folks didn't come here tonight for our baseball commentary." He tightened his strings. "Anybody ready for a little rock and roll?"

Thunderous applause accompanied his opening guitar riff. The music travelled from his fingertips, strumming some strings, through the wires, into the amplifiers, through the air to seep into the fans' blood and pump it full of adrenaline. His music was powerful, it moved people. Fans paid big money for tickets and looked forward to hearing them play all week, hoping to sneak a peek of them backstage after the concert. It was heady. On the stage he was rock star Josh Dunningham...or at least the image of Josh the record execs had helped him create.

He looked from face to face, smiling, making eye contact as he had been taught. But a feeling began to grow in the pit of his stomach. One that had been plaguing him lately. None of the thousands of surrounding faces were familiar. None filled him with the warmth he craved. In the end, it didn't matter. None of them knew the real him. He was just as alone as ever, even in a crowd with people shouting his name. On stage he might be able to forget that. But traveling from one venue to the next left him with too many free hours. Hours spent thinking about how empty he was.

THE MAN AT THE COUNTER grimaced at the line behind her, then glanced at Cassie. "I'm sorry, ma'am. There's really nothing we can do about the wind."

"I know," she snapped. "But I've got a concert ticket to see Money Back Guaranteed."

"I understand, there is simply—"

"Nothing you can do. I know. I know! You've been saying that for the last—" she checked her watch "—eight and a quarter hours." She gave a frustrated snort, blowing air up her face, no doubt messing up her bangs so they better matched the rest of her hair. She had been running her hands through it for the last two hours. She spun on her heel angrily, but stilled, taking a moment to conquer her irritation. She took a breath and came back to him.

"I'm sorry," she said, "I know this isn't your fault. I just...*really* wanted to be there."

"I understand," he called to her as she walked back to her seat. "I'm a huge Money Back Guaranteed fan, too." His fingers flew over his keyboard. "I can maybe get you in there by eleven. You might catch a song or two."

"Thanks," she said, flashing a smile. "I'd appreciate anything you can do."

CASSIE WAS RELIEVED when the security guard at the stadium recognized her name. "Yes, Ms. McCallister. Mr. Dunningham is expecting you." The young, muscular man let her through the line of screaming girls. "Ah-uh-uh, not you!" he shouted to a teen who tried to sneak in with her. "Get back!" He turned his head to look at Cassie even as he pushed the girl back behind the sawhorse. "I'm sorry I can't lead you," he yelled above the scream of the crowd.

"It's okay," she responded. "I'm sure I can find my way."

"It's straight down the hall inside the door. You really can't miss it." He smiled at her brightly, then turned back to snarl at the girl. "I said, cool it!"

Cassie headed down the long, narrow hallway. The stadium was quiet inside, juxtaposed with the furor outside, and she could hear her boots ringing as she walked. The hall started out concrete, but as she neared the back, turned into hardwood. She reached a wide-open spot with several doors in a backstage area. Just as she stopped to figure out what to do, a nearby door creaked open. Out stepped Lancaster Moon, the drummer for Money Back Guaranteed.

"Hello," she said with a smile. She must be close to Josh now.

"Well, hello, beautiful," he dripped seductively.

Not wanting to mislead him, she quickly asked. "Is Josh around?"

Lanny's eyes became sharp. "You must be Cassie," he simpered. "Josh told me all about you. Why don't you come into my room and make yourself at home, and I'll go find him for you? Backstage can be a dangerous place for an unattended lady." He smiled as he looked at her, but she could have sworn she heard an edge to his voice.

Lanny closed the door on her, rubbing his hands and going to search out the blonde he ran off earlier. He found her, as he suspected, still nosing around, looking for Josh.

"Hey, darlin'," he called out. "I think I found him for you."

CHAPTER EIGHT

Josh held out hope until a half-hour after the show. Then he gave up on her. She wasn't coming. He stood, leaning with hands on his dressing table where a half bottle of champagne rested in an ice bucket. But the bubbly had him feeling less than celebratory. He raised his eyes and looked at himself in the mirror. The misery reflected there suddenly enraged him. The bubbles from the champagne turned to popping lava inside.

With a howl he swept everything off the dresser and onto the floor with a crash. Not satisfied, his eyes roamed until he caught sight of one of the champagne flutes. He hefted the delicate glass, and quick as lightning, sent it flying across the room to explode against the far wall. With a snarl, he snatched a second flute, but, thinking better of it, he stuck his hand into the half-melted ice and withdrew the champagne bottle. He filled the flute, lifted it, and let the foamy liquid slither down his throat. Then he reared back and threw it, hitting the same spot on the wall with shattering satisfaction.

He stumbled around the dressing room, drinking straight from the oversized bottle. *What is my freakin' problem? So, she didn't come, so what?* But it hurt more than he liked to admit.

When someone knocked on the door, he was foolish enough to hope it was her. He jerked open the door and a woman with long, straight hair sprang into his arms.

"Oh, Josh. Josh! It's good to see you after so long."

He was surprised by how intimately her hands passed around him and over his backside. They squeezed flesh in a painful way he found at the time, welcome. Still, he grabbed her hands and disengaged them, stumbling back to peer into her face.

"Let me look at you," she squealed in a high-pitched voice. She brought her hands up, his hands still circling her wrists, and stroked his face. "You haven't changed a bit." She pulled his face down and kissed him, her tongue diving into his mouth.

He pulled back, gasping for air, unable to put together a coherent sentence.

Her eyes searched his, and a look of disappointment crossed her face. "You don't remember me, do you?"

Gulping, he shook his head.

"It's Angela. You remember me now?" She stepped close.

Desperately he tried to recall her face, or her name...Angela. He did know her now. She was the one regret he had. *Cassie may be my second,* he thought dolefully. Angela had come to him, like so many others, after a show. But, unlike the others, she was too young to understand he was only interested in her for a quick tumble; when he made it clear afterward, it broke her heart. He thought of her over the years, sorry he had hurt her.

"Angela. You look great." She had grown up and grown up well. Her face was clear, with a hint of freckles, and her long blond hair fell well beyond her shoulders. She had filled out considerably and packaged her body nicely in snug pants and a low-cut, bleached white blouse.

"Oom, baby. I've missed you." She pressed against him, backing him up several feet until his butt hit the dressing table. Caught off guard, he tried to resist her; but after a while, the soft lips, insistent tongue, and the swell of her breasts as she pushed against him were hard to oppose.

Cassie crossed his mind. He longed for her overpowering fragrance, made up, as it was, with the tantalizing mixture of sweet childhood memories and raw desire. He dreamt of the silky pleasure of her skin and the ball of fire she ignited within him every time their lips came in contact.

Damn her. Damn her for doing this to me.

His drunken hands groped the girl in front of him clumsily and found the sides of her blouse. With a burst of temper, he ripped it open, listening as buttons bounced everywhere on the hardwood floor. She gasped, then threw her hair back in triumph as she wedged herself more tightly between his open legs. She wore a lacy black pushup bra which did its job well. "Dammit," he said once, then buried his face in her bosom.

LANNY'S VOICE SOUNDED right outside the door.

"I think he's in here."

Some small part of his mind, which was, as yet, unaffected by the alcohol, registered the fact that the door had opened. He raised his head from the ample bounty in front of him and saw the wide-eyed shock on Cassie's pale face.

"Oh, shit!" he cried out, just as Cassie clapped a hand over her stomach and rushed out of the room. Pushing Angela aside, he hurried after her. Cassie's boots bit into the wood as she sped down the hall.

"Wait a minute." His breath coming hard, he let rage trade places with fear. "Wait one damned minute!"

Cassie had nearly reached the end of the hall when he caught up with her, grabbing her arm and whipping her around. The hurt in her eyes was like a dagger plunged into his chest. It was so strong it took the wind out of him for a second. Unable to bear the thought of what he did to her, he turned his self-loathing around, spewing it out on her.

"We didn't have a relationship—" he began defensively.

Pain seeped out of her face and was replaced with a white-hot fury. "You're right," she returned, her voice dead, "we didn't."

Never had he wanted so badly to undo something he'd done and felt the futility of it. In an effort to erase everything, he reached out to touch her face. His voice faltered. "Let me explain..."

She took a step backward. "No." Her voice raised in pitch and volume. "No. As you just said, you don't owe me an explanation. You don't owe me anything." She ripped her arm from his grip and stormed away, shaking her head.

Scrambling for something to say, he grasped at his earlier anger. "I thought you weren't coming. Maybe if you had been here—"

That stopped her in her tracks. She spun around, her blue eyes like twin blades. "Maybe if you called the airport," she said through clenched teeth, her voice deceptively low this time, "you would have found out all the flights were cancelled out of O'Hare due to high winds."

He had to say something to stop her from leaving. But he had lived so much of his life without emotion, the depth of his feelings for her mystified and alarmed him; he felt himself spiraling into ever deeper confusion. He didn't want this drama. Life was so much simpler before. His mouth seemed surreally disconnected from his brain. "I could have any girl, you know." So why was it he wanted *her* so badly?

The words were like a slap, and, if possible, she looked even more shocked and hurt. "You're right," she said finally, with a blandness he was sure she didn't feel. "You're right, of course, so go ahead." She turned, plodding now as if her feet were weighted with sandbags. "This was a mistake from the start." As she reached the exit door and banged the metal bar, she muttered on a half-sob, "I'm such an idiot."

He stood frozen to the spot as the door closed behind her and the sound of her heels on the concrete faded. The champagne rose in his throat, and he fought to swallow the gorge. Wild with emotion, his brain spun through thoughts of chasing after her and what he would say when he caught her, but jumbled in his mind also was the look of agony on her face, and that thought arrested him. He stood completely motionless, as powerless to go after her now as he was when she left him in Vegas. After a time, with no other recourse, he turned to head back into his room.

Lanny still stood outside his door. "Geez, man, I'm sorry," he said contritely, but even in his state, Josh caught the glint of amusement in his eye.

Sick bastard probably did it on purpose. But his brain couldn't handle one more thing, so he left it for the time being. He reentered his dressing room, closing the door on Lanny's smiling face.

Unbelievably, she was still there. He looked at the girl blankly. Angela walked over to him, taking long, slow strides, her pale eyes locked on his.

"Come on, baby," she cooed. "Whoever she was, let me help you forget about her." She knelt in front of him and leisurely unzipped his pants.

He watched her stupidly, his mind disconnected. Dammit, he deserved a good time as much as the next guy. And he needed to forget what just happened, needed it desperately. He shut his eyes and a teardrop squeezed out, rolling down his face, serving as a wakeup call of sorts. His mind focused in an instant, as if an internal windshield wiper cleared away all distractions.

"No," he said firmly, stepping back and jerking his pants closed. "Get out of here."

"Wh-what?" The girl seemed as shocked as Cassie had been, and that was another thing he didn't need on his conscience.

"You heard me, Angela. Get out of here."

She remained on her knees. "But Josh, you don't mean that."

"The hell I don't!" He yanked her to her feet.

Looking him in the eyes, she knelt again. "Josh, you're just upset." She reached for his belt buckle.

He backed away in a near panic. "Angela." He was bewildered by her persistence. "I'm sorry." He turned away from her, sickened by what he had done. "Please, just leave me alone."

Josh heard Angela struggle to her feet and thought he had at last gotten through to her. Then her arms again snaked around his waist.

"Angela!" He moved away from her and turned with his hands up in a defensive posture. "Please...just leave."

She picked up what remained of her blouse and with shaking hands, slipped it on. "I don't understand why you're so upset." Holding the front of her shirt closed with one hand, she tossed her hair back and sighed. "I'll give you some time. You'll come around eventually." Retreating from the room she murmured, "We'll be happy together." Then she closed the door.

CHAPTER NINE

Josh tossed another piece of sheet paper in the trash with a snarl. Weeks had passed since the incident in San Diego, and if he'd thought he was miserable after Las Vegas, when all he'd been doing was wanting her, he had known nothing about how bad miserable could get. Now, not only did he still want her, badly, he also was infuriated with himself for screwing up so royally and hurting her.

Ryan, sitting across the table from Josh, read a magazine. He glanced over at the growing pile of crumpled up sheet music near the trashcan. He raised an eyebrow. "Uhh...having difficulties?"

Josh angrily scribbled on a new sheet of paper with his pencil. "Other than this all sounding like crap, no. It's all so...lame. Meaningless dribble."

Ryan closed his magazine. "You told me once that music was only good if it came from the heart. What's in your heart, buddy?"

Lanny glanced up from the book he was reading across the room.

Josh sighed. "Confusion."

"Good. Go with that then." Ryan picked up his magazine.

"Write a song about confusion?"

"Yeah, maybe by the time you're finished, you won't be confused anymore."

Josh stared at the back of the *Rolling Stones* magazine his friend held. He sighed, staring out the window. Several minutes of silence passed, and then a noise slowly began to build as the pencil made scratches across the paper. Before long, Josh had filled up a page and reached for another.

The words came pouring out, spilling like his blood, onto the paper.

Ryan glanced over at Lanny and gave him a wink.

"COME ON, CASS, WHAT gives?"

"What do you mean?"

"You never call unless you're upset about something."

"Sarah," she said, pretending to be offended, "that's not true." She giggled. "Well, maybe it is."

"So, what is it this time?" her sister asked with pretend exasperation.

"It's nothing. I just wanted to talk to you. Can't a girl call her big sister without getting the third degree?"

"Absolutely not. Is that guy at work bothering you again?"

"Colin the Perv? No. He's actually dating someone in the office now. So, he only hits on me occasionally, when she's out of town."

"Okay, so it's not Colin the Perv...how's work?"

"Work is good. I just sold a major sportswear chain a slogan idea. The campaign should bring in about a quarter of a million dollars, and over time, the client should net us a whole lot more than that."

"So, it's not Colin the Perv, and it's not work. What's his name?"

"Whose name?" Cassie replied, feigning ignorance.

"The name of the guy who's got you tied up in knots."

Cassie couldn't resist. "Josh Dunningham."

"Well," she laughed, "every red-blooded female is in love with Josh Dunningham. You're going to have to do better than that."

Cassie paused, waiting for her sister to put two and two together. "You met Josh Dunningham?"

"Oh, I didn't just meet him. He licked salt off me."

"He...did you just say Josh Dunningham licked salt off you? You partied with Josh Dunningham? *The* Josh Dunningham?"

"Well, I'm not sure 'partying' is what you would call it."

"You've got about five seconds to explain."

Cassie plopped into an oversized living room chair, swinging her legs over one of the arms. "He came up to me at the bar in the casino—"

"When you went to Vegas?"

"Yes. This would probably go a lot quicker if you didn't interrupt me."

Cassie imagined her sister's pretty, chubby face twisted in a pout, her curly blond hair bobbing as she talked. "Okay. I'll be good. Tell me."

"We talked, and then we did a shot together. Only, instead of licking salt off his hand, he grabbed my arm and...licked it."

She couldn't continue because Sarah was hooting on the other end. She could hear her calling to her husband, "Brad. Brad! Come here. It's Cassie. Josh Dunningham, of Money Back Guaranteed, licked her. My sister's banging a rock star!" She spoke into the receiver again. "I've never been prouder of you."

Cassie heard her conservative brother-in-law's distant reply. "Whoa! Whoa! Too much information. The kids are just outside."

"Ohh, they can't hear me, you poop-head."

She could hear the smile in Brad's voice. "And I definitely don't need to hear about who your sister is taking to bed."

"I didn't go to bed with him. Well, I did, technically, go to his bed, but I didn't...you know."

"Why didn't you 'you know?' I sure the hell would have 'you knowed' with Josh Freakin' Dunningham! Ouch! Brad punched me."

"Well, I wanted to 'you know,' I just...couldn't."

"Ahh. Thus, your dilemma."

"Thus, my dilemma."

"Hmm." When she didn't continue Sarah probed. "What's he like? You know I live my life vicariously through you," her sister whispered conspiratorially.

"Ohh," she sighed. "He's even more of a hunk in person—"

"No way."

"The mind of man hasn't yet discovered a way to capture the green of those eyes...and his bod was *s-o-o-o incredibly hot*."

"You're killing me here, you know."

"Dynamite arms, spectacular pecs, and the abs of a god. A finer six-pack I have never seen."

"Shit. The closest thing I get to a six-pack around here is what Brad has got chillin' in the back of the fridge. Ouch! Just kidding, honey. I didn't know he was still listening. Okay, so let me get this straight...he licked you, you went to his bed, but you didn't 'you know.'"

"That's it in a nutshell."

"Why the hell not, Cass? Are you crazy?"

"Maybe." Cassie's heart squeezed again, and her breath hitched. She tried to rein in her feelings before her sister caught on.

"And you haven't seen him since." Sarah's voice was softly compassionate.

"I wish I could say that."

"You saw him again?"

She nodded, even though her sister couldn't see her over the phone. "He sent me a plane ticket—" A small sob escaped.

"What happened?" Sarah prodded.

"I walked in on...Josh and another girl." The tears were flowing now.

"Maybe you misconstrued—"

"Can you misconstrue a man's hand on a half-naked girl's ass while she's got her hands all over his crotch and his head is buried in her enormous boobs?"

"It's pretty hard to," her sister admitted.

"Then I didn't misconstrue anything. And to top it all off, I've got to go into the office every day and watch a ten-foot-tall version of Josh outside my window."

"Huh?"

Cassie pulled a tissue out of the box on the end table and dabbed at her eyes. "Some radio station's got a ginormous banner hanging right outside my damn office and I have to look at those eyes every morning."

There was another pause while Sarah seemed to absorb the information, allowing Cassie to collect herself. "So, what did you do? When you walked in on them and all?"

"Well, I turned around and walked out. And then he came after me...and blamed me."

"Blamed you? What the hell for?"

"I don't know. My memory of that part is a little blurry. I think I was in shock or something...I remember he said he could have any girl he wanted, and I said, 'go ahead then.'"

"Well, good for you. What an asshole!"

"Yeah...I guess."

"You *guess*?"

"It's just...I know this sounds crazy...but I can't stop thinking about it. All of it. The girl with the silicone boobs—"

"You're sure they were silicone?"

"No, but I like to think of them that way. And the way Josh kissed me."

"That good, huh?"

"It was like the doctor yelled 'clear,' and I didn't have the good sense to get away from the metal table."

"Shit," Sarah breathed appreciatively.

"Yeah, shit."

"Well, honey...I'm so sorry you're going through this. Especially after all you went through with Troy."

"Yeah. I sure can pick 'em, can't I?" She blew her nose.

"I wish I could be there to take you out and get you trashed."

"That's okay. That turned pretty ugly the last time." She smiled, remembering how she and her sister got hammered, and then stumbled home to her irate husband, who had been up for several hours with a screaming baby.

"Yeah. I'm not sure if I'm even out of the doghouse for that one yet."

"Well, now I've had my little sobfest, I think I'll take my wine upstairs and have a nice long bath."

"You do that, girlfriend. Brad." Cassie heard her chuckle. "Brad!" She giggled again. "Stop that! Ohh, my."

Cassie smiled, despite not knowing exactly what was going on at the other end of the line. "What's he doing?"

"*Brad!*" Sarah sounded happily shocked. "You save that for later, mister. He's trying to convince me he's just as good as any rock star...mmm."

"O-o-okay. I'm hanging up now. You two are weird, you know?" she said fondly.

"So, you keep telling us."

"Thanks, sis. I feel better. I knew you would help."

"Glad to be of service, Termite," she replied, using her childhood nickname.

"Good night." Cassie put the receiver down softly, thanking God for a sister who listened, and ambled upstairs to fill her tub.

CHAPTER TEN

Josh sat in an empty auditorium, strumming his guitar. Ryan walked up from behind him.

"Sounds like it's really coming along. Can I hear it yet?"

He nodded silently and Ryan drew up a chair. Josh began singing with the smoky voice which had made them all rich. He started tentatively, but after a while, he became lost in the song. He closed his eyes from time to time and rarely glanced at his notes; the music came from deep inside him.

Before I met you, life was so simple
I knew all the rules of the game.
But now I met you, nothing is simple
And thoughts of you drive me insane.
Before I saw you, from across the room
I had all the moves down pat.
But now it's you who moves me, without even trying,
And everything I do leaves me flat.
What are you doing to my heart?
You came along and gave it a start,
But I liked when it was dead,
Stop playing games with my head.
Don't just move me, then leave me alone, leave me here all alone.
Now I sit all alone in my room,
Having sent yet another girl away.
I was happy before you came,
All right...maybe things just were okay.
But now their kisses leave me hollow,
Making me feel less than shallow,
Making the emptiness grow inside,

You made the light shine, so I no longer have a place to hide.
It pisses me off you think you know who I am,
And pisses me off more that you're right.
I've been the one to move people all these years.
Now I'm a fighter without any fight.
Don't just move me, then leave me alone, leave me here all alone.
But I don't need this, whatever it is,
Geez, what the hell kind of perfume do you wear?
I don't need this thinking of you,
When your scent doesn't hang in the air.
Dammit, life was so simple, life was so pleasant
Before you walked into my sight
Yeah, life was so simple, life was so pleasant
Only I never knew I had no life.
Don't just move me then leave me alone, leave me here all alone.
Don't just move me then leave me alone, leave me here all alone.

He stared off into space as the last note hung in the air. After a second or two, he started a little, like he was waking from a dream. He looked over at Ryan, who sat absolutely still. Slowly, a grin spread over Josh's face. "So...what do you think?"

"What do I think?" He cleared his throat. "I think that was friggin' awesome, man! It was...unbelievable. The lyrics and the music flowed together seamlessly. It is easily better than anything you have ever written before."

"Really? I'm still not happy with the series of chords right after the chorus." He picked up his notes and a pencil.

"No! Don't change it! Don't change anything. It's perfect."

Josh smiled, his first genuine smile in weeks. "Thanks, man." He didn't know what else to say. He chuckled. "I forgot you were there for a minute."

"But she was there. She was there in every note. You need to go see her."

His eyes darted to Ryan's face. Neither of them had spoken her name, but he knew what his friend was saying.

"I want to. If only to apologize. To try to make it up to her somehow. Oh man," he said, slamming his guitar case shut. "I really screwed things up this time. I mean, I know she'll never consider...anything...with me again, but I'd really like for her to know I'm sorry."

"So, go. We've got a two-day break in the schedule after tonight. Go to her."

CASSIE WAS NEARING home after her date with Kevin. He was a dark-haired, good-looking banker who had caught her off-guard when he asked her out one morning after church; she'd had no plausible excuses ready and had regretted giving in to him ever since. She was quiet, considering all of the ways she could get out of the dreaded kiss goodnight. Simply put, no sparks flew between her and Kevin. He was a nice guy and all, but...

He swung his black Mercedes sedan into her driveway confidently, having missed or ignored all of the signals she had sent him throughout the evening.

"Oh, no," she breathed in a choked voice, the blood draining from her face.

Kevin followed her gaze. The tall figure, sitting in the glider on her front porch with his long legs stretched out in front of him, eyed them intently. "Is that...?"

"Yes," she answered flatly.

His voice cracked. "He's in some rock band, right?"

"Yes."

Although Kevin had been obtuse about Cassie's feelings toward him during the course of the evening, he seemed able to read the shocked and horrified expression on her face. "You two got some kind of history?"

Cassie swallowed and managed a nod. Kevin got out, staring coolly at Josh as he walked around the car to open her door. She sat frozen in her seat, her gaze glued on the figure who was now slowly unfolding himself from the wrought-iron seat. Kevin offered his hand to her, and despite being distracted by their unexpected guest, she caught him admiring her legs as she swung them out onto the driveway.

Josh, too, was finding it hard to take his eyes from her as she exited the car. She was wearing a simply cut, sleeveless black dress that came up high on her neck and flared out from her waist. The black, delicate high heels which now hit the pavement made him feel like a frog that just saw a fly and he resisted the urge to check if his tongue needed to be tucked back into his mouth. Her short hair was somehow scooped up and secured in the back, revealing the graceful and tempting curve of her neck.

The joker with the Mercedes slipped her hand into the crook of his elbow, patting it possessively. The hair on Josh's arms stood up. That had been him patting her hand once. Her soft hand that fit perfectly in his. It should be him now, not Mercedes Man. Without words of any kind the guy was still speaking in Male, signaling his ownership of Cassie loud and clear. He bent down to speak to her in a low tone as they strolled up the sidewalk, but Josh could hear him. "You want me to stay? I don't like this guy. Didn't he write that stalker song?"

This, at least, made Cassie smile. "Yes, Kevin, but it's okay. I can handle him."

When he whispered to her and she smiled, Josh's hands clenched at his sides, and he said a silent prayer he wouldn't punch the guy unless openly provoked. But the next second, he decided the way the loser was stroking Cassie's hand was provocation enough.

Kevin and Cassie reached the front porch and stopped, the tension between all parties like hitting a stone wall.

Josh jammed his hands into his pockets and inclined his head toward Kevin. "Who's this?" he growled. His eyes bore into Kevin's, then shifted slightly to Cassie.

She gripped the guy's arm, wetting her lips. "He's a friend from church," she stammered.

"Did you do this to get back at me?" He knew it made no sense, but his swirling jealousy was befuddling him.

Cassie's jaw dropped for a second. "Are you kidding? I had no idea you would be here tonight."

"Yeah. Maybe you should just go," Kevin added.

Josh took a step and Cassie whirled around to her date. "Kevin, thank you for a wonderful evening, but I think Josh and I need to talk. I'll call you later." As she gave him a staid peck on the cheek Josh took another step forward. She disengaged her arm from Kevin's and fumbled in her purse for her key. She moved to open the door, while both men stood locked into position, glaring at each other.

After a few seconds, Kevin muttered, "If you should need *anything*, call me."

"I will, thanks."

He turned his back on Josh, sticking his hands in his pockets and whistling as he strolled down the sidewalk back to his car.

Her date's show of bravado seemed to amuse her. Cassie smiled. But catching Josh's death stare, the smile dimmed. She went inside, leaving the door open behind her. Josh whistled loudly in retribution, giving Kevin a huge smile as he ducked inside her doorway, the message unambiguous; *he* was the one who was going home with the girl.

He followed Cassie into the kitchen, where she dropped her keys on the wooden table with a clank. She grasped the top of a chair pulled up to the table, keeping her back to him.

"Why did you come here?" she breathed.

His answer died on his lips as she turned around. The agony in her eyes was visible; agony he had put there.

Before he could invent an answer for her, she asked, "How did you find me?"

"Well, unbelievably there are only three other Cassandra McCallisters in the phone book, one of whom has a pretty powerful right hook."

By the oven light she must have been able to make out some of the faint bruising around his eye. "Oh." She stepped forward and tenderly felt his face.

Her light touch made his body sigh in response. Glancing up and catching his gaze, she tried to remove her hand, but he caught her wrist. They stood like that for several silent seconds, gazing into each other's eyes. Her arm trembled and tears came to her eyes. He couldn't stand to see the pain reflected there, so he let her go. She rubbed her arm as if his contact had seared her, reminding him of the time he licked her and she did the same thing. She turned away from him.

"If you're here to relieve your guilt, you can go. I'm fine."

Yeah. I can see that. "I'm here..." he said, laboring with his words, "...because I want..." He was frustrated; the verbal skills he made his living from had suddenly become so elusive he couldn't seem to string two words together. "...you."

She spun around, suddenly furious. "You know why you're into me?"

"No, pray tell, inform me."

"It's the thrill of the chase. I should just sleep with you and get it over with. Then we could both go our separate ways."

"Something we agree on." And before she could react, he closed the distance between them, sweeping her into his arms. His lips came down firmly, demandingly on hers, crushing them with their need. He felt her tension melt, and he thought, "Finally, something I can do right." But then her tears fell on his face.

"Josh...please, don't," she begged between kisses. "Josh...*please*!"

Aggravated, he released her, stepping back and rubbing a hand over his face. When he looked up she clutched her arms, shaking uncontrollably. He just wanted to hold her, soothe her, make her understand he didn't want to hurt her anymore. But his touch seemed anything but soothing for her.

The phone rang, and they both looked at it as if an alien just popped out of it. She lunged for the receiver then caught her breath before speaking.

"Hello?" She jerkily wiped tears, turning so her back was to Josh. "I'm fine, Kevin, really."

At the sound of the name, Josh's muscles tightened.

Cassie listened for a second, then glanced at Josh. "Okay." She walked out of the kitchen and into the front hall.

Following her, Josh saw the black Mercedes out the window, still parked in the driveway. "He's still here." He exploded, racing to his right and grabbing the front door handle.

"No!" Cassie screamed, dropping the phone and diving in front of him to press her back against the door. "Josh. Don't do this."

"Cassie," he rumbled. "He deserves a beating."

"*Please*!"

He let out a huff of air. "All right. But make him go away."

"I will. I will," she promised. Keeping her eyes on him, she moved over to scoop the receiver up off the floor.

"Kevin, I'm sorry, I dropped the phone. I'm fine, I swear. We're just going to talk, and then he is going to leave." She looked at him pointedly, then stepped to the window, pulling back the filmy curtains to look out as she finished talking. "But I think it would be best if you left. I will. Thanks. Goodnight." Josh crossed to watch over her shoulder as the sleek sedan pulled away. "Happy now?"

"Thrilled." Although their bodies weren't touching, her heat and her scent besieged him, making him lightheaded. Just as he was about to give into the urge to bend his head and taste her neck, she moved away, skirting him in a wide circle. But as she passed him, he made a quick move, throwing his arm out to stop her and then stepping forward. She had no choice but to back up, and when he took another step forward, he had her effectively pinned against the opposite wall.

Her frightened eyes flew up to his, her lips parted with a small gasp. He smiled down at her lazily, bringing his other arm up to surround her. "What were you saying..." He bent down to nip along her neck even as she brought her arms up to brace them against his chest. "...about how I was to get you out of my system?"

She turned her head to the side, struggling against him. "Josh, don't." But her breath quickened, and her chest rose and fell beneath him as he pressed against her. Once again, the scent of honeysuckle was intoxicating and he brought one hand down to her waist, sliding it to the small of her back and pulling her in roughly so their pelvises were pushed together in a rage of heat.

"Cassie..."

"I want you to leave. You need to leave." And then she quit fighting. Her hands flew to the side of his face, guiding his lips to hers.

He felt the tiny prick of her nails on his face, and then her warm mouth, enveloping him in its sweetness. He put both his hands around her waist and lifted her slightly off her feet as she threw her arms around his neck. "Josh...oh, Josh..." Her moan ripped through him like a bullet, and he set her down, only to readjust so he could sweep her off her feet entirely and into his arms.

"Where's your bedroom?" he asked in a husky voice his vision shaded with lust.

"U-upstairs," she answered breathlessly, and before she could say anything else, he claimed her lips again, his kisses hard, insistent, his tongue commanding. One of her hands stroked his face, then his neck, sliding finally underneath his shirt, running along his shoulders.

He managed the stairs with astounding speed, guessed the correct door at the top, and pushed it open with her feet till it banged into the wall. He dimly registered a big, dark wood, elaborately-carved antique bed with some sort of light-colored cover as he threw her, with a bounce, onto the mattress. He tore through the buttons on his shirt, undoing the cuffs so he could whip it off. She sat up on her elbows, watching him with wide eyes, her lips moist and red, her face flushed. He put one knee onto the bed next to her, then swung his other leg over her, straddling her hips. He gripped her waist with both hands, and then his hands glided up until he was caressing her breasts with an urgency they both seemed to feel.

He fell across her, his tongue and teeth finding the flesh of her neck as she murmured something incomprehensible in his ear. With a rush, he flipped her over, so she now rose above him, her pelvis pressed against his in sweet pain.

Her hands reached up to search her hair for pins, which she flung across the room, and shook her hair out, turning him on all the more. He watched her steadily, holding himself in when he wanted to explode. Without warning, he sat up, running his hands up her back feverishly.

It was to be like this. Little fitful starts. Taking, then holding back, then taking more. He gained control of his unremitting desire for her again, pulling back to look her in the eyes as his hands painstakingly made their way up her back to her zipper, pulling it down inch by subtle inch. He saw just a hint of unease as he let the dress fall to her hips. He sucked in his breath as he looked at her, falling back against the pillows. Man, did God know what He was doing when he made this woman.

Her breasts heaved in the smooth, black bra which was cut low over the swell of her bosom, held in the middle by laces tied in a bow. A diamond-shaped ebony pendant hung between her breasts, and he sent it swinging with a small flick, fascinated by the way it looked against her pale skin. He reached up, first exploring her through the material. Then he peered up into her bottomless blue eyes and brought his fingers to the delicate bow cinching the bra closed. He looked down again, a smile sliding across his face as he tugged until the bow released, then let go of the silky cord so it fell between her curves.

He rubbed the back of his fingers against the inside of her breasts, glancing up again, pleased to see her nibbling on her lip, obviously as turned on as he was. He sat up again, kissed above the laces, then let his tongue dart in between the diamond-shaped openings they created. With a moan, she brought her hand to the back of his head, as if to hold him there, but he had no intention of venturing elsewhere at the moment. He brought his hands up, grasping either side of the material held together by the laces, and abruptly jerked it apart. His tongue began to work lower, where he had now exposed more flesh.

She gave a shuddering breath, closing her eyes and giving into the heat cloaking her. His tongue, his mouth, his hands, his body, hot, beneath her...they were in total control of her now...even the rough hair of his face as it brushed against her skin was highly erotic. He pulled the fabric a little farther apart, revealing her nipples, and his tongue raced to follow what his hands found, circling the sensitive skin with the tip of his tongue, then taking her into his mouth forcefully, his teeth sinking into her flesh.

The juxtaposition of the gentle teasing tongue and the savage feel of his teeth sent her spinning into orbit. He brought the flat of his tongue underneath her nipple, pushing, working the flesh with his mouth and the blood left her head in a whoosh.

She was glad his hands were now supporting her as they grasped her sides. Wanting more of him, but needing to undo all barriers between them, she urged him back against the pillows. Straightening her back to rise above him, she brought her hands behind her to the clasp of her bra, now barely on. She smiled as she shrugged it off. He lifted his upper body and reached to touch her, but before his hands could fly over her flesh, she pushed him back down again.

He looked up at her, confused, but she smiled. She was taking control now. *That's all right with me,* he thought with a sigh of contentment. Holding his gaze, she crossed her hands over her chest, rubbing her arms lazily. Still watching him with a self-satisfied smile, she glided her hands down her smooth skin and over her hips where they disappeared under the fabric of her dress.

He was certain drool was pooling on the pillow, but he continued to lie still and watch the show. She sat up on her knees, shimmying out of her dress and backing up to bring her hands to his belt. He made a move to help her, but she pushed his hands out of the way. *Yes, you are in control of me...only you.* He had never felt so awake before, aware of the smell of the sheets, the feel of her nails scraping against his abdomen as she worked at the belt, the beating of his own heart. Being with her was unlike anything he ever experienced before, so intense, capturing every aspect of him, his body, his mind, his heart, his soul, all of him. With a startling slap of leather, she released the belt. Bending low over him, her nipples grazing his chest, she ran her tongue over his abdomen while her skilled fingers worked at the button of his jeans. Making a mental note to buy jeans with a snap next time, he groaned, hoping she would finish before he was finished. She pulled the zipper down, and her hands slid inside, over his black cotton boxers, feeling how hard and edgy his desire was now.

Then, in a flash, he flipped her onto the bed so he could take control now, so he could conquer her. He found his conquest willing. He peeled off his jeans and boxers, but when he was finally inside of her, they stilled, enjoying the sensation of their coupling, of becoming one. The tension lessened for a moment. He spread his fingers, watching as he laid his hand on hers on the pillow, palm to palm. He looked into her eyes and they laced their fingers. They began to move in tandem, his hips diving to meet hers, hers rising to meet his. Their hands clenched together on the pillows, squeezing with each thrust. He fought dual urges. One to prolong the moment, make it last forever. The other, impatience for the sweet release he knew lay ahead. Sweat slicked their bodies, removing all friction as they slipped smoothly along each other, again and again. She moaned his name in quick succession, louder and higher, and clutched his back to bring him deeper into her. He rose on extended arms as he answered her calls and they came together in one final, blinding, shuddering thrust, falling together in a mass, quivering every few seconds as small aftershocks wracked their systems.

Twilight had descended as they made love, and the room was now bathed in shadows. At last, he took a deep breath and moved to her side, sighing over the loss of their extremely intimate connection. He fell against the pillows, spent, and wrapped her in his arms, fuller of bliss than he had ever been in his entire existence. "Cassie..."

She pressed a sharp fingernail to his lip. "Sh-shh. Please, don't say anything." He tried to decipher the emotion he heard in her voice but settled for pulling her closer and shutting his eyes. Full of contentment, he fell asleep.

Around dawn, Josh woke up to empty arms. He got up and searched for Cassie, calling her name. With a growing dread, he returned to the bedroom, switching on the light. When his eyes adjusted to the blinding glow, he saw what he feared. A note propped against her pillow. She was nothing if not consistent. He walked over and with trepidation pulled the rose-colored page off the bed.

Now you've had me, you're free.

I hope I never think of you again.

Even with sleep-sealed eyes he could tell the paper was made wet by her tears.

CHAPTER ELEVEN

Cassie sat with her head resting on her desk. Her office door was locked to keep out the night cleaning crew. She'd allowed herself to cry for hours before slipping off to sleep.

His face drifted in and out of her dreams. Troy Leary. Father Troy Leary, now. They'd fallen in love when she was eighteen, became engaged when she was twenty. He was everything she dreamed of as a girl, handsome, kind, considerate. He respected her desire to wait to make love until after they were married and never forced the issue. He was the perfect man for her. He proposed to her on one knee underneath the cherry tree in his parents' back yard. She'd said yes without hesitation.

Wedding planning became a happy whirlwind of choosing dresses, flowers and bridesmaids. They'd spent every night together making plans for their future.

Then, one day, it all changed.

They were out horseback riding all afternoon at Troy's. He was from the Leary family which had, at one time, owned *The Boston Sentinel* and now owned most of downtown Boston. Their estate had stables, along with a pool and tennis courts. Troy told the grooms to go home to their families, promising not to put the horses up wet when they returned from their ride.

They stopped in a meadow for a late afternoon picnic and Cassie spread out on a quilt in the fading warmth of the afternoon sun. She was relaxed from a glass of wine, the first she'd ever had. Troy, two years her senior, leaned over her, his sandy-brown hair falling forward as he fed her strawberries. She giggled as the juice ran down her cheek and he bent to kiss it off her.

"Troy," she said coyly. "I want to tell you a secret."

He smiled. "You're tipsy."

"I'm not."

"Yes, you are. But it's cute." He pressed another fat, ripe strawberry to her lips. She laughed and nipped at it.

"I..." she said lazily, tracing the outline of his aristocratic lips with a fingertip, "am wearing the bra I will be wearing when we become man and wife."

"Really?" he said, laughing, and pulled down on the top of her sundress to get a peek.

"Nuh-uh-uh," she said, slapping his hand. He kissed her, pressing her into the soft grass. A whinny startled them, and he turned just as his horse nudged him.

He laughed. "I guess Tracer is trying to tell us something." He patted the old horse's nose. "I suppose you're hungry, too, eh, pal?" He stood and helped her to her feet. "It's probably for the best anyway. The sun is going down pretty fast now."

They packed their things and headed back to the stables, urging their horses to a gallop on the last part of the trail. She edged him out at the last turn, having cut corners to pass him.

"You cheated," he called, swinging down from his horse as soon as it came to a stop and running over to her. Laughing, she dismounted, sliding down into his arms. He kissed her, giving the horse a slap on the rump to get him to move along so he could do it properly.

"Uhh. We promised to rub them down."

"All right." He sighed. "Slavedriver," he mumbled good-naturedly. He grabbed the horses' reins and led them into the stables. She followed, watching him as his big hands expertly brushed the horses and made sure they were watered and fed before closing their stall doors. He grabbed her up in his arms again.

She fought him off. "You smell horsey."

"Well, you smell like a little piece of heaven." He nuzzled her ear. "So when are you going to show me that bra?" He raised an eyebrow.

Emboldened by the wine, she stood back and put a hand to the top of her white sundress. It had multicolored polka dots and oversized buttons from top to bottom. She teasingly undid the top button. Their gazes met, and suddenly they weren't joking around anymore. She froze.

Troy's eyes shone in the fading light. "Come here." His voice was thick.

He took her arm and led her into a clean stall, the sweet smell of hay surrounding them. The door closed behind with a soft click.

"Troy..."

"Come on, Cass. We're going to be married in a couple of months. Maybe it would be a good idea to see if we're...you know...compatible."

"I know we're compatible. You get my heart racing every time we kiss."

"You do the same for me." He stepped close to her and rubbed her bare arms. "I want you to do more for me now." His mouth came down swift and hard. She pulled away, studying him a moment before kneeling in the hay. He knelt before her but then popped up. "Wait." He left and came back with a clean horse blanket, spreading it out on the hay. "It might be scratchy." He laid her back.

She dropped her gaze, rubbing his arm. "It's my first time, you know."

"Well, don't tell anyone because it will go against my manhood, but it's my first time, too. I've never wanted to be with anyone other than you."

"And you want to now?"

He nodded so vigorously it made her laugh. "Very much so. But I can wait, if you want me to."

In answer, she reached for the sides of his face and pulled him to her. What started out tender, quickly became turbulent, a desperate need to share themselves in total. Afterward, they lay in the hay, the blanket wrapped around them. In the quiet he stroked her arm.

After a while, she worked up the courage to speak. "You're quiet. Do you regret what we did?"

"No," he said softly. Several long moments lapsed.

"Was I not...everything you hoped for?"

He sat up on one elbow. "Oh, no, honey. No! You were more beautiful than I ever dreamed of. It's only...I *have* dreamed of this moment, of making love to you, for years now. I wanted it to be...soft, tender." He sat up and began tearing up a piece of straw. "I was like a savage." He sounded disgusted with himself.

"You were just passionate." She stroked his hair, savoring the messiness of it. "I loved it."

"You did?"

"Yes." She gave him a tender kiss. "I did."

"Next time I won't be such a...beast. I promise."

She kept a hand on the side of his face. "Next time it will be just as magical as this time was." She smiled and kissed him and thought their life together would be perfect bliss.

But after their night in the stables, several weeks passed. He made excuses not to see her. Finally, almost frantic, she went to his house unannounced. His mom answered the door. "Why, my dear, how good to see you." Her voice was cool. She had never approved of their relationship. Cassie's parents were entirely too middle class for her. "Troy will be down in a moment." She swept off, leaving her to find a seat in the drawing room. She sat, wringing her hands. Something was wrong. Troy entered, looking a little pale.

"Do you want to take a walk?"

"Sure." She beamed up at him. It felt good to see him after so much time, but he only gave her a weak smile in return, his gaze darting away from her. They strolled out to the same meadow they had picnicked at, the last time they were together. She made small talk that was met with silence. She leaned against a tree and watched him as he picked up a blade of grass and slid his fingers back and forth over its edges.

"I don't quite know how to say this."

"That's never a good way to start a conversation."

He tried again. "Cassie, you're the only woman I have ever loved. The only woman I will ever love."

"Now, that's better," she responded playfully. Smiling, she clasped him around the neck.

He deftly removed her hands and brought them down to hold in front of him. "But I can't marry you. Last week...I joined the seminary. I know I should have told you this myself, instead of you having to come over here and find out like this. But I didn't think I was ready yet."

She took a step backward, stunned, wrapping her arms around herself. The sun poured over his shoulders, making him a silhouette. The light hurt her eyes and she blinked. "I...I...don't understand."

"I'm not the man I want to be when I'm around you."

The tears rolled down her face. "This is your mother."

He shook his head. "She had nothing to do with this. Well, very little."

"But...you said you love me."

"I do love you. Maybe too much."

"You're not making sense. I love you; you say you love me...we're planning to spend the rest of our lives together—"

"Well, plans change, Cass."

Her head whirled. She had her dress. Invitations had been sent out. Flowers were ordered. Not to mention the fact she was head-over-heels in love with him, and she thought, he with her. Not knowing what to say, she took a step forward and tried to take his hands, but he retreated as if he couldn't bear to touch her.

He turned his back. "Dammit, Cassie! I nearly ripped your clothes off in that stable."

"We were simply...sharing each other. It was an act of love. Love that strong breeds passion, but that doesn't make it wrong."

He turned back to look at her, his eyes sad. "I can't be that person. So out of control."

Her head ached. There had to be a way to fix this. "But maybe we can change things. I can change."

He stroked her cheek. "That would be wrong, too. I wouldn't want you to change who you are." She closed her eyes and leaned her head into his hand, the hand of the man who once brought her so much comfort, so much happiness. "I can't do this. I'm sorry." He bowled past her, marching across the meadow and never looking back.

She turned and called after him. "Troy, *please*! I love you. Don't do this to us!"

It hurt. More than she thought possible. And it still hurt. She didn't intend to let anything like that happen again. It was good she'd sent Josh away. Surely it would have hurt more later, although she couldn't fathom how. She needed to quit while she still had a chance of getting out intact.

The phone rang and she jumped, bumping her legs on the underside of the desk.

"Ms. McCallister, I wasn't sure you were in. Dave Collins is on line five."

"Thank you, Denise." And the world went on. She cleared her throat and picked up the receiver.

CHAPTER TWELVE

Josh sat on the glider on Cassie's front porch. He had watched the sun come up, but not with the joy such things usually brought.

It was quiet on Cassie's street; he couldn't remember the last time he'd sat in the stillness of a new morning. He heard only the faint sound of the distant highway, the morning chorus of the birds, and the occasional jogger or dog-walker, saying "good morning." People were friendly—would smile and wave—but not disturb him. It was very unlike his usual encounters with the general public. No one pawing him, asking for his autograph, bathing him with compliments. He was just one of the crowd, and he loved it. It lifted his spirits enough to make him believe if he could only show Cassie their relationship meant more to him than any he'd ever had, maybe she would come around.

His feet were stretched out in front of him, hands behind his head as he closed his eyes and debated his course of action. He wasn't sure how to show her he cared about her. He had spent years only thinking about himself. His parents had never really shown him how to love others. The closest thing he had to a real relationship was his friendship with Ryan.

"Well, I'll be damned."

Josh jumped, not having heard anyone approach. Standing in front of him was the redhead from Vegas in silky, hot-pink jogging shorts and a skimpy sports bra. He was glad, at the moment, to see a familiar face.

"What the hell are you doing here?"

Or so he thought. "Heather, isn't it?" She nodded tersely. It was clear she was not about to give in to any of his charm. He decided to be frank. "I came to see Cassie because I couldn't stop thinking about her."

Her face seemed to soften a little bit. "Is she here?"

"Not anymore."

Heather hesitated, seeming to size him up. She sighed, slapping his leg. "Scoot over."

Grateful, Josh sat up and made room for her on the glider. Without all the makeup on he could see she was actually quite pretty.

"So, I'm getting the feeling there's trouble in Paradise."

He grimaced. "I'd say that's a pretty accurate assessment."

"Well, you're going to need to be patient with our gal. After what she's been through with Troy and all, it's no wonder she's a little gun-shy."

He stared at her.

"She didn't tell you about Troy?" She began to rise from her seat, a panicked look on her face. "Okay, I've said way too much."

He put a restraining hand on her arm. "No, please, wait. Tell me about Troy."

She sat back down reluctantly. "Don't you two ever talk?"

He laughed, feeling sheepish. "To be truthful, when we're together, there's not a lot of talking going on."

"As I suspected."

He rubbed his palms along his jeans. "Most of the communication I get from Cassie is in the form of notes she leaves me when she runs out on me. Like this one." He withdrew the rose-colored paper from his pocket and handed it to her.

"Oooh. Ouch." Heather looked him in the eyes. "You know she's hurting, right?"

"I get that. I just don't know why. I guess I didn't help things much when she came to see me in San Diego."

"No. You sure the hell didn't."

He dropped his head. "She told you about that, huh? I thought when she didn't show up, she decided she didn't want to see me again. And...I got drunk, and this girl basically threw herself at me, and..." He sprang up and strode several feet away, agitated, then came back, sitting down and running his hand through his hair. "No, I shouldn't make any excuses, I was an ass. But I'm sorry about it, I swear."

She studied him. "Okay. I believe you. But a thing like that takes a lot out of a girl's self-esteem. And to *see* you with another woman, in the middle—"

"I know. I know!" He shook his head. "Do you think I have a chance?"

Heather glanced down at the paper in her lap. "I take it from the note you two...were together last night?" she asked, with a rare sense of tact.

He nodded.

"Listen, I probably shouldn't tell you this, but...you're the first man she's let into her bedroom since Troy. That's got to count for something." She patted his knee, handing him the page as she rose.

He thought about what she'd said for a moment, then sprung up. "But you didn't tell me about what happened with Troy," he yelled as she started to jog away.

"That's something you'll have to discuss with her." She jogged in place, her breasts bouncing wildly. "Of course you'll have to stop boinging each other long enough to have an actual conversation."

He grinned at her as he leaned against the porch rail. "I'm not making any promises."

She gave him a wide smile then jogged off, only to make a circle and come back. "Be patient with her, Josh. She's worth the wait."

"I figured that out. Besides, she doesn't give me much of a choice. I'm pretty crazy about her."

"That's my boy," she called out. She waved over her shoulder and took off up the street.

CASSIE PULLED INTO her garage, shut off the engine, and laid her head down on the steering wheel. Her half-hour commute had turned into a two-hour commute from hell, due to the owners of a pair of stylish BeeMers, both thought they had the right of way. The ensuing accident created the mother of all traffic snarls. She was sweaty from being stuck in the car for so long, on what just happened to be the hottest day of the summer so far. On top of that, she was tired from her night of sleeping on her desk, not having enjoyed waking up with a pencil stuck to her forehead.

Opening the door to the house, she stumbled in, carrying her portfolio and wishing she were eating something other than a frozen meal tonight. Was her hunger spurring on her imagination, or did it smell like...Italian? A loud noise startled her, and then some mumbled cuss words. Someone was in her house. Before she could flee, a tall figure came around the corner.

"Aaaahhh!"

"Oh, geez." Josh set two glasses of wine on the front hall table, spilling some on his hand. "I'm sorry, Cass."

"Oh, my gosh. You scared me." Her hand over her heart, she tried to bring her breathing back to normal. He took her by the shoulders, and steered her into the living room, into the oversized chair.

"Here, let me take your things for you."

Cassie sat dumbfounded while he placed her briefcase by the door and brought her a glass of wine.

"How about some wine? You look like you could use it."

"Thanks." Why was he still there? And was he wearing her black apron? As if reading her thoughts, he whipped it off and stuffed it behind him as he sat casually on the arm of the couch.

His foot bounced up and down. "Err...how was your day?"

"It sucked. How was yours?" Cassie was astounded at the turn of events. Why was he acting as if this was a perfectly normal conversation?

"It was good." He seemed to relax a tad. "I called for a rental car and then went to the mall to get some new clothes—"

"I like them," she couldn't help but comment. He wore some very sharp tan pants and a dark burgundy button-down shirt with a wide collar. He looked fantastic. He even had on what appeared to be some very expensive shoes.

"Thanks." He gave her one of those slow grins of his which made her gut clutch. "Then I went to the grocery store and got us some stuff for dinner."

"You made dinner?" She took a deep drink of her wine; she thought she may need it.

He grinned. "Well, I tried anyway. And I think it just might be edible."

"I'm sure it's great," she found herself saying. "Josh, what..." She knew she had a question. *What the hell are you still doing here?* came to mind.

"You know what? You must be tired." He jumped up and took her wine glass from her. "Why don't you go upstairs and take a shower, and I'll put the finishing touches on dinner?"

"O-okay..." was all she could muster. She plodded up the steps, turning around at the landing to see him smiling at her from the foot of the stairs. She kept imagining Rod Serling stepping out of somewhere and introducing tonight's episode of "The Twilight Zone."

She entered her bedroom and gazed in the mirror. She was a mess. Her hair was disheveled; her blouse plastered to her with sweat and the bags under her eyes had bags under them. In stunned silence she unbuttoned the fuchsia blouse she wore. He was there. Josh hadn't left. Why? She wiggled out of her tailored black skirt, letting it lay where it landed. In a daze, she wiped a hand over her sweaty upper chest and wished he hadn't taken her wine from her. She ambled into the bathroom and reached in to start the shower, removing her undergarments before stepping into the soothing spray.

The water felt absolutely wonderful. She sighed, letting it fall over the back of her neck as she leaned against the wall with both hands supporting her. The sudden thought of him joining her in the shower had her head jerking up. She listened, but heard no noise, only the *pssshhht* of the water as it hit the shower wall and the loud *tha-tha* of her own heartbeat. Unsure if she was disappointed or relieved he hadn't come up, she quickly finished her shower and changed.

When she came down to the kitchen, he was rushing around.

"Uhh...dinner's almost ready." He handed her another glass of wine. "Why don't you have a seat and I'll bring everything out to you." He gestured to the dining room. Despite his efforts to block her view, she spied the premade spaghetti sauce jar on the counter.

"Are you sure you don't need any help?" she offered, with a hint of a smile.

"Oh, no." She pretended to examine a basket of garlic bread but watched out of the corner of her eye as he tried to discreetly snatch the jar from the counter and slide it into the trash.

She snagged a carrot from the salad as he went by. "Everything looks delicious."

When she turned the corner into the dining room, she hardly recognized it as hers.

"Wow! This is fantastic." Her eyes swept over the china and crystal and the splashy bouquet of red orchids and white calla lilies in a beautiful, but unfamiliar, rectangular vase. "Oh, Josh..." she ran a finger over the graceful curve of a lily, "...they're lovely." She took a sip of her wine to hide the fact she was getting choked up, but the tender look on his face told her he noticed. She looked away again, running her hand across the surface of the table. "I don't remember having a red tablecloth," she mumbled.

"You don't. I picked one up while I was at the mall."

"And the candlesticks and candles?"

He shrugged with a smile, pulling a chair out for her. "I wanted everything to be just right."

"I could get used to this."

"Good," he said, bending in to give her a quick peck on the neck which sent goose bumps up her arm. "I'll be right back."

While he was gone, she allowed a smile to dance around her lips; he did all this for her. She no longer thought about how strange it was he stayed, or about what a bad day she had, or even, about what might lie in their future; she simply basked in the warmth he provided. He talked to her as he filled dishes and brought them out to the table.

"I hope this is okay. I tried to remember how my mom did things, and then I fooled around with some of the spices in your cabinet. I really don't cook much on the road." He set a heaping plate of spaghetti down in front of her. "Okay, I never cook on the road," he admitted with a grin, "but there's a first for everything, right? If it's no good, I'll call for carryout."

"I'm sure it's delicious."

He watched her as she took a bite.

"Mmm. This is...*really* good. I think we may have discovered your true calling, Dunningham. You'll need to give up the whole rock star thing."

He grinned, sampling his own. "Wow. It's not bad. I didn't know I had it in me. See, you bring out all kinds of good things." He grinned, reaching over to rub her hand for a second before continuing to eat.

Her heart fluttered and she dropped her eyes before he could catch her staring. "Man," Cassie said wistfully, "I should have thrown on a dress or something to go along with this fancy fare." She had thrown on only a rumpled white T-shirt and pink flannel boxing shorts.

"You look perfect," he said softly as he brought his wine to his lips. He studied her over the rim of his glass. She looked much more relaxed now. They avoided the argument he thought was inevitable, because she was so shocked, he guessed. He hoped the rest of the evening would go off without any glitches. He was really enjoying himself. Who knew cooking dinner for someone could be so much fun? "Oh. I should have had music," he exclaimed, angry with himself for missing this detail. He started to get up, but her hand restrained him.

"No. Everything is wonderful just the way it is." She surprised him by leaning over and giving him a kiss. He was surprised even more when the kiss rocked him to his core. The staggering effect made him feel like a boxer who just pulled himself up the ropes at the sound of the bell. He cleared his head with a slight shake and got out of his seat to cross to the stereo in the adjoining room.

"But...without music..." He fiddled with the knob until the sound of Nat King Cole's, "When I Fall in Love," filled the room, "...how could I ask you to dance?" Strolling over to her side, he offered his hand. She pushed back her chair, slipping her slender hand into his. He pulled her to her feet and into his arms in one quick move. She laughed as she fell against him. Despite their differences in height, they fit perfectly together. As soon as their bodies met, they seemed to sigh and melt, as if all of their lives they had been waiting for this one moment, this one touch, this one person.

"Who knew the guy who wrote 'I'm Sick of You' could be such a romantic?"

It was one of his more violent songs, written about a friend's hellish breakup which ended with his possessions being set on fire by his psycho girlfriend on his apartment sidewalk. "That's—"

"Yeah, yeah. Really about someone else, right?"

"It's true."

She smiled up at him. "Do you ever write things about your own life?"

"I did last week."

"You wrote a new song?" Her eyes lit up. "What's it about?"

He brushed the hair back from her face, amazed by its softness, debating whether or not to tell her. "You."

Her feet stopped moving. "Seriously?"

He nodded.

Her face froze for a second, masking her emotions, and then she lowered her head to his chest. He started moving again, in slow, mesmerizing circles. They were silent as he rested his cheek alongside her head, lulled into a sort of peaceful trance.

"Can I hear it?"

"Hmm?"

She pulled away to look up at him. "The song...can I hear it?"

"I'd rather sing it to you when I have my guitar."

She nodded, rest her cheek against him. When the song ended, she lifted her head to gaze into his eyes as they continued to rock back and forth. A new song started. It was one of his favorites, "The Reason" by Hoobastank, but never had the words hit home so much. He knew he wasn't a perfect person, that he'd hurt her. But she had given him a reason to try harder, to make more of himself. He found he was singing along to the music. The painful memory of what happened in San Diego seemed to fill the room.

When the music ended, both of them had damp eyes. "Cassie, I never meant to hurt you—"

"No, you don't need to say anything." She would have wriggled out of his grasp, but he foresaw her response and held on. "You don't owe me an explanation." The words came out sharp.

A flicker of fire leapt through him, but it was doused with remorse. "But I need to tell you. That's why I came here in the first place, so I could explain things to you." He let her go and rubbed his face and the stubble along his chin, working up the nerve to talk about it. She started to protest again, but he spoke over her. "I didn't think you were coming. I knew you got the tickets because you signed for them, and when you didn't show, I automatically thought the worst. I was upset, and started drinking, and then...that girl showed up. Ahh!" he yelled in frustration, throwing up a hand and turning away from her. He gazed at the ceiling for a moment then took a deep breath and spun to face her. "I'm not very good at this, Cassie. I've never even had a date with a girl before. In high school, I chased after them. After the band took off, they chased after me. But it never meant anything to me." He was more and more lost as he continued. "I'm not very good at showing I care. I've never wanted to before. I've never needed to before."

Cassie stepped up and placed a finger on his lips. "Josh, I think you're doing a pretty damn good job of it." She looked at her finger on his lips, and then removed it, peering up into his eyes. He bent slowly in and kissed her; not the fast, fiery kisses that usually ignited between them, but deep, tender kisses. He released his heart with each one, squeezing her in his arms. She laid her head down on his chest again and they swayed together, holding on to each other like a lifeboat in a storm.

The radio commercials ended and Orleans' "You're Still the One" permeated the air waves. "I haven't heard this song in forever," Josh commented. Then, wondering about the variety of music they had heard, he asked, "What radio station is this?"

"It's WTIM, Tim 94.2, their concept is no format radio. They play a little bit of everything. But I hate this station."

"You do? Why?"

"Because," she fiddled with a button on his shirt so she could avert her eyes, "when I returned from Vegas, this station put a big, obnoxious billboard on the building across from mine with a huge picture of *you*...and the band."

His laugh rumbled up from deep inside his chest. "You're kidding? I swear, I had nothing to do with it."

"Oh, I know. I know." She smiled a little, smoothing down his shirt.

He lifted her chin with his fingertips. "And you were thinking of me then."

"Well I couldn't help but think of you, you were constantly staring over my shoulder," she joked. She tried to look away, but his steady gaze brought her eyes back to his like she was following the little flashlight at the eye doctor's office. "And I would have been thinking of you, regardless," she ended quietly.

"Good." He bent to kiss her again. Then, suddenly in a playful mood, he took both of her hands and twirled her until her back was against his chest. He swayed with her like that for several seconds, whispering into her ear. "I was thinking about you, too." He felt her tremor and was filled with a sense of power. On a whim, he spun her out to the end of his arm then yanked her back like a yo-yo.

She twirled into his arms, laughing. "Maybe this radio station isn't so bad."

"Maybe not," he said lightly, kissing the tip of her nose. He released her to move over to the couch. "But now it's..." with an exaggerated drum roll he produced a DVD from a plastic bag, "...chick-flick time."

"You got us a movie?"

"I got *you* a movie," he corrected, "which I am going to sit and...enjoy with you. The girl said this was 'like the best movie ever,'" he said, imitating her high school tone. "*Pride and Prejudice*, have you seen it?"

"About a half dozen times. But that's okay. I can't wait."

Josh popped it into the DVD player. "I'm going to, real fast, clean up the dishes and make us some popcorn."

"I'll help."

He brought her hand to his lips and kissed it. "Not tonight. It'll only take me a second. I'll be in before the feature presentation begins."

CHAPTER THIRTEEN

Josh hurried through the cleanup and was beside her on the couch before the first shot of the moors. After a few minutes, he yawned exaggeratedly and stretched his arm behind her, pulling her close. She smiled and jabbed him in the ribs then leaned into him for the rest of the movie. It felt so good, so right, like some old married couple. She stole a few kisses, and he slid his hand up and down her arm, and held her hand, kissing it from time to time.

While she watched the movie, he watched her and wondered. Wondered about the person he had become with her. His parents would never have sat like this, together on the couch watching a movie. They were each involved in their own thing. His mother played Bridge and Pinochle; his dad bowled. Neither ever had much time for him; it was like three complete strangers living in the same house out of necessity. They didn't even share their meals often. Birthdays and holidays weren't celebrated. He'd never received a gift from Santa Claus. But when he met Ryan, that's when he discovered what family was all about.

Ryan, his mom and dad, and three sisters showed him what love was, and he was grateful for it. He speculated on how much more warped he would be if he hadn't had them. Cassie stretched like a cat beside him. The movie was over. She looked up at him, her blue eyes a little sleepy, and the need inside him growled like a hungry cat. He kissed her and her wine-sweet breath filled him. She slipped onto his lap so they could kiss more comfortably. She ran a hand along his shoulder, and then under his shirt.

"I do like your new duds," she purred, sending his pulse up another notch. Apparently, chick-flicks were a huge turn-on. Her tongue seduced his into a new dance, creating a fresh excitement in him he needed to control.

He cleared his throat. "How 'bout dessert?"

"You made dessert, too?"

"Are you kidding? No way." He slid out from under her hurriedly. "It's frozen cheesecake."

"Cheesecake. Oh, my gosh!" She followed him into the kitchen. "You are a prince. That's my favorite."

"Hmm," he said, retrieving it from the refrigerator. "And they say the way to a *man's* heart is through his stomach."

"It is," she said, grabbing plates. "The way to a woman's heart is through her ring finger."

She said it in jest, but it made him think. Was it possible he could have a marriage? A real marriage. Not like his parents', cohabitation without any love. Strangely, the idea'd never occurred to him before. His thoughts were interrupted by Cassie suggesting they eat their cheesecake on the porch.

They sat on the glider he'd spent a good deal of the morning on by himself, setting the wine down carefully so they could eat their cheesecake. It was better with her there. A storm was rolling in and brought a cool breeze.

"Man, it's beautiful out here now. Nothing like earlier today," she said.

"Yeah."

"You're quiet. Either you're really into that cheesecake, or something's on your mind."

"This cheesecake is really good," he answered evasively.

"So...how come you're not playing anywhere tonight?"

"We've got a two-day break in our schedule."

They rocked back and forth on the glider. "What would you normally be doing with your free time?"

"Well, normally I would be back home, in Cedar Rapids, visiting my parents."

"Oh. I'm taking you away from your family. You probably don't have much time with them." She collected his plate and set it aside with hers so she could snuggle up next to him better.

"No, it's okay." He paused. How was he supposed to explain his relationship with his parents, or more accurately, non-relationship? "We're not...close...at all, really."

"I'm sorry," she said quietly. "A family fight?"

"No, nothing like that. We just were never close. I think my being born was a big mistake in their eyes."

She sat up. "Oh, Josh. Don't say that. I'm sure your parents love you a great deal."

He twirled the stem of his wine glass in his fingers, looking at the deep burgundy color in the light pouring out from the kitchen windows. "No. It's okay. I've come to an understanding of it. Strange thing is," he mused, "you don't really miss something you never had. I didn't even know how strange we were until I spent time with Ryan's family. *They're* what family is all about."

"Tell me about them."

"His sisters are all dolls...and pains." He smiled. "They could be helping you out with homework one minute and knocking you up side your head the next."

"I'm sure you deserved it."

"Oh, no doubt. Natalie—or, as Ryan and I used to refer to her, Nat the Brat—is a hoot. She's...oh, my gosh, she must be legal now...yeah, she was twenty-one in March. Brenna is studying law at UCLA. And Chridder...or Christy, will be a senior this year at Xavier High School, where Ryan and I went. She's a cheerleader so we'll probably try to catch one of her games this year."

"You enjoy spending time with them."

"Yeah." He laughed, thinking about them. "They're pretty cool. And his dad was...what a dad should be. Always there for Ryan. Sometimes it ticked Ry off, but I really admired his dad. And he was the kind of man you could tell was in love with his wife. They used to waltz around the kitchen, or sit at the table and play cards, laughing and teasing each other. And every other Friday night was date night for them. They'd get all dressed up and go out to dinner somewhere, and we'd eat pizza and watch that fabulous television duo, "The Love Boat," followed, of course, by...?"

"'Fantasy Island.'"

"Da plane. Da plane. Gotta love Tattoo." He shook his head with a grin.

"Sounds like you really loved them."

"Who? Tattoo and Mr. Rourke? Who didn't?" She jabbed him neatly in the rib cage. "Oh, the Sandovals." His voice was soft. "Yeah, I do." He caressed her arm in long strokes. Thunder rolled low in the distance, and in the stillness, it seemed they were the only two people in the world. "I was amazed by how quiet your street was this morning. You'd never know you were in Chicago."

"Yeah. It's a nice neighborhood. I'm very lucky. Our neighbors across the street, Tammy and Kevin," she gestured to a white ranch, "and Cheryl and Roger down in that brown two-story, and then Dave and Doreen, right next door, we like to sit out, when the weather is nice, at the end of Dave's driveway and have a drink or two. Heather will join us, too, straight across the street. You met her in Vegas. But she and I are the only singles on the block."

"Heather lives right across the street?"

"Yeah. That's how we met and became friends."

"I saw her this morning, but I didn't see what direction she came from."

Cassie sat up quickly. "You saw Heather? Oh Josh, I'm sorry for whatever it was she said or did. She didn't hit you or anything, did she?"

"No." He laughed. "She was actually very sweet."

She looked mildly shocked. "Are you sure it was Heather? I mean, I've heard people call her a lot of things, but generally sweet doesn't top the list. I mean, she just says what's on her mind, just blurts it out there without thinking sometimes, and people either like it or they hate it. There's no two ways with her."

"She's a good friend to you, and I respect that."

"So she did tell you off."

"No. Actually, she sat right down on this glider where you are sitting right now and had a chat with me."

"Okay. Now I'm really scared. She knows more about me than anyone, including my sister. What did she tell you?" She reached down for her glass of wine, searching for reinforcement.

"Why, Miss Cassie," he said as he took a strand of her hair to play with it, "you don't have any deep, dark secrets you need to tell me about, do you?" He spoke teasingly, but his eyes pierced through the dim light.

She gulped her wine, suddenly uncomfortable. She put her glass on the ground, then subtly moved so he couldn't see her face and read her emotions there, turning her back to lean against him. She quieted, and he didn't press her. They didn't speak, each taken with their own thoughts, and then, as if someone turned on a faucet, it began to rain. She listened, the sound of the wind rustling the leaves, replaced by the gentle tapping of raindrops on their surface.

"Cass, come here." Josh shifted so she was lying across his lap, supported by his arm. He stroked the side of her face, and down her neck, trailing it across her upper chest before tucking it into her waist. They gazed at each other without speaking as the rain fell about them, dripping from the leaves to the ground lazily. "You know..." he said, quoting the movie they just watched together, "...you 'bewitch me, body and soul.'"

It was too much for her. He was listening after all. He stayed, made her dinner, danced with her, and quoted *Pride and Prejudice*. Her breath caught in her throat as she peered into his beautifully sculpted face, and it passed between them, that raw current that had become familiar. The breeze blew his hair and pressed the fabric of his shirt against his chest, bringing with it the mist of the rain. Moisture covered their skin as it swept in under the eaves, and through the porch rails. The rain didn't chill them, it felt refreshing, and it certainly didn't match the storm raging inside her. She reached for him, her hands on his face when his lips met hers, parting them even as she invited him in.

The kiss contained both tenderness and passion, a need for him on several levels at once. And suddenly, she wished the rain would whip through them, drench them with its zeal. She wished he would touch her body, there, on her front porch, knowing her neighbors were just behind their curtains, watching TV or making love themselves. One of his strong hands still held her at the waist, the other in her hair, clutching her as their kisses became more heated, and then, inexplicably, he pulled away from her.

With a look of confusion, he stuttered. "Well, I guess I should go now."

"Go?" Her mind leapt with an old fear. "What did I do?"

"You didn't do anything." But his actions belied his words. He pushed her up to a sitting position and rose. He walked a few feet across the porch, his hands shoved into his pockets.

Maybe it was because she was so tired, but tears were rolling down her cheeks again. When he turned, Josh rushed back over and squatted down, his hands on her arms. "Oh, Cass, honey, you didn't do anything." He wiped the tears from her face. "Man, he really did a number on you, didn't he?"

"Who?"

"Troy," he answered quietly.

"B-but...how did you know?"

"Heather told me. She didn't mean to, she just said something about after what you had been through with Troy. But when I asked her for details, she said I needed to talk to you about it. She wouldn't tell me anything. And you don't have to tell me anything either, not until you're ready to."

"Then...why are you leaving?" she asked tentatively.

"I'm just trying to give you time. Time to trust me. Time to be comfortable with our relationship. I want to make you understand what's going on here between us, while new for me, and a little confusing at times, it's important to me. What we have here is special." He cupped her chin, looking her straight in the eye. "You are not just another girl to me, Cassie McCallister." She smiled through her tears, and his shoulders relaxed. "Now," he said rising, and pulling her up to her feet, too, "I got a hotel room for me tonight. So, no matter how hard you beg me, I will *not* be seducing or attacking you this evening, even though I want to very much." He kissed her and then hastened down the two porch steps, still holding her hand. "I will see you tomorrow." He sighed loudly then stretched up to give her another kiss. The rain speckled his shirt and hair. He turned to leave, groaning. "This whole chivalry thing is for the birds."

He was halfway down the sidewalk when she called to him. "Josh, wait."

"Oh God, Cassie. Don't do this to me. I'm a weak man."

She smiled at him. "There's no reason for you to go to a hotel. I have a guest room all the way at the opposite side of the house," a grin split her face. "Although it does share a wall, so that's not saying much, but you can stay there."

He seemed to waver. "Are you sure my virtue will remain intact?"

She grinned, leaning against the porch railing as he had done that morning, her arms crossed. "I'm not making any promises."

"Good enough for me," he answered quickly, running back and grabbing her by the waist to swing her off the porch in a circle.

They got ready for bed, both exhausted from the emotional day they'd shared. She stood on her tiptoes outside his bedroom to kiss him goodnight. He was bare-chested, with pants on; she wore a white linen nightgown. They parted and he stood with his hand on the doorknob, watching her leave. She looked back as she entered her door, closing it softly behind her. With a sigh, he entered his own room.

In the middle of the room was a large, antique brass bed. He hung his pants over the bed rail and slid beneath the sheets, his body welcoming the rest. A streetlight shone through one of the windows, but he didn't bother to get up and close the heavy curtains. He lay on his side, looking at the shadows on the wall, well aware that she lay on the other side.

After about twenty minutes of restlessness, his door cracked open, spilling light from the hallway. Her shadowy figure drifted in the doorway as he raised his head. "Will your virtue remain intact if I just sleep beside you?" she asked.

His only response was to raise the sheet and the comforter so she could climb in. She shut the door and ran the short distance to the bed, hopping in with a bounce. She giggled as he pulled her close, comforted by her warmth and her scent, and they fell asleep within minutes.

CHAPTER FOURTEEN

When he woke, she was gone, but he could smell the coffee brewing downstairs. He rolled out of bed and pulled on his new pair of jeans, along with a white, Adidas T-shirt.

On the kitchen table, he spotted a piece of the now-familiar rose-colored paper held in place by a coffee cup. Cautiously, he inched toward it until he could read the bold print.

Gone for a run. I'll be back soon.

Help yourself to coffee and anything else you can find. ~Cassie

He smiled, taking the mug to fill it up.

When she jogged into view, he was sitting on the glider. She looked more modest in her running attire than Heather had, tight black shorts with a white stripe running down each side, and a matching, formfitting, sleeveless top. Her hair was pulled back in a stubby little ponytail. A few shorter pieces had fallen out and were sticking to her sweaty face. She smiled at him as she came up the sidewalk. He stood, leaning against the porch post with his coffee in hand. "Hi," she called, slowing her breathing down.

"Hey, beautiful," he said, his voice deep still from sleep. She climbed up the steps, stretching to give him a quick kiss. He set his cup on the top rail and pulled her in for a better one.

"Oooh, I'm still sweaty," she said, squirming.

"I don't care," he replied, taking the kisses deeper until she melted against him.

When he pulled his lips slowly away from hers, he asked, as he stared down into her breathless and somewhat dazed face, "How was your run?"

"Good." She kicked her foot up on the railing next to his coffee, bending over her leg to stretch it. He swallowed, taking in the smooth curve of her legs and the ease with which she bent herself in half. "Can I get you some breakfast?" she queried. She acted so naturally, he was sure she was oblivious to the effect she was having on him.

"Sure, sure...I mean, no. I'm not much of a breakfast eater," he answered, distracted.

"Me either, how about some toast?"

"Sounds good."

As he entered the house behind her she asked, "So, what's on the agenda for today?"

"Well, I want to do whatever it is you would normally do on a Saturday morning."

She hunted in the refrigerator. "Ahh...well..." She pulled out a plastic container, "...do you like strawberries?"

"Sure."

"Okay." She turned to find a cutting board. "If this were a normal Saturday morning, I'd probably be out there weeding, but—"

"Let's weed, then."

She froze, then turned from the sink with a strainer in her hand. "You want to weed with me?" she asked, in a tone which clearly pointed out the strangeness of such a statement.

"Yes. It doesn't matter what we do, as long as we spend time together."

She turned back to her strawberry washing. "But there's probably a million things we could do that would be more interesting than pulling weeds...a gazillion even."

He crossed and stood behind her, his hands on either side of her on the edge of the sink while he nuzzled her hair. "But I want the Day in the Life of Cassie McCallister Experience."

She picked up the paring knife and began to thoughtfully slice the strawberries. He got a bowl down for her. "So...Mr. Mega-Rock-Star wants to try on the life of your average slob."

"*You* are no average slob."

"Okay. So, the above-average slob. Let's face it, I'm just a jingle-writer."

"Don't do that to yourself." He grabbed her by the waist and twisted her around. "Don't sell yourself short. My job puts me in the limelight, but that doesn't mean it's any more important than what you do, or you are any less creative..." he kissed her nose, "...or brilliant than I am. I'm certain you are good at what you do."

"How are you so sure?" she asked skeptically.

"Because your creativity shines through in everything you do. For instance, those photos upstairs in my bedroom...they're not your average landscape photos. They're taken at interesting angles or centered on an odd object most wouldn't focus on—a leaf on a bench instead of a pile of leaves, or the fallen tree trunk, instead of the mass of trees. You find beauty in the unusual items that others would disregard. That shows creativity." He plucked a strawberry from the strainer and ate it, throwing the stem into the sink. "It shows whenever I talk with you. You're quirky—"

"Some people would see that as a negative."

"Not me." He snatched up the last whole strawberry just as she reached for it, their hands brushing. As she turned with the bowl, he fed it to her.

He saw a shadow cross her face, but before he could ask her what was wrong, she recovered, saying, "Well...obviously the man wants to weed, so who am I to stop him?" She was quiet during the rest of the meal, and she didn't eat any more strawberries. In fact, she only ate about half her toast, shredding the rest as she listened to his small talk.

She took her plate with his to the sink, rinsing them and putting them in the dishwasher. She stood for a moment, staring into the empty sink. She jumped a little when he approached her from behind. "What are you thinking about?"

She gave her head a shake. "I'm thinking about which weeds to attack first. I must warn you, though, I'm somewhat of a Weed Nazi."

He smiled. "Show the way, oh, Fearless Leader."

AS THEY HEADED OUT the front door, Josh stated, "Okay, I've never weeded before, so you may have to give me some pointers."

She spun around. "You've *never* weeded?"

He shrugged. "We lived in places where weeds were welcome. Apartments. Trailer parks."

"Never?"

"Never."

She picked a long stick up off the ground and thwacked it loudly on the steps leading to the porch. "Sit down," she ordered, though he could see the playfulness in her eyes.

Josh sat, grinning.

"Wipe that smile off your face, weeding is serious business."

"Yes, ma'am." He sat up straighter. "May I say the whole drill sergeant thing is kind of a turn on for me?"

"You may not."

"Yes, ma'am," he responded with a frown.

She smiled. "Better. Now. The veeds, they are verwy, verwy cleva." She strode back and forth, her stick behind her back, like a member of the Weed Gestapo. "They will disguise themselves to look like a nearby plant. You must be smarter than the weed."

"Piece of cake."

"You think it isn't hard?" She brought her stick down on a plant in the landscaping to the right of the sidewalk as if it were her riding crop. "This." He nodded, gulping. "Weed?" she said slowly. "Or plant?"

He studied the surrounding foliage. He could see some clover and one massive dandelion, and a low growing vine with small dark green leaves and purple flowers which took over most of the bed. She was now lifting the specimen up with her stick so he could get a better look. It was viny with green leaves. "Well, weed or plant?" she prompted.

He stretched his legs out in front of him, folding his arms behind his head, confident in his assessment. "Plant."

"WRONG!" She brought the stick down across his thigh sharply.

He sprang up. "Oww!"

"Oh, did I hurt you? I'm sorry. I didn't mean to do it that hard."

"No. No." He laughed. "Go on, Professor."

She smiled, backing up and lifting another vine with the stick. "*This* is vinca." She returned to the first. "*This* is a weed." He could see now it was slightly darker in color, with leaves a little broader.

"Ahh." He nodded. "I see now."

"Now, come with me." She crooked her finger at him.

He grinned. "Gladly." She hustled down the sidewalk, laughing as he chased her. She stopped, holding up a hand and pointing to another landscaping bed with her stick. "More weeds?" he whined.

"If you don't want to..."

"No, I'm in." *This better be worth it.* But with one look at her tight tush as she leaned over the landscaping bed on the other side of the driveway, he reassured himself it was.

She was pointing to a purple, spiky flower with wide, dark reddish-purple and green leaves. "This is ajuga."

"Wait," he interrupted. His eyes scanned the bed. Then he moved to take a closer look. He examined a purple stalk which was much thinner than the others, with smaller, green leaves. It could be a baby ajuga...or... "Weed?" he said tentatively.

"That's right." She smiled at her pupil. "Now, all you have to do is remove them."

Josh took another glance at the bed. "No problem."

"I'll work on the vinca."

Josh got down on his hands and knees to work. At first it didn't appear like it would take long, but the more he pulled, the more he found. A half hour later, he was sweaty, grimy, and only halfway done.

"Hey, Rog." Cassie called out.

Josh looked up to see a tall, slender man walking up the slope of the street from a neighboring house, one Cassie pointed out the night before. Welcoming any distraction from his labor, he got up and followed Cassie over to greet him.

"Roger Frey, this is Josh Dunningham."

"Pleased to meet you," the man said easily, extending one of his large hands; but Josh knew when he was being sized up. The newcomer was about six feet tall, with extremely short, graying hair, and twinkling blue eyes. "Oh," he said now, becoming more animated, "the Josh you met in Vegas? Heather started to talk to us about him before you shut her down." He looked teasingly at Cassie, a smile playing over his lips.

"Yes, just like I'm going to shut you down now, Roger. So, what can I do for you today?" Her warm smile contradicted her stern tone.

Roger chuckled, low. It was obvious the two had a good relationship. Josh could see a debate in Cassie's neighbor's eyes. He was wondering, should he rib her more, or should he just get down to business. The latter won out. "Well," he let his eyes travel over to Josh again, unable to resist a final opportunity to make her squirm, "I just came up to see if it was okay if I cut your lawn on Wednesday instead of Tuesday? I've had something come up."

"Roger and his sons run a lawn mowing service," Cassie explained to Josh. "Sure, Rog, no sweat. Whenever you can make it up here."

"So, you own a lawn service," Josh said, thoughtfully, looking at Cassie. "Do you do weeds?"

"No way." He grinned. "That's hard work." He gave Josh a wink as he shook his hand. Ambling back toward his house, he called back over his shoulder, "Nice to meet you."

"You, too." Josh looked at Cassie. "Seems like a nice guy."

"The best." She slipped her hand around his waist. They walked over to his landscaping bed. "How's it going?"

"Pretty good," he commented, surveying his area critically. He had to admit, it did give him some pleasure to see the progress he made. She squeezed his hand, standing on her tiptoes to give him a kiss on the cheek. "You must be ready for a break. How about some lemonade?"

"Sounds fantastic."

They sat on the steps, downing tall glasses of the beverage. He studied her pile of weeds. "It looks like you got a lot done."

"Yeah." She set her glass on the steps and put her gardening gloves back on. "I'm about to go tackle the ivy bed on the side of the house. It's a bear."

He slung a hand over her shoulder. "Why don't I help you out over there? I can come back and finish this up later." He gestured to the far side of the driveway.

"Okay." As they walked around to the side of the house together, she questioned, "Are you sure this is how you want to spend your time off?"

He looked down at her. "Couldn't think of a better way to spend my time." He squeezed her closer to him. "Actually, I'm kind of enjoying it. It feels good to get sweaty and dirty every once in awhile, and it's been far too long since I've done any manual work. It's sort of satisfying to see how good everything looks when you're done."

She nodded. "Well, we'll see what you think about that after we deal with this." They rounded the curve. The whole side of the house sloping down to the neighbors' lawn was covered in ivy. He tried not to show his dismay. "I can't get grass to grow in this shade, so I planted ivy. It's usually beautiful, but I've been neglecting it lately." She stomped right into the vines. "The problem here is this strawberry vine." She lifted a vine with little flower-like berries growing on it. "Actually, I'm not sure what they call this, I just call it strawberry vine, and it's incredibly invasive. In fact, there are some areas where it has taken over the ivy." She fell to her knees, and he knelt beside her. "The trick is," she started digging through the vines, "you have to tunnel through all this stuff until you find the root. See? Luckily, they are red, where the ivy's roots are green, but sometimes you have to go through several layers to find them."

He found a vine beside him, and started following it back to its root, several feet away. Prying through masses of ivy, he got his fingers to the very base of the weed, pulling steadily until the root released.

They worked side-by-side for several more hours, each occupied by their own thoughts.

Josh's thoughts wandered back to Lanny outside his dressing room in San Diego. He started wondering if Lanny might be like a weed, growing alongside him and Ryan, seemingly innocuous. But maybe Lanny was actually winding his way around them, leading them along while trying to harm them like the weed was strangling the ivy. The funny thing was, just as it was sometimes hard to tell the weed from the plant, sometimes it was hard to tell the true friend from the false one. He sat back on his heels while he contemplated this.

"What, is Mr. Pampered Rock Star getting tired?"

In a flash, Josh grabbed one of the wrists supporting her as she kneeled in the weeds and yanked her off balance so she fell into the vines. Quickly he climbed on top of her, while she tried, weakly, to dislodge him, squealing. He looked down into her laughing eyes. "Woman." He wrestled her arms over her head and held them there. "You're pressing your luck." He bent and kissed her, long and hard, in her ivy bed, allowing her to liberate her arms. She brought her hands to the back of his head, playing with his hair as she kissed him.

"Miss Cassie?" someone called from the front of the house.

"It's the neighbor boy! Get off me!"

He laughed at her sudden sense of propriety but quickly disengaged himself, following her around to the front while she picked leaves out of her hair. He removed one which still clung stubbornly to her ponytail.

"Hey," she called out. "Joseppi. Wassup, dawg?" She strolled over to a young man with a blond crew-cut astride a bike, initiating a complicated handshake with him. Josh recognized the similarity between the boy and the Roger he met earlier. "Joe, this is my friend Josh. Josh, this is Joe, the youngest of the Frey boys."

"Oh. Then I guess that makes you a small Frey then, eh?" He laughed at his own cleverness, only to receive a dark look from the boy, who was short. "It's just a joke. You probably have never heard of the expression, 'small fry,' have you?" he said, trying to dig his way out of the hole he created. "A 'small fry' is a—"

"Fish," he said blandly. "I know."

Cassie changed the subject. "Been up to the Casey's, Joe?"

"Yep," he responded, smiling as he turned toward Cassie.

"What did you score?"

"I got Bubble Yum—" he pulled out a container fashioned like a reel of measuring tape "—and a Twix bar."

"You can never have enough measuring-tape-shaped gum, I've always said." She snatched it out of his hand. "So, where's mine?"

Joe just grinned even bigger, an award-winning grin, Josh judged. He watched the exchange with interest, enjoying the way Cassie got along with the boy.

"I didn't get you any."

She handed his gum back. "Man-n-n. You let me down, Joe. You said the next time you went, you'd take my order before you left...and here you leave me, high and dry..." She gave an exaggerated sigh.

"I'm sorry," he responded, his face still bright. "I'll remember next time."

"You better."

"Got time to shoot some hoops?"

Cassie glanced at Josh. "How about bringing Matt up so we can play a little two-on-two? You can be on Josh's team, and Matt and I will team up."

Joe took one more look at the giant beside her and seemed to decide he might have a chance at beating his big brother this time. "Sure." He put his feet to the pedals and sped off downhill.

Josh wrapped his arms around her. "I think he's sweet on you."

"I have a way with junior high boys."

"I just bet you do." He kissed her but then moved away as they heard the distant sound of a basketball thumping on the street. He slid his hands around her waist as they watched the two brothers coming up the street. While Joe was barely five feet tall, his brother was a good six-two, six-three. "That's Matt?" Josh said weakly.

"Uh-huh." Cassie gave him a wicked smile. "Game on, Dunningham." She turned to walk up to her driveway, and he smiled after her.

"So this hoop's not just for show, then?"

She bent to tighten her laces, suddenly all business. "No way. You're going down."

He walked over to her, straightening out to his full height. She came up to his chest. "That's pretty big talk, squirt."

"I'd keep my voice down if I was you," she said, shooting a look down the street. "You've already pissed your partner off once this morning. Besides," she said, turning back to look at him, "I'm not easily intimidated. As far as I'm concerned, the bigger they are, the harder they fall."

When Josh turned around and Matt got a good look at him, his jaw fell open. "Y-you're—"

"Josh. Nice to meet you."

"Coool!" Matt slid his eyes to Cassie.

"Yeah. It's pretty sweet." She gave Josh a pat on the ass.

"I feel so used," he mumbled so only she could hear.

She gave a low, sexy laugh.

"Joe," Josh called out. "Come on over here so we can discuss our secret plays." He laid his hand on the boy's head, marveling at the softness the crew cut provided, and then bent to huddle with him. He looked over to where Cassie stood with a hip cocked, arms folded, Matt next to her with his hands on his hips. "Don't you think you guys ought to discuss strategy?"

"We don't need strategy," Cassie replied sweetly. "Do we, Matt?" She looked up at him and he shook his head with the same slow smile his dad had.

Josh pretended to growl, saying to Joe, "I hate it when she gets all cocky."

"Yeah. Women!" he agreed, seeming to have forgiven him already for his earlier indiscretion. Josh looped a hand across his shoulder, turning his back to their opponents. "Okay," Joe queried, "what are our secret plays?"

"We don't have any," he confided in a whisper. "We're just making them nervous." He glanced over his shoulder and smiled at the pair by the garage.

"Matt will never fall for that. My dad tries that stuff all the time."

"Yeah, but Matt doesn't know me, so it'll make him wonder. Does he have secret plays or not? All we need is to get inside his head, mess with his game a little."

"Yeahh," Joe breathed with approval.

"All right. Look over there and laugh on three. One, two, three." They yucked it up, but Matt and Cassie only smiled and nodded.

"We're ready now," Josh said confidently.

Cassie winked at Matt. "I'll take Josh."

Josh snorted. "Oh, yeah?"

"Yeah. Cut the small talk, Dunningham. Let's play some ball."

"Is she always so bossy?" he asked the boys. Being smart boys, they didn't comment. "Do you know how to check the ball?" he asked as he tossed it to her.

She sent it rocketing back into his gut causing him to exhale loudly. "Yeah. I do."

He smiled. This was going to be fun. Her hands were out and moving up and down to try to block his pass, but he bounced it into Joe, who fed it back. Josh took the shot, and just like that, they were in the lead.

"Nice shot," Cassie commented evenly. She took the ball to the point, and he checked it for her, being kinder than she had been. Matt set up almost on the street. She hummed a pass to him, and he took a fade away shot from about eighteen feet out and hit nothing but net. Josh turned to look at her in shock. "*Really* nice shot," she called with a huge smile, not taking her eyes from his.

"Joe," he replied humorlessly, "take the ball out."

Joe proceeded to take the ball to the point, where his brother harassed him enough to cause him to almost throw the ball away, but Josh stepped up to get the pass. Cassie was all over him, bumping him, pushing him, with her pelvis, with her chest...he never knew basketball could be such a turn on. Joe cut toward the basket, and he threaded a pass into his hands as he swung by. The ball was up and in.

Now it was Matt's turn to bring the ball in.

"I'm on you, McCallister," Josh growled.

"In your dreams," she replied pleasantly. Matt got the pass into her, despite Josh's flailing arms. Pushing her cute little butt into his midsection, she bumped him off, then bounce-passed to Matt, timing it so she hit him after the first step of his layup. "Two more points for the good guys."

Josh bent, his hands on his knees, laughing and huffing as he tried to catch his breath. "Joe, I think we're in trouble." Joe nodded. Matt, who retrieved his own shot, passed it to Josh. Cassie checked him, and the two brothers began squabbling about an alleged foul. Josh spun the ball around in his large hands, looking at Cassie intently. "*You* set me up."

"I thought, being a rock star and all, someone needed to keep you humble."

"And that little someone was you, huh?"

"Yep."

He smiled. "How are you at baseball?" He dribbled the basketball by his side as threats to "tell Mom" were exchanged between the two Freys.

"I don't know. Why don't you try me?" She raised her eyebrows in challenge, and Josh's heart squeezed in his chest. He didn't think he could love a woman more. One who liked sports and could keep him in his place; now that was a find. He leaned in as if to kiss her, and she responded in kind. At the last second, he broke for the basket, rolling the ball off his fingertips and into the net.

"Not fair!" she cried in unison with Joe, who was still arguing with Matt. Sensing something was up, they both turned to see Josh had scored. Joe ran across the driveway and knuckled him.

"I'll bring it in," Matt told them. Joe checked him and, again, he got a slick pass into Cassie.

With a hand on her hip, Josh taunted, "Go on, Cass, take a shot, or are you going to let a high schooler do all the work for you?"

"Well, he does seem to be wiping the floor with you." She tried to back him up to get a better shot, but he wasn't giving an inch. So, she took the shot. The only shot she could take and be successful. With flair, she sent up a sky-hook Kareem would have been proud of. It arched enough to avoid Josh's hands and circled around the rim; then, inexplicably, it fell out. "Damn! Oh. I mean, darn."

"He's heard worse." Matt grinned. "Great shot. You were robbed."

Josh's voice rang out. "I'll bring it in, Joe."

He handed the ball to Cassie, and she checked him, a grim look of determination on her face. "Where did you learn to shoot like that?"

"The oldest Frey, Drew. He's in college now, but he's six-eight. And stop talking to me. You're distracting me."

"Okay," he returned, amused by her tenacity. Out of the corner of his eye, Josh saw Joe fake his older brother out and drive toward the basket. He almost lost the handle on the pass from Josh but was finally able to pull it in and make the shot.

"Way to go, Little Joe." The two exchanged grins and high-fives.

Matt walked over to Cassie. "Go for the alley-oop," she instructed him out of the side of her mouth.

"You got it," he replied, just as grave. "Nice shot, Joe," Matt said begrudgingly, looking down at his little brother as he took his position.

Josh and Cassie exchanged the ball wordlessly. She stood staring into his eyes, but at the same time following the action on the court out of the corner of her eye. When Matt made his move, she shot him the perfect alley-oop pass, high, and right to the basket. He timed it right but brought the ball down a little too hard and it ricocheted out and across the lawn.

"Time out," Cassie snapped. They were down two baskets; it was time to take some serious action. She and Matt huddled under the basket, discussing their options.

"You're dating a rock star? How cool is that?"

"Hey, Frey. Eyes on me. Focus!" She drew two fingers from his eyes to hers then laughed. "Just kidding." She eyed Josh. "It is pretty neat. But not because he's a rock star," she amended, "because he is a great guy."

"How much longer are you going to take, McCallister?" Josh yelled as he leaned against a tree smugly.

She grimaced. "Most of the time. Got any ideas?"

"Yeah. I got one." Matt looked her straight in the eyes, gripping her arms. "You need to distract him by using your womanly ways."

Cassie slapped his arm. "Matthew!" she said, shocked. "Well, I guess you are a high school junior, but you still shouldn't be thinking like that. I've known you since you were Joe's age."

"You want to win, don't you?"

"Of course, I want to win."

"Okay." He walked away and motioned for Josh to give him the ball.

Joe walked up to the point, and Josh strolled onto the court. If Cassie had been uncertain, the cockiness in his jaunt cemented her resolve. "Can I have just one more minute, please, to make a minor wardrobe adjustment?" Everyone agreed, Matt with a big smile on his face. Cassie reached up and pulled the rubber-band out of her ponytail, arching her back a little as she shook her hair out. She gathered the extra material from her top together, securing it with the rubber-band so it rode high above her waist, barely below the bra line, exposing her midriff. "There," she said coyly, "that's better."

"Ho-ho-ho," Josh chortled. The move had its desired effect. When Matt passed the ball to her and Josh began to guard her, his hands accidentally skimmed the skin of her waist and it threw him off enough for her to make a second hook shot; this one good for two points.

Josh collected the ball and went to the point. He started to hand the ball to Cassie so she could check him, but he stopped. "Would anybody mind if I just made a little 'wardrobe adjustment' myself?" Not waiting for a response, he set the ball down and held it in place with his foot while peeling his T-shirt off. The sun shone on his bronzed, sweat-glistening pecs and abs, and Cassie had to swallow to breathe. He handed the ball to her, and she simply stared. "Uhh...you're supposed to hand it back to me," he prompted.

"Oh, yeah." She gave the boys an apologetic smile.

Matt's face fell.

"Are you ready, Cass?"

"Hum? Oh, yeah."

"Good." He rose and took the shot from the point, swishing it without even looking.

"That's game," Cassie called out. "Who wants some lemonade?" She headed to the house, muttering, "Cause I sure the hell need some."

CHAPTER FIFTEEN

Cassie poured the lemonade and excused herself to take a quick shower. When she came back down, feeling refreshed and rejuvenated, she heard the slow strumming of guitar and Josh's voice.

"That's it. You've got it now."

She walked in to see Josh standing behind Matt, who was playing guitar, while Joe sat trying to hide the fact he just took his fifth cookie from the plate Cassie put out, covering it with his palm.

She smiled at Josh. "What's going on?"

"Uh...Matt said he was struggling with a few chords, so I thought I'd see if I could lend a hand."

"Sounds good, Matt." She looked on wistfully. "I wish I'd taken lessons when I was little, but my mom said it wasn't 'ladylike.'"

"You're joking?"

"I wish I was." The phone rang, interrupting her thoughts. "Hello?"

"Hey, this is Cheryl. Are Joe and Matt still there?"

"Yes, they're here." Cassie turned around to see, belatedly, Matt and Joe signaling her to deny their presence to the caller, who, they must have already guessed, was their mom. She shrugged and mouthed, "Sorry," to the boys.

"It was nice of Josh to help Matt with his guitar."

Her eyes slid over to Josh. "Yes, it *was* nice of him."

"Well, could you send those two knuckleheads down here? They have swimming practice in like fifteen minutes."

"Oh, sure. I'll send them..." Cassie had to turn her back to the boys to avoid laughing, as Matt and Joe began flailing wildly and mouthing, 'NO!' "...right down."

"And you behave yourself with your little rock star."

"I will. Bye." She giggled and then hung the receiver up to a chorus of, "No way! That's not fair! Oh, man! That stinks."

"Sorry guys, she said you had swim practice."

"Swim practice sucks," Joe stated succinctly.

"That may be, but if I keep you guys here, she may not let you come again."

After a lot of good-natured grumbles, the boys pushed their chairs back.

"Matt," Josh asked, "could I borrow your guitar for a little while? I could run it back to your house later."

"*You're* gonna come to my house?" His eyes were wide as he grinned.

"If it's okay with you."

The smile on his face could have lit an entire neighborhood for a year. "Yeah, man. That would be cool."

Once the boys hit the outside, they sprinted in a race for home. Josh and Cassie watched from the front door as Joe tried to jostle for position and lost his balance, falling, but rolling across his lawn. He hopped up quickly to put on a burst of speed to pass Matt, who stopped to make sure he was okay. They both disappeared into the depths of the garage at about the same time.

Josh, who stood behind Cassie, laughed. "Those are some nice kids."

"They are," she sighed with contentment. "The whole family is nice."

Josh slid his arms around her waist, breathing in. "Mmm," he groaned. "What kind of perfume do you wear?"

She giggled. "I don't wear any. Why?"

"Cause the smell of you is driving me crazy."

She squirmed as he kissed her neck. "Maybe it's the honeysuckle body lotion I put on."

"That's it. Mmm," he murmured again. The stubble on his cheek as it brushed her neck and shoulders made her body respond with a single warm shiver and her desire for him caused her to suck in her breath a little. The corners of his mouth turned up. "U-um. You like that, huh?" He gave a sexy chuckle which had her reaching out to grab the door frame for support before he stepped back inside.

When the door closed behind them, he took a step toward her and reached out to brush the backs of his fingers down her cheek. She didn't realize she was holding her breath until he spoke. "I have something I want to show you."

He took her hand and led her into the living room. He pulled over a dining room chair as he gestured for her to sit in a plush, red club chair, and then disappeared into the kitchen. He came back with the guitar. "I thought I'd sing you that song now."

"The song you wrote about me?"

He nodded, tightening a guitar string.

She fidgeted while he worked on the guitar. He wrote a song about her. A song about a one-night stand gone awry? Or was it something more than that?

She didn't have much time to think about it as he sat in front of her and started to play.

Cassie's heart lodged in her throat while Josh played. The beauty of the music merged with the moving words he'd written, consuming her, along with the passion she felt for the gorgeous man who sat in front of her, staring into her eyes. Never before could she remember when so much emotion was stirred up inside her at once. As the music continued to pour out of him, she fought for control over the whirlpool of thoughts and sensations swirling within her. It was like she couldn't think at all, only be, and listen. The idea of him feeling things for her which would have compelled him to write a song was overwhelming. And to see the pain in his eyes, and know she caused it, twisted her heart until she could hardly breathe. She wanted it to stop; but at the same time, she wanted it to go on forever.

As he strummed the final chords, she could no longer keep the tears in check. They slid down her cheeks unfettered, and she searched for words to explain to him how much his song moved her.

"Oh, Cass, don't cry. You're not supposed to cry." He swung the guitar to the floor and stood, just as she did. He wrapped her in an embrace, holding her as she shook with emotion.

"Oh, God! I'm sorry," she got out. "I didn't know... I was just so confused. I never meant to hurt you."

"I know. It was just so much, so quickly for both of us. I am just as much to blame as you are, even more so. That's why I decided to slow things down, so we can get to know each other. So you can become comfortable with your feelings and my feelings for you."

She squeezed him harder. She didn't know what to say. All she could manage was to whisper. "That song was beautiful, Josh. Just beautiful."

"I'm glad you liked it. And happy I could share it with you. Now," he said, pulling away, trying to lighten the mood, "can we get something to eat, cause I'm starved."

She wiped the tears from her face. "Oh. We worked right through lunch."

"And played." He grinned.

"I'll get something started right away."

"No. Don't do that. Why don't we go somewhere nice and have dinner?"

"That sounds great. But it's my treat. You made dinner last night."

"We'll see."

"No now, I insist. Just because you make more money than I do—okay, a lot more money than I do—that doesn't mean you should pay for everything. I want to take you."

"Okay, okay. Can I at least call and make the reservations?"

"Sure. You can do that," she said with a smile. "What do you want to eat?"

He shrugged. "I'm game for anything...except maybe Italian. It would be hard to beat the fantastic meal we had last night," he added, grinning.

"You're right. Well...there's a place called 'Le Radis Rouge.' It's funny how they can make even 'red radish' sound expensive in French."

"All right. I'll call and make reservations, and you go finish getting dolled up."

Josh looked up the number, hoping that eating late would discourage interruptions from fans.

"Le Radis Rouge, Dixie speaking."

Josh almost laughed as the southern drawl uttered the French words. "Hi. I was hoping to get a reservation for two for dinner. Would you have anything available at, say, eight o'clock?"

"Yes, sir, not a problem."

"Good. I was wondering if you could do me a special favor and reserve the most private table you have. I'd be *very* appreciative..."

"No biggie, honey. You want privacy, you got it."

"Thanks, Dixie. The last name is Dunningham."

"Dunningham? Just like Josh Dunningham, right?"

"Exactly like."

"Okay. We'll see you at eight then, Mr. Dunningham."

Josh hurried upstairs to spruce up. He pulled another new purchase out of the bag. It was the same style as he wore the night before, only this time it was black pants with an electric blue shirt. He wished he had grabbed a sports jacket, too, but this would have to do.

He paged through a magazine while he waited for Cassie and was surprised by a picture of himself and a redhead, with a blurb about him getting "hot and heavy" with the actress, whom he was barely introduced to at a party a month ago. He turned as he heard Cassie coming down the stairs, closing the magazine and tossing it onto the coffee table.

First, he saw the shoes, silver, strappy affairs which made his heart go *zing*. His eyes slowly traveled up her legs. The high hem made them look like they could go on forever. The dress was what he would call "swooshy," flowing about her legs with a sheer hem of turquoise-blue fabric, then rising with a splash of the same-colored silk to kiss her hips and nip at her waist. It was a sleeveless number, crisscrossing at her chest leaving a V-shaped opening where a white crystal necklace hung tantalizingly between the tempting curves of her breasts. She had pulled back her hair, curling the few strands which hung near her face, alongside slim columns of silver and crystal hanging from each ear. He stood, unsure his legs would support him, temporarily deprived of the ability to speak.

She furrowed her eyebrows, and her eyes darted from his expression to her dress. "Wh-what?" Adding after a few seconds, "I should change." She turned to head back upstairs, but he lunged at her, grabbing her arm. She was spun around and found his face inches from hers.

"Don't you *dare*." He pronounced each word clearly, although his voice held the slightest tremble.

She realized, after a moment, the look wasn't one of disapproval, exactly the opposite. He liked what he saw; he liked it a great deal. She breathed out a sigh of relief and a surge of raw power flowed through her, making her feel almost giddy. This was how she'd always wanted a man to look at her, as if he would disintegrate if she so much as moved a fraction away from him. They stood frozen a second more, a knowing smile spreading over her lips, a tremulous one across his. His eyes roam over her again, without relinquishing an inch of her, and then let out a shuddery, devastated breath. At last, he let her go, stepping back. "Cassie...man!" He shook his head.

She stepped down on the hardwood, then leaned a hand against the wall, and kicked a heel behind her to pull a silvery strap up which had fallen when he spun her. He watched the strap slide over her ankle and closed his eyes for a second. He cleared his throat, "Uhh...you're ready, then?"

"Oh. I forgot my purse."

She flew up the stairs and he sank onto the arm of the couch with a schoolboy sigh. He was never going to be able to take things slowly with her like he promised, if she kept doing this to him. It was definitely her fault. No woman should have the right to look that hot, and cause a man to have such lurid thoughts, just by entering a room. Just when he thought he was regaining his composure, he saw the heels coming down again. But this time she skipped down the last several steps and sprang into his arms with a laugh.

Laughter and love bubbled up out of him as he grabbed her around the waist and they giggled, nearly falling into the armchair together. "Let's go, you big goofball."

She handed him a bundle of turquoise as she slung a silver beaded bag from her shoulder, the long straps allowing it to hang nearly to her hips. "Could you put my shawl on for me?" she asked coyly, shooting him a flirtatious look over her shoulder.

He chuckled again and stretched the gauzy material out to its full length, stepping up, and hesitating a second before dropping it over her perfect shoulders. Then he gave his hands permission to briefly run the course from her neck to her shoulders underneath the fabric he just draped, bringing his lips to her ear. "You don't play fair, you know," he said, his voice a low rumble.

She flipped the end of her wrap over her shoulder, almost hitting him in the face, and said imperiously, "I don't know *what* you're talking about," before striding out of the room with another playful glance back.

"The hell you do," he said to the air, but hurried after her all the same.

CHAPTER SIXTEEN

Forty-five minutes later, after a brief stop at the mall, where Josh purchased the sports coat after all, Josh pulled Cassie's car into the parking lot of the restaurant. "Wait. Let me open your door for you."

"Ooh. Such manners."

"Just because I play rock and roll," he replied with a grin, "doesn't mean I don't know how to treat a lady." He kept his eyes on her as he crossed in front of the car. Helping her out, he crooked an arm, and she slid hers through it.

Her eyes twinkled. "I've got to say, that jacket looks good on you. And you wear it well. I swear you look as comfortable in it as you do in T-shirts and ripped jeans."

He felt an unfamiliar heat in his cheeks. "Well, I do have to attend award shows and schmooze with record label execs from time to time." He tugged on his lapel. "But don't let this get-up fool you. I may be polished around the edges, but underneath it all I'm still the same old boy from Iowa leashed to a thousand-watt amp."

He was grateful for the fading light which would allow them a degree of anonymity. Fancy restaurants usually had fairly dim lighting as well, and when they arrived, he was not disappointed.

Even before they got close enough to read her name tag, he knew the bleach-blonde older lady behind the hostess stand had to be Dixie. Her conservative black and white uniform was unbuttoned a little farther than the others, and the pink, fuzzy ball rubber band holding her hair in place was a dead giveaway.

"Hi, Dixie."

"Holy shit!" she said, accidentally letting her pink bubble gum fall out and onto her reservation list before clapping a hand over her mouth. "You're—"

Josh put a finger to his lips, shaking his head.

The hostess came over, whispering loudly, "Do you know who you are?"

"Most of the time, yes. But the night is still young."

She laughed, a hand over her heart, going back to her first assessment. "Holy shit!"

A barrel-chested man in the same black and white uniform rounded the corner, looking red-in-the-face and ready to explode on lil' Miss Dixie. Catching Josh out of the corner of his eye just as he raised a finger to scold her, he stopped, finger in midair, blinking at Josh.

"You're—"

"Josh Dunningham," he said hurriedly. "Nice to meet you. Now, Dixie, do you think we could get that table now, before there's a scene?" Other eyes were beginning to turn from the dining room.

"Sure thing, sugar." Grabbing menus, she escorted them through the bar on their left, avoiding all the eyes in the dining room, to a smaller room behind French doors. They were in a corner, so, after holding Cassie's seat out for her, Josh was able to turn his back to the rest of the diners. Dixie continued to bustle around the table, straightening things that didn't need to be straightened, with the manager moving in her wake.

"Mr. Dunningham, let me buy you and your lovely lady here, a drink."

"Thank you anyway, but I was feeling a little extravagant." Josh took the wine list from the center of the table and perused it quickly. "Could we please get a bottle of the Omni Noir?"

"Yes, sir," the manager answered happily, no doubt sensing a big night. He shooed Dixie off and left.

"The wine is on me," Josh said sternly. "I felt like splurging."

"So you said. What's the occasion?"

He picked her hand up off the table and kissed it. "Dinner out with a beautiful lady."

Cassie smiled at him then looked up questioningly at a man who was now standing over Josh's shoulder. He was a tall, middle-aged man who wore pristinely starched, expensive clothing and had black hair plastered in place with hair spray.

"Excuse me," began the man with a game show host's smile, "but can my wife get a picture with you? We're huge fans."

Why do people think saying they're 'huge fans' excuses any behavior?

"Actually—" Josh started to respond.

"Thanks, thanks." He began setting the scene. He gestured at Cassie, impatiently, "Could you move over there, babe?" Before she could respond, he stepped in front of her, almost knocking her off balance. "Just sit on his lap, honey," he added to his wife, who climbed onto Josh's lap and threw her arms around him. Her bottled-blond hair fell to her shoulders, where it curled up perfectly, just above the pink cashmere jacket she was pressed into.

"Wow, you *are* nice looking," she said in a scratchy voice, running her fingertips through his thick hair.

Josh had moved past annoyance and was well into aggravation. "Listen—" The camera flash blinded him for a moment in the dim room. "We're trying—"

The man looked up from his camera and addressed Cassie. "How about you, sweetheart? Are you someone special?"

"Me?" she said, seeming surprised he had spoken to her at all. "No...I'm not—"

"She damn well is special!" Josh shouted, jumping out of his seat. He would have dumped the man's wife on the floor, except for the fact she still had her arms locked around his neck. He reached up and separated her hands as he talked, his jaw clenched and his eyes firing as hot as his mouth was. "You need to apologize to the lady for being rude. NOW."

"Josh," Cassie said quietly, "it's okay. He didn't mean to—"

"No, Cassie. It's not okay," he snapped. The rest of the restaurant had become quiet.

"Hey, I didn't mean to insult your little..." he looked Cassie over contemptuously, "...*date,* here. Just because you're some big rock star—" The man was either drunk or stupid because he took a step toward Josh who took a step toward him.

"Sir." Perhaps seeing smashed tables and dark headlines, the manager stepped between the two with his back to Josh. "Mr. Dunningham and this fine young woman are trying to enjoy a nice evening together. Don't you think they deserve that? You got your picture. Why don't you let these folks get back to their dinner?"

"Yeah, well..." the man muttered. He acted as if he was giving the matter some debate then slid his arm around his ditzy wife's waist. "Come on, baby," he crooned as they turned to walk away. "Let me take you home and show you what a real man's like." He looked balefully over his shoulder. Josh made a move to follow him but was blocked by the manager.

"I have your wine, sir." He snapped his fingers, and a waiter appeared who had apparently been hanging back to avoid the fray. He held an ice bucket with the wine. Josh looked over his shoulder when the blonde squealed, squeezing her husband's muscles as he flexed them for her.

"Josh," Cassie said mildly, "I could use some wine."

He turned around to look at her, an apology on his lips. Her hands shook as he moved to pull her chair out for her. They sat and the waiter poured each a glass, skipping the whole smelling and tasting portion of the program in his haste. Josh glanced around uneasily, noting many pairs of eyes trying to look at them, while appearing to not look at them. He slid down a little in his chair, his elbows resting on the table, his hands laced together at the fingertips with his palms spread apart. He looked darkly over them at the bottle for a minute.

Cassie sipped nervously, seeming unsure of what to say next. Josh's gaze flicked up to hers.

"I'm sorry, Cass.'"

"No. No," she reassured him. "That wasn't your fault."

"Well, I didn't exactly handle it with the diplomacy of Ghandi, either."

"You're not Indian. You're Irish. You're entitled." She raised her glass to clink it with his.

He picked his glass up with a smile and tapped it against hers before taking a sip. It soothed as it traveled down his still-tight throat. Suddenly all he wanted to do was kiss her. "Hey, I've kind of lost my appetite. What do you say we take our wine and go for a walk along the shore? Unless you're hungry...?"

"I lost my appetite as soon as that woman put her hands on you," she replied. "Let's get out of here."

They stood, and Josh pulled a money clip out of his pocket, peeling off four hundred- dollar bills and tossed them on the table. He lifted the bottle from the ice bucket and dried it off with a napkin, hooking his fingers around the stems of their empty glasses. He held his other hand out to her with a smile and led her away. The manager approached as they headed for the door.

"You're not leaving?" He sounded sincerely disappointed.

Josh nodded. "I left money on the table for the wine and the glasses." He tipped his head at the hostess station. "Goodnight, Dixie."

"Goodnight, handsome. You make sure you come back and visit us again sometime."

"I'll do that."

Without another word, they rushed out, giggling like truant school kids as the restaurant doors closed behind them. A fresh breeze greeted them.

"M-mm," Cassie sighed appreciatively. "Taking a walk was a good idea."

"Hold on," Josh requested, setting the wine and glasses down on an empty wrought-iron table on the patio. "I have another good idea." With surprising quickness, he cradled her face in both hands and crushed his lips against hers, backing her up, at the same time, against a brick column supporting the restaurant's overhang. His thumbs caressed her cheeks as he ravaged her mouth, hungry for the feel of her body next to his. "I've wanted to do that ever since you came down the stairs in that dress."

She looped her hands around his neck. "So why did you wait so damn long, Dunningham?" She pulled him in so it was her lips claiming his, with equal fervor, and he tasted the sweet wine on her breath. They parted as a couple left the restaurant, but he never took his eyes from her face. She leaned, with her hands behind her, against the brick, smiling up at him, the light from the parking lot bathing her in its glow.

When the couple was out of earshot he brushed the back of his hand across her soft cheek. "My gosh, Cassie. You're so beautiful, you take my breath away." Her eyes searched his as if the answers to the Universe lay there. "I think I'm falling in love with you."

Her smile twitched on the ends, and she dropped her eyes for a moment. Just as he started to ask her if something was wrong, another couple approached to enter the restaurant.

He smiled. "Let's take that walk."

They passed Cassie's car in the parking lot on their way to the beach. She leaned against the hood and slipped off her shoes. Looking around, she discreetly tried to roll her stockings down. He watched the sheer hem of her short dress as it skimmed up her leg. *Ummm. Thigh-highs.* She rolled them into a ball and stuck them in the toes of the silver heels she hooked on the windshield wipers. *What makes those things so damn hot? Maybe it's because they travel the length of those incredible legs and then just stop, right there, near The Promised Land.*

He scolded himself for his dirty thoughts as he pulled his own socks down and put them in the shoes he had already taken off, which were now lying on the hood of the car. She wrapped her shawl around the antennae, and he rolled his pant legs up. She walked in front of him in the sand, holding his hands from behind her back, until she got close to the water's edge. She dropped his hands and ran the last several feet to splash in the waves like some kid. He stood there and watched her play for a minute, mesmerized by her, until she turned around and caught him.

"Come on down here, you big chicken. It's not that cold."

He stuck the wine and glasses in the sand and strolled toward her, his hands in his pockets, stopping in front of her. She gazed at him, an impish grin on her face, and then slipped her hands between his arms and his body, grabbing his behind. He laughed, putting his hands on her shoulders, and kissing her again, softly. He felt the goose bumps on her arms. A chillier wind was blowing off the water. "You're cold." He slid his jacket off.

"That's okay, Josh. I can run back and get my shawl."

"No. Just wear this. I don't need it, and, besides, you look cute in it." The hem was down to her knees, shoulders halfway to her elbow. He put his hand around her waist and they ambled down the beach. "I really am sorry about the way I handled things back there."

"The guy was being a jerk. And if that woman hadn't stopped pawing you I was going to have to start tearing her hair out, and that would have been really embarrassing."

His gaze slid sideways. "You sound jealous."

"Damn right, I am. The only one who should be pawing you is me." She spoke naturally, as if conversing with herself, and then seemed embarrassed she spoke the words aloud.

Noticing her blush, Josh stopped walking and captured her in his arms again. "Good. Cause you're the only one I want pawing me anyway." He kissed her on the nose and then picked her up off her feet, swinging her around. He set her down and they walked again, hand-in-hand, faces lifted to the breeze. After a while he asked, "Okay, so you know who I watched 'Fantasy Island' with. Who did you watch it with?"

"Mostly my sister, Sarah. There was just the two of us."

"Your parents didn't watch it with you, too?"

She stopped in her tracks. She stooped to pick up a seashell, turning it over in her hands. "Sometimes," she said softly, staring out over the horizon to where the sky met Lake Michigan. "But they were killed in a car accident when I was sixteen." She tossed the shell into the waves, watching it disappear.

Josh couldn't find words for a second. "That must have been rough."

She reached for his hand and turned to continue strolling up the beach. "Yeah. It was. It was storming. They'd gone into town to have supper at a local restaurant. When I got off work at the movie theatre, I passed the ambulances on the way home. Didn't even recognize the old truck my daddy had since I was a little girl. Just drove right past it." He rubbed her hand in an effort to comfort her as she spoke. "Sarah was away at college. She's five years older than me. She came home to take care of me and finished her degree at Madison Community College so I wouldn't have to switch schools."

"Madison, Wisconsin?"

She nodded. "I was born there and lived on my family's farm until my parents died. Then Sarah and I had an apartment for a while before I left to attend college at Wash U. in St. Louis."

"So you're one of those 'Midwest farmer's daughters' the Beach Boys wrote about."

"Uh-huh. My dad had a large dairy farm, not exactly an oddity in the state of Wisconsin, and I did my fair share of milking. It was hard work. I can't say I missed it too much when we had to sell it off. But I did miss the cows. Still have a fondness for cows, in fact. And cats, plenty of barn cats..." She stared off, lost in her reminiscing. She stirred. "Do you think we should head back? We still have a very expensive bottle of wine buried in the sand, I hope, and all this talking is making me thirsty."

He nodded and they made their way back toward the car. It was interesting hearing her talk; like getting little bits of the puzzle which was Cassie McCallister that he could lay out on the floor and piece together.

"It must have been scary moving away from Sarah to go to school."

"Not really. Sarah and I weren't really getting along then. My fault entirely. She was doing her best to be a mother to a teenager at the ripe old age of twenty-one, and I resented being bossed around by her." She paused, thinking. "Actually, I think I resented more not being able to be bossed around by my mother." She was silent, and the only sound for a while was the waves lapping against the beach, oddly mixed with the unnatural sound of the cars on Lake Shore Drive.

Josh was quiet, trying to imagine what it must be like to lose a parent, one you were actually connected to. He pictured it like losing Ryan's mom and dad, and that was horrific. "What was your dad like?" he asked quietly. "Or maybe I shouldn't—"

"No. It's all right." She gathered her thoughts. "Hank McCallister was a...portly man," she smiled. "Round, an older parent—he was forty-five when I was born—my mom was thirty-seven. He was a cradle-robber. When I was in school, he was balding. What hair he did have was gray. People would always mistake him for my grandpa, but it didn't bother him a bit, he'd just tell them proudly I was his little girl. And I was proud of him." She stopped, looking down the beach wistfully.

"And your mom?"

Cassie sighed. "Dame Judy McCallister. She was...fabulous, utterly fabulous. Having come to motherhood late, she seemed determined to make up for lost time...or maybe she somehow knew her time was limited... Anyway, she was head of the P.T.O. for...gosh, I don't know how long...forever. She coached my volleyball team to two back-to-back state titles."

He raised his eyebrows. "Mental note: never challenge Cassie to volleyball."

She gave him a funny smile, her top lip slightly curled. "I know, I know. I don't look much like a volleyball player, do I? Don't have the legs for it."

"I love your legs."

"Oh, now you're just blatantly flattering me. I have...woefully inadequate legs. They're so short."

"It's not the length," he said, reaching down to run a hand up her leg, "it's the shapeliness."

"Ahh. No one's ever told me that."

"Well, it's true. You have *great* legs."

She glanced down to evaluate her legs in the mixture of moonlight and streetlight then looked up quickly. Grateful for a change in subject, she called out. "Look! There's our wine."

When they reached it, he pulled it out of the sand. "Hey, it's still cold." He poured her a glass. "Do you want to sit down? We could spread my jacket out and I could go get your wrap."

"That's okay," she said, swinging the jacket from her shoulders. "You can keep me warm."

"Even better," he purred, stretching the jacket out for her.

She sat, giving her legs another brief inspection while he poured his own glass of wine. Catching her at it again, he lowered himself next to her and, this time, slowly trailed his fingers from her ankle to the hem of her dress, then pulled it up a little.

He thought back to when he kissed her under the restaurant's overhang. During their walk, he hadn't let it bother him. She did not respond when he told her he loved her. It was enough he was able to say it, enough he was able to feel it, since he was a man whose own parents never chose to say it to him. But, he had, in any case, seen and felt love with Ryan and the rest of the Sandovals. Now he found he wanted, badly, to hear her say it. He wanted to take her home and make love to her slowly, to show her how he felt. Instead, he withdrew his hand, taking a long drink. "Tell me more about your mom."

"Well...she loved to sew. Made all our clothes, much to Sarah's and my eternal mortification. Although...there was this one really sweet dress she made me. Stoplight yellow with a red bubble gum dispenser on the bottom near the hem, with a bunch of different colored gum balls in it." She smiled again when he raised his eyebrows. "Yeah, I know. Majorly sweet."

He tried to picture her in it; could, for the most part, except for the hair. What her hair would have looked like then was a mystery to him. He reached out and touched a strand. He could smell her now that they were so close, the sweet honeysuckle scent of her skin. He wanted her. Now that she had given him the bits and pieces of her life, he suddenly needed all of it.

"Tell me about Troy."

She looked away, and he was afraid he'd asked too much, that she would pull away, but she started speaking. "I met Troy in college, my second semester freshman year. He was in law school at Wash U. and we met running across the quad in the rain." A small, sad smile stole across her face. "He had an umbrella, I didn't. We hit it off right away." She took a long drink of her wine, sighing as she continued. "I was eighteen, he was twenty-two..." She paused and he was about to ask another question when she began again. "Troy was from a very wealthy family back East, studying to be a corporate lawyer like his father, Banton Leary. But—" She took another sip.

"Wait. Banton Leary? The Boston power broker?"

She raised her glass. "The one and only. But, miraculously, he is nothing like his father, or his mother, for that matter. His father is clever and calculating, Troy is sensitive and sincere. His mother is cold and haughty, Troy is warm and genuine." She stared out over the waves. "We were happy. He proposed to me on his family's estate in Connecticut when I was visiting over break."

Josh didn't want to hear it, desperately didn't want to hear her talk about another man. But he needed to know. He wanted to look away as her face softened when thinking of him, wanted to plug his ears when she spoke his name with tenderness. He didn't want to picture them together, but he knew, definitely knew now, for them to go forward, they had to deal with whatever it was that happened between her and Troy.

Her finger skimmed around the edge of her glass for a moment. "We planned everything together, from the font on the place cards at the reception, to the color of my garter belt. The flowers were ordered. I had only one final fitting remaining for my dress, the invitations had all been mailed...all four-hundred-twenty-seven of them." She drained her wine, and he reached to fill her glass again. "It was all a huge headache. His mother second-guessed every decision I made and one night I overheard her telling Troy she didn't understand why he 'was thinking with his penis and not his head.' I had no 'people' for God's sake, what was he thinking? But he loved me, so it was all worth it. Every insult she hurled at me, every menu she rewrote...because, eventually, at the end of it all, I would be married to the man I loved. Six weeks before the wedding, I was back for another visit. We went horseback riding and had a picnic, where I had my first glass of wine." She looked down into her glass now, as if reading the words she said in its depth.

"We ended up back at the stables. He wanted to make love to me. We'd agreed to wait until we were married." Her voice was tight now, her face etched with pain. She blinked back her tears.

He felt a rage boiling up. "He forced you to, didn't he?"

She shook her head vehemently, and a hot tear landed on his arm. "No. No. It wasn't like that. It was my first time, his, too." A small sob tore from her and she covered her mouth with a trembling hand. "I'm sorry. You don't want to hear this." Agitated, she made a move to stand up. But he laid a hand on her arm.

"Please, Cassie, finish this."

She sat back down but looked away from him. Her voice was small and hollow when she spoke next. "He didn't call me the next day or answer my calls. Or the next day. Or the next. Two whole weeks passed, and I couldn't take it anymore. I missed him. He was my best friend. And I didn't know what was wrong. I went to his house." Her face became hard, her voice, flat. "He told me he joined the seminary." She laughed, a strange, high-pitched laugh. "Funny, isn't it? The man makes love with me, and the experience is so traumatic for him he has to become a priest."

Josh didn't know what to say. This wasn't at all what he expected. The man made love to this beautiful woman, and chose to become a priest? It made as much sense as a blind man performing surgery.

Suddenly she sprang up and ran toward the waves. He pushed up and sprinted after her, unsure about what she was doing. But she stopped when her feet hit the water, stood, her legs spread apart, her hands clenched by her sides, not making a sound. He moved toward her, intending to comfort, but she spun around in a fury. "So, you can just go now." Her eyes flashed with anger and tears. "I'm damaged. Too much baggage. A real whack job." She stumbled back a few steps, and he reached for her, afraid she would fall. She crossed her arms over her chest, rubbing her arms and rocking.

And then she fell apart. "Josh," she cried out, breaking his heart, "I don't even know how you can stand to look at me."

"Cassie." He stepped closer and folded her into his arms.

"No. Let me go!" She tried to free her shoulders, but kept her head buried in his chest as the sobs began to break loose. "Please, Josh...just let me go." Despite her words she clung to him, shaking.

"Let's go sit down," he whispered to her, leading her back to his coat, which had blown into a heap. He stretched it out and sat with her again. She leaned on him, and he rocked her, patting her hair as she cried, letting her get it all out of her system. When she calmed some, he tried to talk to her. "Cassie, what happened back then—"

"I know. It was a long time ago, four years ago, I should be over it. Everybody's been through a bad breakup. But they don't let it scare them off relationships forever, they get over it. I should be over it by now."

"That isn't what I was going to say. And give yourself a break. You were together for two years and were planning to get married." He was torn up over losing her after knowing her for less than four hours. "And, he didn't leave you for another woman, who you could hate," he tried to lighten the mood. "Or take a picture of, which you could then turn around and throw darts at. He didn't give you someone you could call and hang up on. He left for the church. A noble and downright nasty thing to do." She chuckled a little. He pulled back so he could peer down into her face. "What I was going to say was, what happened back then doesn't affect the way I feel about you right now. Not one little bit. Except, maybe, it helps me to understand why you pull away every time I get close."

"I'm s-sorry. You see..." she looked up at him, her brokenness written in her eyes, "...I'm messed up. And I don't blame you if you run as far away from me as you can. I really don't."

"But, you see..." he crooked a finger underneath her chin to lift her face, as he did the first night they met, "...then it would be me who would be messed up. I need you. And for the life of me, I can't understand a man who would want to leave you after making love to you. Because ever since I've made love to you, all I want to do, is do it again."

"H-he said he couldn't be the man he wanted to be with me. What we did, he felt was so out of control. He couldn't be like that. He couldn't love me like that. I told him I'd change. I could change..."

"If the man couldn't accept the wonderful woman you are, that was his problem, not yours. You didn't do anything wrong."

So this is why she doesn't trust my love, and why making love to me is painful for her. This is why she runs away, a sort of preemptory strike. She thinks if she leaves, maybe it won't hurt her as much as when I do. Add to this the fact he came on to her like a man just released from prison when they first met, it was amazing she hadn't run the minute he licked her arm. *But then again,* he remembered, *I didn't give her much of a chance.* When she needed someone to be gentle with her, he had been anything but. What could he say to her now to make her understand he loved her and didn't want to do anything to hurt her again?

He was saved from figuring out an answer to that question by an odd source. His stomach rumbled. Loudly. Cassie, whose head was still resting against his chest, jumped back, startled, and they both laughed.

"I guess I'm hungry after all."

She sniffled. "There's a place...up on the pier," she said hesitantly. "It has these really greasy, really incredible hamburgers."

He hopped up, offering his hand. "Lead me to them." If he was going to figure things out between them, he had to do it on a full stomach.

CHAPTER SEVENTEEN

He liked the place immediately. It was loud, a little dingy, and it reeked of greasy French fries. The sign outside read "Shorty's," but the proprietor was anything but. The African American bar owner played for a short stint with the Harlem Globe Trotters, and he still retained an air of showmanship. "Welcome to Shorty's, Home of the Best Damn Burgers in Town. What can I get you two?"

"I'll have a beer. Cass?"

"Huh? Oh. Just water, please."

"Coming right up."

A big-chested, brunette bartender, who had been eying them since they came in, stopped incessantly wiping the bar down. "Has anyone ever told you, you look like Josh Dunningham?"

"A few. My mother especially."

Cassie snorted.

"Well, we mothers have the right to have an overinflated opinion of our sons."

Josh was amused. "So, you think it's overinflated, huh? I'm not as good-looking as Josh Dunningham?"

"Well, no offense, you're gorgeous and all, but Josh Dunningham...he's hot. Am I right?" she asked Cassie.

"Absolutely." She smiled up at Josh.

He kissed her.

"Hey, you two." They turned and saw Heather, dressed to the nines in tight jeans, stilettos, and a barely-there tank top.

"Heather." She threw her arms around her friend. "What are you doing here?"

"Where else would I be? It's Karaoke Night."

"Is it, really?" Cassie said innocently.

"I've been set up."

"What, afraid of a little karaoke, Dunningham?"

"No. Did you forget, sweetheart, I do this for a living?"

"Oh, yeah. But the thing is," she winked at Heather, "we get to pick your song out for you."

"Another attempt at keeping me humble?"

"Uh-huh."

"You're something else."

"I bet you say that to all the girls. Come on, Heather, here's the list." They moved off to a table, he following with their drinks.

"This works two ways, you know. If I have to sing what you pick, then you have to sing what I pick."

Cassie's head snapped around, a look of surprise on her face. "If I'm going to sing," she said slowly, "then I'm going to be needing some tequila."

Five minutes later, the waitress dropped off the shots, salt, and lime. Josh and Cassie looked each other in the eyes, then locked hands.

"What?" Heather asked, looking from one to another. "You guys have an arm-wrestling thing?"

Without breaking eye contact, Cassie turned Josh's hand over, and licked his wrist to sprinkle it with salt. Josh did the same to hers, and then they took turns licking the salt off and simultaneously downed their shots.

Heather stared. "O-o-okay."

"Our first singer tonight," the announcer began, reading the name off a slip of paper, "is Josh. Josh, come on up here."

"Here goes," he said with a smile. He stepped onto the stage to a polite smattering of applause.

"Okay, Josh, what are you singing tonight?"

He smiled down at Heather and Cassie. "I have no idea. It's a surprise."

"Okay. Well, let's get started then. The words will come up on that little screen in front of you."

Josh stared at the monitor and started laughing. "You've got to be kidding." The words to Aretha Franklin's, "Respect" began rolling along the screen. He began to sing, and pretty soon found his comfort zone with the song and had the crowd behind him. Heather and Cassie started off laughing and ended up begrudgingly high fiving him as he returned to the table.

"Do we have a Cassie in the audience?"

She stood and prepared to face the challenge.

"Wait, Cass...the song I picked's too hard. Let me find another one."

But it seemed her liquid courage had really boosted her spirits. "I can take anything you can hand out, Dunningham."

The host held his hand out to help her onto the stage. She twirled the microphone around, her eyes looking laughingly at Josh's. The title came up on the screen, "Hard to Handle" by The Black Crowes. "I love this song!" she squealed.

"This will be interesting," Josh commented to Heather.

Cassie converted the lyrics, which was written for a male, as she sang. She kept her eyes on him and belted the song out with a sexy little smile. As her comfort level increased, so did her animation. Soon, the crowd was into her song and catcalls and wolf whistles filled the air. She threw a wink at Josh as she sang to him.

"You go, sugar!" Shorty called from the bar. Josh noticed all work had stopped and everyone was watching her. By the time she was done, the crowd was whipped into a frenzy. Two guys offered her their hands to help her off the stage and she strolled over to kiss Josh, who was giving her a standing ovation.

"I'm not sure we've ever had a performance quite like that before," the host called out excitedly. "Thank you, Cassie. Now, I know that was a hard act to follow, but I'd like to call David to the stage."

A middle-aged, overweight man took the stage and sang a very off-key version of "Feelings," which the crowd enjoyed for its over-the-top badness. Meanwhile, Cassie snuggled with Josh.

"You were incredible."

"Yeah, girlfriend. You really kicked ass," Heather added with glee.

Josh and Cassie turned to her and said, at the same time, "Your turn."

"No way. I'm not goin' up there." But, after another couple of shots, Heather did a rollicking rendition of "I've Got Friends in Low Places." She left the stage to roam through the crowd while she sang, much to the delight of the males in the room. Then, she realized she didn't know all the lyrics and started making up some of her own.

When she returned to the table, a dark-haired twenty-something muttered to Josh, "Dude, you're hogging all of the fun women. Not to mention the cute ones. Haven't you ever heard of sharing?"

Josh laughed. "Get your own, dude," he returned, looping his arms around both girls' shoulders. "I'm not into sharing."

"Speak for yourself," Heather interrupted, jabbing him in the ribs. "Come on over here, cutie."

The newcomer joined them, and Josh and Cassie enjoyed each other's company, while Heather got to know her new friend better.

Twenty minutes later, Josh and Cassie heard their names. The host announced, "We've had a special request for a duet." They slid their eyes in Heather's direction and noticed she was now giggling, ready to fall out of her seat.

They looked at each other. "Come on!" people shouted from the crowd. Josh shrugged and stood, offering his hand to Cassie, to the cheers of the bar patrons. She rose with him and they took the stage together.

"Can we get two more shots of tequila, please?" Cassie said into the microphone to a chorus of laughter.

"Okay, Josh...is that your real name or are you just using it while you're singing tonight because of your resemblance to Josh Dunningham?"

"It's my real name." Shorty delivered the shots.

"No kidding? You even sound like him, a little. And Cassie, where are you from, hon?"

She swallowed the tequila. "Whoo! From right here in Chicago."

"Well, lucky for you, you have a good voice. Some of these people are going to wake up tomorrow and have an office mate say, 'I saw you at Shorty's last night. You weren't doing any better there than you do around here on a daily basis.'" The statement earned a round of snickers and finger pointing. "Now, let's see what your friend picked out for you. Ahh...Sonny and Cher's, 'I Got You, Babe', a classic."

Cassie consulted with Josh. "Since I'm short, I think I should be Sonny. You be Cher. You have the right hair color."

"O-okay," Josh said slowly. He threw back his shot as the music started, Cassie launching into her best imitation of Sonny's scratchy voice. When it got to his part, the audience hooted at Josh's imitation of Cher, and as he warmed to the role, he threw in an imaginary hair-flip which sent them rolling. When the song was over, he smiled and hugged her, as the crowd roared their approval. "Do you want to go home now?" he yelled over the noise.

She smiled. "Yeah."

They high-fived their way out of the bar, waving goodbye to Heather who was too engrossed with the guy she was with to take much notice of their departure.

When the bar's door closed behind them and they were in the quiet again, Josh offered, "Do you want to take a walk down to the end of the pier?"

"Sure." They strolled arm-in-arm, enjoying the stillness after the pandemonium of the bar. They ambled to the end of the weathered pier and looked out over the crashing water. After several minutes, Cassie tried to boost herself up to sit on the top of the rails. Josh helped her up then stood with his hands on her hips for balance. The wind was lapping her hair against her face, and she brushed it back as she asked quietly, "When do you have to go?" She stared at her feet, swinging loosely below her.

He looked off a moment, and then back at her. "Well, I have a concert scheduled for tomorrow night in Cincinnati."

"Oh," she breathed out. He barely heard her above the sound of the wind and water.

"But I don't have to go. I can cancel."

"No. You can't do that."

"Come with me."

"To Cincinnati?"

"Yes."

She thought about it. "Well, I guess I could drive back after the show. It's not that far..."

"No. I wouldn't want you driving back at night. Couldn't you take a half-day off work or something?"

She smiled. "I could probably do that." She kicked off the ledge and slipped down into his arms. "Let's go home."

He nodded and kissed her, happy they wouldn't have to say goodbye, just yet.

THEY ENTERED THROUGH the door leading from the garage and Cassie went to the kitchen to hang her keys up on a hook. Josh put his arms around her waist. "You're tired," he murmured in her ear.

She nodded, leaning back against him. "It has been a long day." She turned in his arms and hugged him, laying her head on his chest.

He kissed her hair. "Let's get you to bed."

They trudged upstairs together. She slipped on a shimmering, blue nightgown and met him at the edge of the bed, where he sat with his pants still on, unbuttoning the cuffs of his shirt. She had washed her face, and taken off her makeup, with very little change in her appearance. Her lips were more natural but still inviting. Her eyes were still as dazzling, made more so by the blue of the fabric she wore. She stepped between his legs. His hands went around her, sliding over the silky nightgown, coming to rest on her tush. She placed her hands on his shoulders.

"Thank you for tonight. For listening. For this whole weekend. It's been unbelievable."

He smoothed his hands along her backside, trying to ignore the fact it was turning him on. "I know it is hard for you to...believe in anyone anymore, but I love you." His fingers flew to her lips. "And it doesn't matter if you can't say it back to me right now. I intend to prove it to you." He was going to say more, but almost involuntarily, his finger on her lips began to trace the outline of her mouth. He breathed in, steeling himself to put all thoughts of her aside so they could just go to sleep, but she grabbed his palm and guided it to her mouth. At first she simply kissed it lightly. Then she began to run her mouth and tongue along his palm, and down his wrist as she kissed. Weakening, he looked at her shoulders, bare except for a thin strap. He pushed the strap off her shoulder and kissed her there. He breathed out, pulling back with resignation.

"Don't stop," she whispered, her eyes beseeching him.

He stood to kiss her, turning to lay her back on the bed. He took the rest of his clothing off by the light of the lamp as she watched, and then reached up to push her nightgown up, caressing her legs for several minutes. Then, he stretched out beside her and began massaging her all over, his hands wanting to be everywhere at once. They cruised over the soft skin of her stomach, over her breasts, squeezed her shoulders, her arms, her legs. When she pulled him down to kiss him, he responded to her, but always pulled back and watched his hands in the lamplight as they explored her body.

His touch voiced his love for her, his need for her, telling her tonight was all about her. He pulled the top of her nightgown down to expose her breasts and cupped them with his hands as his mouth came down on them. A pleasured noise escaped her throat. He pulled her to a sitting position to pull her nightgown off over her head, then nudged her onto her stomach, to let his hands wander more...over her back, her arms, her shoulders...diving down to feel her breasts again beneath her. He pulled her panties down and turned her again, caressing her, watching her face as she closed her eyes. He took her slowly up, stroking her as she moaned, her hands clutching at the covers underneath her. His fingers alternately probed and stroked as her back arched until she cried out and stilled.

Then he rose above her, plunging into her even as she reached for him. Her body quivered with fresh excitement. He made love to her, looking into her eyes as he took them both to new levels of ecstasy. He learned there was such a thing as toe-curling sex as his body was just so tensed before their shattering release.

When he finally rolled away, she laughed. "Wow."

He chuckled in return, still catching his breath. "Yeah, wow."

"Oh, my gosh. That was incredible." She lifted to kiss him. "*You* were incredible." She lay over him for a minute, her bare breasts against his chest, a hand running down his arm. He stroked the small of her back, moving his hand lower, where the skin was perpetually cool, like the opposite side of the pillow, and they drifted off.

When he took in his first waking breath, it was drenched with her heavenly fragrance. He was lying on his side, and Cassie was curled up beside him. He wondered over his newfound happiness with her, and how, after such a short time, he knew this was what he had wanted and longed for all of his life. This was where he belonged, where his lonely heart found its rest.

She took a deep breath beside him, then snuggled closer. He squeezed her and she sighed with contentment. "Mmm...good morning," she murmured, without turning. He could hear the smile on her face.

"Good morning to you." He kissed her neck.

"Oom...I don't want to get up. It feels so good lying next to you." She stretched from her head to her toes, her sleep-warmed body like sweet syrup flowing beside him.

"Do we have to get up?"

"I have to get ready for church. You can sleep as long as you want to, though."

"No. I'll get up and go with you."

She rolled over to look at him. "Really?"

He nodded, smiling down into her pretty face, thinking this was the only way to wake up in the morning.

"Do you go to church?"

"No," he admitted. "My parents never took me. But every once in a while, I would go with Ryan and his family."

"Are you sure you want to go?" She wrinkled her nose up as if doubtful, looking unbelievably cute.

"I'm sure." He rolled her over and slapped her rear. "Now get your booty up. I need to get ready." He slid out from beneath the sheets.

CHAPTER EIGHTEEN

Cassie was glad they hit the early Mass. Most of the parishioners who attended eight o'clock Mass were older and completely unaware of Josh's fame. Still, they received a number of looks as people were simply interested in who "the young man who had come to church with Cassie McCallister" was. Thus, Josh was introduced to several elderly ladies, who found him "quite charming." But the only person he seemed truly glad to see was Kevin. He was entering the building as they stood chatting with a circle of older women. Cassie felt uncomfortable, maybe even a little guilty; but Josh apparently had no such qualms. However, he did stop himself from giving Kevin a shout out on the church steps, although it appeared to be a struggle if his dancing eyes and twitching smile were any indicator.

They walked to the car holding hands. "Thanks for coming with me," Cassie said, squeezing his hand. "And for not waving at Kevin. Although I know you wanted to."

He sighed, giving her a sidelong look. "I did show remarkable restraint."

She smiled. "You did."

They went back to Cassie's, packed their bags, and pointed the car toward Cincinnati. It was a beautiful, late June day, and they breezed along, listening to her eclectic choice of music.

Josh gave a low chuckle.

"What?"

"I just find it amusing we just went from Andrew Lloyd Weber's, *Jesus Christ Superstar*, to AC/DC's, 'Shook Me All Night Long.' From J. C. to AC."

"And now we've got The Black Crowes."

"B.C.," they said in unison.

"You just have a wide variety and taste in music, and it cracks me up one minute we'll be listening to a Christian artist, the next Led Zeppelin."

"Yeah. But it was 'Stairway to Heaven,' so they are loosely connected."

He snorted. "Very loosely." He reached over for her hand to give it a squeeze. "I have so much fun with you."

"Yeah? Well, you're all right, too, ya know." She turned to look ahead again, the corners of her lips curling. "For a rock star, that is."

"Gee, thanks. Hey, this is a good song." The music was shuffled to one of Money Back Guaranteed's hit songs.

"Yeah. It's okay, I guess. But I heard the lead singer's a real ass."

"You did, did you?" He switched his blinker on.

"Where are you going?"

"To find a nice place to dump your body."

"No, don't," she said, laughing. "I'll be good. I promise." She raised his hand to her lips and kissed it.

"You're lucky you're cute," he remarked dryly.

She gazed out the window but sang along to his music...quietly at first, but by the end, she was really into it, which seemed to amuse him. The miles rolled along under their wheels as they listened to everything from The Irish Rovers, to Christian rock.

"Do you realize you not only got me to go to church today, but also introduced me to Mercy Me? I didn't even know such a thing as Christian rock existed. You're going to ruin my bad boy reputation, you know."

She winked at him. "That's the goal, Dunningham."

They were nearing the stadium when they pulled up to a stoplight next to a small green sedan. Josh glanced over and smiled broadly. Cassie looked, and recognized Ryan Sandoval. He had a goofy smile on his face and was gesturing, but before she could figure out what was going on, the light turned green, and tires began to squeal. The engines snarled as the two cars kept pace down the abandoned stretch of road. Cassie saw the look of sheer determination in Josh's eyes and the grim smile which still shadowed his lips. She was amused, angry, and terrified all at the same time. She saw the heavy iron bar fence that surrounded the stadium's parking lot whizzing past his window. She turned to look at their competition. Ryan's jaw was set with the same self-confident sneer plastered to his face. The pretty brunette at his side braced herself, looking petrified as speeds approached ninety-five miles per hour. Ahead, Cassie saw a large gate in the fence. Josh maneuvered Ryan to the outside so he could make the turn. Both cars burst through the gate at the same time, slamming toward the building at top speed. Like Hollywood stunt drivers, each slammed the brakes at the same time and steered away from each other to circle one-hundred-eighty degrees and come to an abrupt halt. Dust settled around the cars in the eerie silence that followed the roaring of the engines, now hissing like dogs panting after a race.

Josh turned to look at Ryan in triumph and must have caught the expression on Cassie's face. "Oh, gosh, Cass. I guess I shouldn't have done that with your car. I'll pay for new tires...and anything else that might have been damaged."

She glared at him, still slightly amused, but doing her best to keep it hidden; he needed to squirm a little bit more. Releasing the seat belt, which clanked against the door, she got out of the car. She stood on unsteady legs before leaning on the car. Josh hurriedly exited on his side. Ryan's passenger got out of the car on her side, appearing a little queasy, and he followed, a sheepish look on his face, stammering through some kind of apology or explanation. Shakily, with one hand on the car's hood for support, the brunette walked around the car to stand in front of Cassie, mimicking her pose by leaning against the car, catching her breath.

"What a pair of morons," Cassie quipped.

"You'd think they were still in high school," her opposite exclaimed, the frustration making her southern drawl all the stronger, which added to the humor in the situation.

She spun around, holding out her hand. "The keys, Dunningham," she growled, letting a hint of a smile show. He relinquished them with a guilty expression over the roof of the car. She turned to see the brunette holding out one hand to Ryan with the other hand on her hip, wearing a feigned air of disgust. He handed over the keys, but then, grabbed her, swung her against the car, and kissed her. Seeming not to want to be outdone, Josh came around the car and spun Cassie around to press her up against the car next to the pair and locked lips with her.

A group of roadies exited the stadium, catching the band members in hot embraces. They whistled and hooted. Cassie glanced in their direction, a little embarrassed, but then laughed and laid her forehead on Josh's. He still had his hands on her hips, and he pulled her in to kiss her again, long and deep. Her body responded to him. Even though no one else could know what she was feeling, she still felt a tinge of shame laced with the passion he was sending surging through her system.

Ryan turned to their audience. "He's always trying to upstage me."

Everybody laughed, and Cassie fanned herself in an exaggerated manner, even though, in reality, she was extremely worked up. The band members swung their hands over their girlfriends' shoulders to lead them inside, still receiving looks of admiration from the boys in the crew. They were eating it up.

Cassie offered her hand to Ryan's girlfriend. "I guess I should introduce myself. I'm Cassie McCallister."

"Nice to meet you, Cassie. I'm Paige O'Neal."

"I'm Ryan, by the way." He took her hand. "I'm glad to see you're not just a figment of his imagination." He jerked his head in Josh's direction. Josh reached around Cassie to bop Ryan in the back of the head, and then the two started sparring with each other.

"Oh. Good grief. Come on, Paige, let's go find us some men who know how to behave around women." Taking her hand, Cassie walked in the direction of the roadies, who noticed them approaching and looked up hopefully.

"Nuh-uh." Josh grabbed her arm and spun her around. Before she knew what was happening, he scooped her up in his arms and carried her toward the building.

"Josh, put me down!" Cassie, ordered, laughing and kicking.

"Not on your life."

He pushed through the door and practically ran into Lanny on the other side.

"Oh," Cassie tried to smother her laughter.

"Sorry, Lanny." He put Cassie on her feet. "This is Cassie."

"Yeah," his jaw was set to one side as he studied them. "I remember from the last time." He gave her a crooked smile.

"Have you met Paige?" Josh asked quickly.

"No, I haven't." Lanny gave her an apathetic once-over before adding. "Nice to meet you," in a saccharine kind of way.

"Nice to meet you," she answered sweetly. "Ryan has told me so much about you guys."

"Yeah...well don't believe everything old buzzard-breath has to say," Josh teased, taking another swipe at Ryan, who dodged.

"Yeah," Lanny added, with a low, humorless chuckle.

"Well, we'll be out in a few for sound check. We're going to drink a cold one before we get started," Josh told Lanny.

He watched them with slitted eyes. "Okay, see you in a few then."

LANCASTER MOON WAS not the only one watching the two couples. Angela Sabolti saw them arrive from her car parked across the street. She had been wondering why Josh hadn't called her. She gave her phone number to a roadie to deliver to him after seeing Josh in San Diego. She had to assume the roadie hadn't passed on the number, because he hadn't called. After having seen her again, he wouldn't do that, she surmised. Josh was just a little overwhelmed by his feelings for her. And he did have feelings for her; she could see it in his eyes and feel it in the way he kissed her.

So, that was why she was so totally blown away when he showed up with that girl again. Who the hell was she? And why was she messing around with *her* Josh? The girl was obviously a slut. Why else would she be throwing herself all over him and forcing him to kiss her?

I mean, it's clear Josh isn't into her. He's just hurting...feeling bad for the way we left things together. But he'll come around...he'll come around. And no bitch from Illinois is going to get in between the two of us. Not after I have waited all these years to feel his arms around me again.

After the two went into the building, she put her binoculars down and picked up her cell phone. Her father was the police chief of the small Nebraska town she grew up in. He'd run the slut's plates, and then she would know who the little blond whore was, and where she lived. She scooped up a pen and spiral notebook, adding a "DIE BITCH!" to the cover full of "Angela Dunninghams," and "Mrs. Josh Dunninghams" while she waited for her daddy to get the information. One thing was for sure, she wasn't going to play dead while someone else took Josh from her.

CHAPTER NINETEEN

Josh raised his eyebrows. "Your dad is here?"

"Yeah," Ryan answered with a grin. "He's here on business. That's where Paige and I were when you guys pulled up outside. We got dinner catered in for tonight. We rented tables and chairs and stuff. You guys will join us, won't you?"

He looked at Cassie.

"You should. But I don't want to horn in on—"

"Don't be silly," Paige drawled. "Ryan here got enough food to feed his dad and the entire crew. You'd be doing us a favor taking some of this food off our hands." She checked her with a hip. "Besides, I need another female presence, or I'm going to be in testosterone hell."

Ryan grabbed her from behind. "Oh, baby, I thought you liked my testosterone."

"I do." She giggled. "But I'm not so sure about all the others, especially that Lanny. He makes me feel like he wouldn't mind seeing me face down in some dark alley."

"Who, Lanny? Lanny's okay. He just takes a little getting used to. Anyway, Paige is right, Cassie. I ordered way too much food. Besides, I'd love the opportunity to get to know you better."

"Well...if you're sure I won't be interfering with family time..."

"No way."

"Okay, then." She smiled. "Is there anything I can bring?"

"Oh, Ry. We forgot to pick up the wine."

"I'll get that," Cassie offered.

"No, there's no need for you—"

"I insist."

"She's certainly stubborn, isn't she?" Ryan said out of the side of his mouth to Josh.

"You're telling me. Ouch. And violent." He kneaded his shoulder, where Cassie had punched him. "Despite that abuse, I'll take you to the liquor store."

"No way, Dunningham. I'm not letting you near my car again." She laughed. "I can get it. You stay here and spend some time with your family. I'll be back before you know it."

WHEN SHE ENTERED WITH the wine, Josh rushed over to take the box with the bottles in it and give her a peck on the cheek. An older man rose from his seat.

"Mr. Sandoval, I'd like you to meet Cassie McCallister."

"Josh, I think since we are both adults now, you can call me David." He extended his hand. "Nice to meet you, Cassie."

"It's nice to meet you, too, Mr. Sandoval. Josh has told me a lot about you."

"Really?" He seemed genuinely surprised. "And it's David, please." They all sat, and Josh began to open the wine and pour it.

Cassie put her napkin in her lap. "This is lovely, Ryan and Paige. Thank you for asking me to join you." They managed to dim the lighting in a conference room in the basement of the stadium and the caterers set up a big, round table with a green tablecloth, china, and crystal.

"We wanted to have a little privacy. Sometimes that's hard to achieve when we're out in public. Especially with pretty-boy, here." He snapped his napkin at Josh.

"Cassie got to experience that firsthand the other night." He finished pouring wine and set the bottle on the table.

"Oh?" Ryan grimaced.

"It was no big deal," Cassie tried to downplay it. "But I'll tell you," she said, in an aside to Paige, "if it would have gone on much longer, I would have had to drag some woman out of there by her hair."

"I know what you mean."

"So, Cassie," Ryan's father began, "Josh said you are in the advertising game?"

"Yes." She sipped her wine. "I'm kind of the idea person. I think up a concept, and my associates make it look good so I can pitch it to the client."

"I see. I kind of do the opposite with my job. I'm the detail guy, an accountant for a firm in Cedar Rapids. If I get too creative with my work, somebody goes to jail."

They all laughed, except for Lanny, who had been sitting back, taking it all in. "So, Lanny," Cassie asked, trying to get him involved in the conversation, "I understand you grew up with these guys, too. Did you play ball with them as well?"

He studied her. "Yep."

"What position?"

He took a drink of his wine. "Shortstop."

Cassie nodded politely, unsure of how to proceed after having received such curt answers. She was saved from figuring it out by David's question.

"Cassie, how did you and Josh meet?"

She had trouble swallowing her wine and her face became hot. "Well," she said slowly, "Josh tried to pick me up in a bar."

Ryan snorted.

"And, I see he succeeded," his father said.

"Well...not at first."

"I'm sure there's a story behind that, but I won't embarrass you by asking." He gave his son a meaningful look.

Ryan threw up his hands and mouthed, "What?" in an exaggerated manner. He went back to eating, but a few seconds later, put down his fork.

"So what, may I ask, did the two of you do while Josh was in Chicago?" Ryan's eyes twinkled.

"Well," Cassie glanced at Josh. "Josh made me dinner."

Ryan spit out his wine, causing a near chain-reaction around the table.

As he dabbed at the spewed wine on the table he asked, "He did WHAT?"

"He cooked me dinner. And it was excellent. In fact, after his illustrious career as a rock and roll singer has come to an end, I think he might have a job as a chef." Lanny sat up but didn't contribute anything to the conversation. “Oh, and Mr. Sandoval,” she looked at Ryan teasingly, “did you know Ryan wants to become a professional stunt driver?”

Paige hooted loudly and high-fived her.

“Is that so?” Mr. Sandoval asked, eyeing his son. Ryan chuckled, giving Cassie a look of newfound respect. “You two been hot-roddin’ by any chance?”

“Oh, no. No,” they both answered. Josh kissed Cassie’s hand.

“And then we sang karaoke,” Cassie continued.

“Isn’t that a bit unfair? You being a professional singer and all?” Ryan pointed out.

“Oh, no, man. No one believed I was me. One lady even told me I wasn’t as good-looking as Josh Dunningham.”

They all laughed again. “You’re kidding?”

He laughed. “I wish I was. It was somewhat insulting...sort of.”

“Oh, honey,” Cassie cooed, squeezing his cheeks. “I think you’re *just* as cute as Josh Dunningham.”

Dinner continued in the same vein. Josh sat back at one point, listening to the mindless chatter and laughter, and leaned over to whisper in Cassie’s ear, “This is what family is.”

CASSIE COULDN’T BELIEVE the deafening pitch of the crowd, even with earplugs in. The band was rocking the building; she could feel the bass humming through her body like a pulse. She stood in the wings with Paige and David, and the older man was splitting his time dancing with each of them. She was having the time of her life. She was surprised to find Ryan’s dad was really cool, despite his self-deprecating remarks about being “the nerdy accountant.”

Watching Money Back Guaranteed perform on stage was mind boggling. It was like they were completely different people than those she dined with hours before; they were true showmen, playing their audience as well as they played their guitars. The crowd seethed at the edge of the stage, and far back into the dark corners of the auditorium. Ryan and Josh poured so much of themselves into their music, by the time they left the stage for good, after their two encores, they were wiped out. Josh slung his hand over her shoulder. He walked with her, but didn't talk until they were far away from the stage area and behind some double doors.

"So," he breathed out, "what did you think?"

"I think," she said seductively, "you were *amazing*." She kissed him in a way that she hoped would instantly arouse every part of his tired body. "*Absolutely amazing*."

"You're not so bad yourself," he growled, rocking back and forth with his hands on her hips and his knees bent so he could see her better. He returned her impassioned kiss until the rest of the crew interrupted them by bursting through the door.

"Get a room," Ryan teased, throwing a towel at them.

"Hey, Mr. Sand—" Josh began, forgetting to call Ryan's dad by his first name, "David, I saw you hittin' on my best gal here while I was up there working for a living. I think I'm gonna have to ask you to step outside."

"Anytime, Dunningham. Anytime." David smiled. "The show was phenomenal. I'm blown away every time I come and watch you guys play. But it's way past my bedtime, so I think I'm going to head back to the hotel."

"Believe me, we're not far behind you, Dad."

AND THEY WEREN'T. THEY were able to exit from a little-known garage under the stadium and avoided the fans. Since he hadn't taken the time to shower in his dressing room, Josh told Cassie he was going to hop in quickly when they got to the hotel room.

When he came out, she was kneeling on the bed in black lingerie, silky on the top, then sheer the rest of the way to her waist, where it ended in a line of fur that met the top of her lacy underwear.

"Wow." He whistled. He stood frozen, a towel around his waist and the other hand holding another towel in mid-rub on his hair.

She crooked a finger at him and smiled. He looked so good, clean and hard, with just a little, ol' tip of the fabric tucked in, holding the towel in place below his well-developed abs. He tossed the towel he was drying his hair with carelessly on the floor and moved toward her as if in a daze. Though outwardly she tried to seem in control of the situation, her heart was racing. When he got close enough, she put out a hand to stop him, looking him in the eye for a long moment. Her glance strayed to where her hand lay on his firm stomach muscles. She twirled the soft hair there with her fingertips, prolonging his anticipation, then, took hold of the towel. Looking up at him with a playful grin, she yanked it off as he fell into bed with her, laughing. She climbed on top of him, and his hands wandered up to her full breasts. His cool, strong hands felt delicious as they slid their way up from her waist and she groaned. She bent over him, kissing his neck and nibbling on his ear.

"Ooh. Woman. The things you do to me."

"Oh, baby," she whispered, her hands sliding down his chest. "I'm just getting started."

"Mmm...," he closed his eyes, "...and I was thinking I'd be too tired."

"Don't worry about that," she said, trailing her mouth and tongue across his chest as she journeyed lower. "I'll do all the work."

He felt like he left the atmosphere for a moment as a sudden explosion of sensations near his groin area assaulted him. And just when he thought he was going to do some very unmanly whimpering, she rose above him, removing her panties to straddle him and take him into her smoothly. With each subtle movement of her hips, each twirl and gyration, he moaned. He flipped her onto the bed.

"I thought you were tired." His only response was to crush his lips to hers and thrust until he took them both over the edge. Exhausted, he fell to her side and was almost instantly asleep.

Hours later, he woke to his most erotic fantasy come true; she was stroking him awake. As he breathed in, she giggled.

"You're insatiable," he groaned.

"Some say that's my best feature."

"Some would be right. Wait a minute...just *who* says you're insatiable?"

"Never mind," she said, pulling him to her. "Kiss me, you big jerk. You know," she added between kisses, "you were incredibly hot tonight."

"Was I now?"

"Mmm-hmm." And that was the last of the conversation for the night.

CHAPTER TWENTY

Cassie smiled at the ten-foot-tall Josh for the first time. She was glad to be on good terms with him at last, although he did make her miss the real thing. It was late Monday morning, and she had driven straight to the office from Josh's bedside in Cincinnati. It helped a great deal to know, by the end of the week, he would be playing in Chicago, and they'd get to spend some more time together. A soft knock on the door interrupted her musing.

"Come in."

Julie, a young girl who had just started working for Cassie and was still finishing up her degree at night school, stuck her head in. "Ms. McCallister," the new secretary began, "apparently a package was left for you at the front desk in the atrium. I'm just going to run down and get it."

Cassie smiled. The intern, though only a couple of years younger than her, made her feel old. "Hmm...that's odd. Why didn't it come with the regular mail?"

"They said it was hand-delivered."

Hand-delivered. Could Josh be downstairs waiting to surprise her? "In that case, I'll go and get it myself. Oh, and Julie, please, just call me Cassie."

"Yes, ma'am."

She just had to add "Ma'am" on there; it was a losing battle. Cassie hurried out of her office and into the elevator. On the lengthy ride down, though, she came to her senses, realizing it probably wasn't Josh. Even if he'd left Cincinnati shortly after she did, it would only leave him about an hour before he needed to turn around and head back for practice. But, maybe he sent her something.

The elevator doors dinged open and she crossed to the large, crescent-shaped desk in the middle of the glassed-in atrium. She spoke to the prim-looking woman behind the desk. "Hi. I'm Cassie McCallister and I have—"

"Oh, yes," she said crisply. "Ms. McCallister." She handed her a regular, business-sized envelope with her name on red tape across it. It was the kind of red tape she remembered from her youth. It came from a gun shaped apparatus and moms used it to label everything around the house. She hadn't seen it in years. *Odd.* She ran her fingers over the embossed name.

"Thank you," she said, turning with her envelope toward the elevator. On the long ride up, she tapped her nails on the top of the envelope and ran her finger along its edges. By the time she got to her office, she was dying of curiosity. She tore open the envelope and removed the paper inside, unfolding it. The note had the same red tape, spelling out, "STAY AWAY FROM JOSH...OR ELSE!"

Cassie stared at it, bewildered. She felt an odd mixture of happy, nostalgic thoughts of her childhood, and the ominous vibes the message brought. Who, exactly, knew she and Josh were seeing each other? And who would send her such a message? The envelope still had some weight to it, so she reached in again, jerking her fingers back when she felt a jab of pain. A bright red splotch of blood hit the paper the letter was written on, just below the red tape. She peeked into the envelope. A single, flat razor blade lay within its depths.

"Ms. Mc—I mean, Cassie—"

She dropped the letter on her desk and spun around, trying to hide it.

"Would you need anything—" Julie's question changed as Cassie turned and she saw the blood-red stain on her white blouse. "What happened?"

"Umm," Cassie stared at her for a moment. "I seem to have cut my finger. Would you mind looking for a Band-Aid for me? I think Dori left some in the top drawer of her desk," she added, referring to her former secretary, who was at home on maternity leave.

"Sure, sure." She rushed out, leaving her alone in her office again.

She didn't even know why she felt the need to hide the note from the secretary. *I guess I just didn't need her asking a bunch of questions. Especially when I have so many myself.* Hearing Julie rifling through desk drawers, Cassie hurriedly swept the letter into the trashcan. She warily lifted the envelope and dumped it into the receptacle, too, with a *plop* just as Julie reentered the office.

"Here, let me help." She took Cassie's finger and bandaged it like a mother would, tender and professional.

"Thanks."

"Are you sure you're okay? You look kind of pale. Or are you one of those people who can't stand the sight of their own blood?"

"Yeah. Something like that."

After Julie left, she sat at her desk, staring off into space for several minutes. She picked up the phone and dialed the front desk. "Hi. This is Cassie McCallister. I was down a few minutes ago to pick up a package that was hand-delivered. I was wondering if, by any chance, you might remember what the person who dropped it off looked like?"

The person on the other end asked her to wait, and then the cool voice of the receptionist she received the package from earlier came on the line. "Josephine Donnelly, may I help you?"

"Yes. Ms. Donnelly, this is Cassie McCallister—"

"Yes. I remember. What can I do for you?"

"Well, I was just wondering if you happened to notice what the person who dropped off that package for me looked like. I know you see a lot of people, but I thought I'd try—"

"Oh, yes, Ms. McCallister. I certainly do remember what the woman looked like. She was about your age, maybe a year or two younger. Long, straight, blond hair. She had a few freckles across the bridge of her nose. Attractive, I guess, and big-chested and not afraid to let everyone know it. Does that help?"

Cassie took notes. "Yes, thank you. You're very observant."

"Well, it was such an unusual package. I guess I just noticed her more than I normally would."

"Well I'm certainly glad you did. Could you please do me another favor? If you see that young lady again, please call Security and have her detained."

"Of course, Ms. McCallister."

Cassie hung up and got back to work, feeling a little better. At least someone would be on the lookout for the delivery girl if she showed up again. She worked past quitting time to make up for her late arrival. She tried to forget about the message on the note, chalking it up to a simple prank. Then she shuddered, fished the paper out of her trashcan and locked it in the top drawer of her desk, just in case. Her day had been a busy one, one in which little real work was accomplished, other than trying to sweet-talk a client who was perpetually in a huff about something. This time, he felt one of her coworkers had slighted him. As she walked through the parking lot to her car, she massaged the back of her neck, trying to relieve the tension bundled there.

As she yanked on the handle of the driver's door, her eye caught a flash of white tucked under her windshield wiper. She looked around the empty garage, feeling vulnerable. It was vacant. She tossed her briefcase into the car and slid in, closing and locking the door behind her. She stared at the white envelope, her heart beating rapidly, for several seconds. "Oh, this is ridiculous," she told herself. "It's just a friggin' envelope." She thrust open her door, snatching the envelope and sitting back down in her seat as she pulled the door to. The same red tape was blaring across the front, but this time the writer used just her first name. She cautiously slid her bandaged finger under the flap. Having learned her lesson, she opened the envelope wide to look inside before reaching in. She squealed. Cuddled next to the note was a squashed bug, a cockroach. In her surprise she dropped the envelope, knocking the bug out and onto her skirt. Screaming louder, she hopped out of the car.

Very good, Cassie, she chastised herself. *Real mature reaction.* Angry now, she reached over her seat to grab a Kleenex. She gingerly lifted the bug into the tissue and deposited the whole bundle into her car's mini trashcan. Breathing slower, she brushed imaginary bug germs from her skirt, and sat, if not quite serenely, at least more put together. She eyed the note. Deciding to just ignore it, she started the engine, only to stop it again and grab the envelope. This time the message was simply, "DIE BITCH!" A chill ran down her spine and her eyes flew to her rearview mirror. Seeing nothing, she turned to look into the back seat. Empty. Her hands trembling, she restarted the ignition, and pulled, with a squeal of tires, out of her parking space, racing out of the garage.

She glanced in the rearview mirror again. A yellow sports car with black racing stripes pulled out behind her. It stayed behind her for several blocks but then peeled off at a corner and she sighed. *This is making me paranoid!*

By the time she got home, she'd pretty much convinced herself it was all a childish prank, even though she couldn't help but glance in the rearview mirror from time to time to see if anyone was following her. *You watch too many crime shows,* she told herself. When Josh called later that night, she didn't even mention it to him; she just told him she missed him and couldn't wait until Friday.

THE NEXT DAY WHEN CASSIE returned to her car after grocery shopping, she found another envelope under her wiper. She spun around to scan the area around her. Her eyes zeroed in on a familiar yellow sports car. Tinted windows went up immediately and the car pulled away from the curb and exited the parking lot in a hurry.

By the time the weekend arrived, Cassie had received two more notes, one taped to her front door. That had freaked her out enough to call the police; the person threatening her knew where she lived. She also gave them the license plate number of the yellow car she had seen in the grocery parking lot, and they ran a scan. But it turned out to be owned by a police chief's daughter from Nebraska. She was sufficiently frustrated by that to try in earnest to put it all behind her. She hadn't told Josh, knowing he had to concentrate on his performances. She would talk to him about it after the Chicago show.

She was distracted all Friday, anxious to be with him again. *It's been less than a week, but it seems like a lifetime.* She left work and drove straight to the stadium.

Just as she entered the hall to the dressing rooms, Josh came out of his. She squealed with delight and ran toward him. He grabbed her, wrapping her in his arms and breathing in as he squeezed her tightly. They didn't speak for several moments.

"Hey," he said at last, sounding a little choked up. He pulled back to look her in the eyes and stroked her face.

"Oh, I've missed you." She buried her head in his chest again.

Lanny's door opened, and they broke apart guiltily. "Hey, Lanny," Cassie said, clearing her throat. "How are you?"

"Fine," he returned slowly, with a suspicious air.

Josh turned back to her. "Are you hungry? They've got a whole spread for us down the hall."

"Starved. I've been so anxious to see you all day I haven't eaten anything."

He put his hand over her shoulder. "Well, we need to do something about that." He let Lanny pass them then pulled her in to kiss her quickly. She beamed up at him. "We're going to get some privacy later," he whispered to her, "and then you better look out."

"Promises, promises," she teased.

"Oh, I'll make good on that one. You can bet on it." His hand slid over her backside. They reached the doorway of a reception room.

"Hey, Cass,'" Ryan called out with a grin. He headed over and gave her a kiss on the cheek. "Good to see you."

"You, too, Ryan. You been watchin' out for my guy here?" She reached up to pull Josh down for another quick kiss.

"Been doin' my best."

"Then I owe you. How's Paige? When's she coming to a show again?"

"I'm not sure. We only have a few left."

Everyone chatted while they ate, except for Lanny, who seemed as reticent as ever. "Get you another beer, Josh?" he asked as he got up.

"Sure, Lan. Thanks."

When dinner was over, a member of the crew stuck his head in the door. "Josh, Mike has a question about the timing of the pyros on 'Dressed to Kill.'"

"Okay, I'll be right down." He turned to Cassie. "You go down to my dressing room and make yourself comfortable and I'll be right back."

"Okay. Do whatever you need to do, I'll be fine."

JOSH MARCHED DOWN THE hall, determined to put the pyros to rest so he could get back to her. He knew he was anxious to be with her, but it seemed like his heart was thundering in his chest even more than usual.

"All right." He grabbed his guitar and headed over to Mike. "I thought we had this all worked out in practice, man," he said irritably.

"Yeah," the technician snapped back. "But excuse me if I want to make sure I don't catch you on fire."

"Okay. Okay. It goes da, da, da, da, hit the first flame." He demonstrated with his guitar. "Da, da, da, da, hit the second flame. I don't think I can make it any easier than that." He was annoyed with the man, which wasn't like him, but he suddenly found himself strung so tightly, even the guitar chords grated on him. His head was pounding, and the stage lights seemed hotter than usual, going in and out in intensity. "Do we have to have those fucking stage lights on?" he growled.

"No." The technician studied him. "Kill the lights. That better?" Mike asked sarcastically.

"Peachy!" Josh slammed his guitar in the stand and stormed away, calling over his shoulder, "Try to fucking get it right next time." He patted his arms as he walked. They felt twitchy. In fact, everything felt jumpy. He'd calm down as soon as he could spend some time with Cassie. He was just anxious to see her was all, he told himself.

When he walked in, she was on the phone. He nodded in her direction. "I'm going to get an aspirin. I have a headache."

He didn't know how much time had passed when he heard a knock. "Josh," she called. "Are you all right?"

"Yeah, yeah. I'm fine. I'll be out in a minute." But he was not fine. He sat on the toilet holding his head so it wouldn't explode all over the bathroom.

When he finally stumbled out of the bathroom, Cassie was gone. Lanny sauntered into the room. "Where's Cassie?" His voice had an edge.

"Well, partner, she seems to have skedaddled. Listen," he draped his hand over Josh's shoulder. "I don't want to be the one to tell you this, but...I overheard a conversation your little girlfriend was having with some Sarah, and I don't like what I was hearing."

"What are you talking about?" *And why are you talking so damned fast?*

"Well, I hate to be the one to break the news to you, but...we've been friends for a long time, and—"

"Dammit, Lanny! Spit it out!"

"Okay. Okay. Well, Josh, I heard her telling this Sarah person she would have the money she needed soon. She had you wrapped around her little finger, and you'd be willing to give her anything she wanted. Said something about bailing Sarah's husband out. I got the feeling he'd been cooking the books for his company or something from what they were saying. Do you know a Sarah?"

"Cassie has a sister named Sarah."

Lanny seemed to be thinking this over. "Do you know what her husband does for a living?"

"I think he's an accountant."

"That's it. He's doing some phony accounting and they're all using you to get themselves out of trouble. The more I think about it, the more I think this was a setup from the start. It was no accident she was in that bar in Vegas. And she didn't sleep with you that night, because then she'd be just another roll in the hay. She's been playing this smart all along to get you on the hook. At the end I heard her laugh and say, on top of that, you were a good lay, so it wasn't even much of a sacrifice."

Josh looked at him, stunned. "She said that?"

Lanny nodded. "It made me sick to hear it, Josh. But she's taking you for a ride. She doesn't give a plug nickel for you." Footsteps approached. "I've got to go get ready for the show. Sorry, man." He hurried out as Ryan and Cassie rushed in.

"Hey, bud," Ryan started. "Cassie says you're not feeling well."

"What the fuck would she care about that?" Josh barked, eying her coldly.

Their jaws dropped. Ryan looked to her, but she shook her head, as if to say, I have no idea what he's talking about. "Josh...what's going on?"

"Can you get out for a second? I need to have a talk with Cassie."

"I'm not sure that's such a good idea."

"Ryan," he said menacingly, "you can either get the fuck out of here, or I can send you out on your ass!"

Now the fire was in Ryan's eyes. "What the fuck is your problem?" He took a step toward him and Josh did the same.

"Wait. Wait a minute!" Cassie stepped between them. "No one's throwing anybody out of here."

Josh switched tactics. He draped his arm casually over Cassie's shoulder, which had the added benefit of helping to steady him, and told Ryan, "I just want to spend a little time with my girlfriend here."

"I'll talk to him," she said, nervously.

"I'm not sure this is a good idea." Ryan hesitated a moment longer, studying Josh's eyes. "Okay, but I'll be right outside if you need me."

As soon as he left the room, Josh removed his hand from behind her neck disdainfully and crossed to the couch. He lounged with his arms spread across the back of the couch and plopped his heels on the coffee table with dual *thuds*, watching her.

She hesitantly crossed to sit on the coffee table. "Are you feeling all right?" she said, reaching up to feel his forehead. As quick as lightning, he viciously slapped her hand away. "Ouch," she cried out. Covering her hand, she jumped up from the table and backed away. "Josh—"

Even as he did them, he knew his actions were wrong. It was as if he was watching himself from a distance, and the anger he gave into felt so good, so justified. He bolted up. "Don't give me that crap, Cassie!"

Hearing the noise, Ryan burst through the door. "And if you don't get what you need from me, are you going to sleep with him?" he screamed, gesturing wildly in his friend's direction.

Ryan came around to stand in front of Cassie. "What the hell are you talking about?"

"*Did* you call your sister?" Josh snarled.

"Wh-what?" Cassie asked, confused, tears in her eyes.

"You heard me! Did you call Sarah?"

"I..." He took a step forward and she screamed, "Yes! I called Sarah."

With a roar, he threw over the coffee table and Ryan and Cassie scrambled to get out of the way as beer bottles crashed to the floor. "Get out of here, you whore. And don't you *ever* come back again." He made another move toward her and Ryan grabbed him by his shirt, restraining him.

"Cassie. You'd better get out of here," Ryan warned, as his feet began to slide backward.

She grabbed her purse and ran from the room. When the door closed behind her, Josh pushed Ryan off but didn't advance on him. Instead, he moved to a cabinet and pulled down a bottle of Scotch.

"I don't know what your problem is—"

Josh waved a hand to cut him off.

Ryan shook his head. "You messed up, pal! The best thing that ever happened to you just walked out the door and it's your fault." He gestured at the door then pointed to him accusingly. "*Your* fault!"

Josh made no answer, just added ice to his glass, dropping them from up high, with a loud clink. Ryan turned to walk out. Just before he closed the door, he said, "We have a show in one hour. You better not be drunk, or I'll walk off the stage and that's the end of it."

When the door closed behind him, Josh set the glass of scotch down after a long swig. He leaned his hands on the counter, dropping his head. What had he done? What the hell had he done?

CHAPTER TWENTY-ONE

Josh bumbled his way through the concert, but it was one of their worst performances ever and was touted so by all the local papers the next day. Money Back Guaranteed was probably going to have to live up to their name. When the show ended, he came back to his dressing room and flopped face-down on the couch and fell asleep for nearly fourteen hours. Ryan left him alone for the first ten, then he came in occasionally to see if he was breathing. Each time he found him in the same position, snoring loudly, his mouth wide open.

When Josh woke up in the dark, alone in the dressing room, his head hurt even more than the previous night, if possible. The blinding pain was gone, replaced by a remorseless, throbbing ache. What happened? He remembered the events of the night before clearly but could not understand what had driven him to act the way he had. He knew Cassie was not the type of person to use people...but Lanny told him... He sat in silence, trying to make sense of it all. Why would Lanny lie about that? They had been friends forever. He would never do anything to hurt Josh on purpose. Maybe he misunderstood what he heard.

He fumbled around for the phone.

"Hello?"

"Mr. Sandoval." He let out a sigh of relief.

"Josh? Oh, my God, what's wrong with Ryan?"

"Nothing. Nothing. Ryan's fine, Mr. Sandoval." There was a long pause. Josh hung his head, overwhelmed with emotion.

"Okay, Josh," Ryan's father said slowly. "Then why did you call?"

"I respect your opinion..." He wasn't sure why he needed to tell him now; he just needed to. "I need your help. I need to know...how do you know when a friend is really your true friend?"

"Josh, what are we talking about here?"

"I'm just so confused."

"Well, let me try to help you, son," the older man said compassionately. "I remember a time when someone backstabbed me at work."

"Mmm-hmm." This sounded interesting. Ryan's dad told him the story about office politics, one-upmanship and competition. It made Josh glad, for the umpteenth time, that he didn't have to live his life that way.

"I think you need to look at the person's motivation, the fruit of their actions. You can't tell by their words, because people who set out to deceive you are always smooth. Look at their actions. Do they look out for others? Or are they just out for themselves?" He didn't respond. "Josh? Are you still there, son?"

"Yes," he sighed, rubbing his eyes. "I think I understand now."

"Well, I'm glad I could help. And Josh, you can call me anytime you need to talk, you know."

"Thanks, Mr. Sandoval. Goodbye."

"Goodbye, son."

Josh hung up the phone. He thought about Cassie, saw her as she knuckled the boy from down the street, saw the tender look on her face when they made love, remembered the look of fondness she had in her eyes for Heather, and the way they sparked whenever she talked about her sister.

He thought about Lanny. He could not come up with one thing Lanny had ever done for anyone else. How could he have been such a fool?

THE DOOR CREAKED OPEN, and light flooded in from the hallway. Josh put a hand up to block the light and saw Ryan's figure silhouetted in the doorway.

"You okay, buddy?" he asked tentatively. Josh nodded and Ryan crossed to sit next to him on the couch, leaving the doorway open for light.

"I really messed up this time, Ry."

Ryan placed a hand on his friend's knee.

"Lanny told me..." Josh started.

"Lanny?"

"He said he overheard Cassie on the phone. Heard her say she was using me to get to my money—"

"Cassie would never do that."

"I know that now. I was just so..." His head began to clear a little from its fog. "I yelled at the pyro man..."

"Huh?"

"My head was racing, things ricocheting like crazy inside my skull...Lanny gave me my last beer. Oh, God! I think Lanny drugged me!"

"What?"

"He drugged me, Ryan. I'm sure now he did. Then he lied to me about Cassie, to make me upset. He knew I would blow up. He's trying to ruin things for me, but why?"

"I don't think that's the most important question right now. I think the most important thing is for you to find out if Cassie can forgive you for what you did."

They were both silent. "Will you help me? I still feel like my head has been rolling down a bowling alley straight into some pins."

"Sure thing," Ryan said with a grin, rising from the couch.

They were ready to leave the building when Lanny walked out of his dressing room. "Hi, guys—"

Before he could finish his sentence, Josh grabbed him and threw him up against the wall. "You son-of-a-bitch!"

"What the hell's your problem?" Lanny pushed back. He was stronger than Josh believed him to be. Ryan tried to step between them.

"You drugged me. You drugged me and lied to me!"

"I don't know what the hell you're talking about," he answered with a sneer.

"The hell you do!"

"Josh! This isn't helping things right now. We need to go find Cassie. Let him go."

Josh loosened his grip but bit off his reply to Lanny. "When this tour is over, we're over, Lanny. Got it? This whole thing is over."

"Yeah, right, Joshie. Like you're gonna give up the stardom, and the drugs, and the women."

"Drugs are your thing, Lanny. And as for women, there's only one woman that matters to me, and you helped me drive her away. You better damn well hope I can get her back, or I'm coming after you, and that's a promise!" He released him and strode away, throwing over his shoulder as he banged through the outer door, "Either way, at the end of the tour, the band dies."

LANNY COULDN'T BELIEVE it. After all his efforts, the whole thing blows up in his face. It had been easy to find information about little Miss Cassandra McCallister. She worked for that stupid ad agency in Chicago, she had filed for a marriage license before. He so wanted to use that juicy little tidbit, but decided Josh may already know about it, and then he'd end up with egg on his face. She had one married sister with three kids. The husband was an accountant. And BINGO, he'd come up with the whole scenario. And Josh bought it, too, with the help of some pharmaceuticals. Hook, line, and sinker, the idiot. The girl would never take him back. But, somehow he'd figured things out; so now he was going to have to talk Josh down from his decision to break up the band. The band was Lanny's whole life, and he wouldn't give it up because of some girl. He just needed to think up another plan.

CHAPTER TWENTY-TWO

Josh peered in the window from Cassie's front porch while Ryan waited, parked on the driveway, but it was evident from the house's silent stillness that she wasn't home.

He shuffled back to the car and put his hands on the roof, leaning down to talk to Ryan through the window. "She's not at the office. She's not here."

"Do you have any idea where she might go?"

"Yeah," Josh said, looking across the street. "I'll be right back."

He strode across the street purposefully. Heather came to the door and seeing it was him, started swinging and cussing in equal measure. He was able to hold her off at arm's length where she couldn't do much damage.

"Listen, Heather. I know I'm a screw-up. Believe me, no one knows that better than me. But, I'm telling you, my friend—or so-called friend—drugged me." She stopped swinging at him, and encouraged, he continued. "I wasn't in my right mind. I love her. That's why I was so upset when he told me those lies. And the drugs made everything...murky for me. I was so strung out..."

"Well, you're not going to be able to fix this like before. It's worse. She fell for you this time, really fell for you, and you—"

"I know! I know what I did."

She crossed her arms, staring at him. "She's torn up, Josh."

"I know that, too," he said more quietly. "Heather, please." He could tell by the set look on her face he would have more luck cleaning the bugs off his bumper by ramming his car into her garage door than getting information out of her. *If she wasn't with Heather...* "She's at Sarah's, isn't she?" He saw the flick of alarm and turned immediately to march back across the street.

Heather chased him and grabbed his arm, but he shook her off. "Shit! Wait. Don't do this!"

"I have to."

"ACCORDING TO MY LAPTOP and my GPS, this is the right house."

"Thanks, techno-geek." Before Josh could offer Ryan genuine thanks, a green minivan, that had what he easily deduced to be bicycle handlebar scratches down the entire passenger side, rolled down the street. They each watched in their respective side-view mirrors, then slid down into their seats as the van approached them. "Why are we hiding?" Ryan whispered.

"I'm not sure." They stuck their heads up enough to peek across the street. The minivan was waiting for a garage door to rise in the driveway to the house Ryan said belonged to Cassie's sister. "It's them!" They watched as a blonde hopped out of the seat, and three towheaded children disembarked like circus clowns, spilling out of the seats and onto the pavement.

"Nah-ah. Get back here. You help me with these groceries, boys."

Josh watched as she opened the back and handed bags to each of the children, grabbed a few herself, and pulled the liftgate down enough to be able to kick her leg up sideways and push it closed with her foot while still balancing the over-full bags. A can dropped out of a bag, and she muttered, "Shit," but retrieved it, remarkably, without further loss of her cargo.

"Cassie's not with her."

"Maybe she's inside."

"Right."

"Aren't you going in?"

He turned to him. "Maybe Heather is right. I should just leave her alone."

"Do you believe that?"

"I'm not sure."

"We drove over a hundred miles, and now you're not sure?" Ryan said in mock disgust. He put his hand on Josh's knee. "Seriously, I think you owe it to yourself to give this a chance."

He grinned. "Thanks, Ry."

Josh opened the car door and when he trotted around to the other side of the car, Ryan called out. "Maybe you should be wearing a sparring helmet."

Josh turned, "I'll just keep my hands up." He mimicked a defensive posture before crossing the lawn. As he got close to the house, he could hear voices through the open windows.

"Did you get any sleep, hon?"

"A little. There was a phone call, but I let it go to the machine." Josh's heart rate bumped up to a full gallop as he recognized Cassie's voice.

"Okay, no biggie."

He sucked in his breath and resolutely knocked on the door.

"I'll get it."

As the door slowly opened, he got a clear shot of Cassie. Glancing up and recognizing him, a look of shock, anger, and sorrow crossed her face in an instant and she quickly tried to close the door. Without forethought, he stuck his arm in the doorway just before it closed, trying to wedge his hip in the opening as well.

"Leave me alone, Josh. I mean it. Get out of here!"

"Kids, go play in the backyard!" Sarah snapped.

"But Mom, we want to—"

"NOW!" she shrieked.

"Cassie, please." He tried to force his way in, but she at last pushed him out and bolted the door. He slapped his palm against the door. "He drugged me," he pleaded.

After several seconds of silence, he turned to trudge away, his hands on his hips, shaking his head. If she wasn't going to listen to him, what choice did he have? He couldn't kick in the door. That wouldn't exactly work in the favor of his argument. As his feet hit the grass, he heard the deadbolt draw back.

"What are you saying? Who drugged you?"

Her sister called out from behind her. "You're not really going to believe this sack of shit after what he said—"

"Shh."

"Fine. It's your funeral." She threw her hands up and marched farther into the house, but not too far. Josh heard her mutter, "Never listens to a word I say."

He was breathing heavily after the struggle. "Lanny." He stared into her eyes, stepping forward and explaining, "Remember that last beer he got me? He put something in it."

He could see she was torn. She wanted to believe him; he could read it in the way she was leaning toward him. She opened the door to let him pass.

"Perfect," her sister yelled. "Fucking perfect!" She stormed off into the kitchen, leaving them alone.

Cassie remained silent.

"Cass." He tried to reach for her arm, but she stepped back. He sighed. He needed so badly to embrace her. To see her, to know she was in pain, and not be able to touch her, not be able to be touched by her, to comfort his own misery, was almost unbearable.

"I started feeling weird the minute I got up from the table, but I had no inkling of what was going on. I yelled at Mike, the pyrotechnics guy, for no reason...then came back to the room. When I came out of the bathroom, you were gone, but Lanny was there. He told me he overheard your phone conversation with Sarah." Sarah turned from the kitchen table and stared at him. He returned her gaze, then shifted to look at Cassie again. "He said you told her you had me wrapped around your finger. You would have money to give her soon...and implied...our relationship was...well...you said some not very flattering things."

"No," she said, stepping forward. "You tell me what he said." Her voice was fierce.

"I don't want to hurt you."

"Well, it's a little too God damn late for that, now, isn't it? Tell me!"

He glanced up at Sarah again and she dropped her eyes. "He told me that you said at least I was a good lay."

She drew her breath in sharply and a tear flew from her eye. "He said that?" Her voice trembled and she laid a hand over her stomach and took a few steps back, shaking her head in disbelief and reaching out to the piano for balance.

"But I know the things he said aren't true."

"You weren't so sure last night."

He hung his head. "You're right. I don't know what to say. The drugs made me edgy, paranoid...but I know that I was terribly, terribly wrong. I believed him. I never thought he would—" The hurt of his friend's betrayal brought him up short, but then he looked into her eyes earnestly. "I should have believed in you, in us."

"Oh. Come on! That's rich!" Sarah scoffed. "You're not actually buying this line of crap, are you?"

She searched his eyes. "Shut up, Sarah."

"Unbelievable. Your pillow is still damp with your tears, and he brings his tight little ass and his beautiful green eyes in here and you just melt."

"Shut up!"

"No. I'm not going to shut up. You know, you may have made the dean's list every semester, but when it comes to your heart—"

Cassie spun around. "I know. I've brought it to you broken more than once." She got a grip on her emotions. "I'm sorry. I'm sorry to disappoint you. I'm sorry to have gotten you caught up in all this. But if this is a mistake, then it's *my* mistake to make."

"So, you've already decided then."

Instead of answering, she scooped her purse up off the couch and walked past Josh to the front door.

"Cassandra Joanne McCallister, if you walk out that door, don't be comin' back here again for my advice, 'cause I'm through."

Cassie hesitated in the doorway, then left the house without looking back. Ryan was leaning on his sedan on the opposite curb. He straightened up hurriedly as she approached, but she didn't even seem to notice him; she simply opened the door and got in the back seat, leaving it open for Josh. Ryan shot Josh a look of surprise, but then motioned for him to climb in beside her, as Sarah had now stepped out on the lawn with her arms crossed, giving them a death stare equal to no other.

Cassie sat leaning against the opposite door, chewing her nails and staring off into space. Josh tried to think of something else to say but could not come up with anything. After a while, he bookended her position, leaning against the other door, and looking out at nothing. A half-hour later, he chanced a glance over and found she had fallen asleep, huddled against the door. It struck his heart. She looked so tired and beaten. He had done that to her.

When Ryan pulled into her neighborhood, she woke up but said nothing. When the car slid into her driveway, she reached up to squeeze his shoulder. "Thank you, Ryan," she said softly.

He covered her hand with his own. "Anytime, Cass."

She got out on her side, and Josh caught Ryan's eyes in the rearview mirror. "What do I do?" he mouthed.

Ryan shrugged and mouthed, "I don't know."

Josh got out, watching her as she trudged up to her front door. He gripped the edge of Ryan's rolled-down window. "If I need a ride, I'll call a cab," he said quietly. "Thanks again."

"Good luck," Ryan whispered, looking at Cassie's back. He put the car in reverse, slipping away up the street.

She was searching in her purse. He walked toward her and she fished out the key, opened the lock, and headed in, leaving the door open for him to follow. Watching for a reaction, he crossed the threshold and turned to close the door. She kicked off her tennis shoes, plopped her purse and keys down, and headed upstairs. Josh waited a beat, uncertain of what he was supposed to do, but then followed her. He walked to the door of the guest bedroom, where she lay, flopped stomach-down, on the bed, one hand trailing nearly to the floor. He stood, leaning against the doorframe, watching her.

"Hold me," she murmured sadly.

He crossed to the other side of the bed, using one foot to wedge the opposite shoe off as he leaned on the bedpost. She flipped over and watched him. He pushed the other shoe off and stretched out beside her on his side, offering his arm, she curled up next to him, shifting so her back was against him, his arms around her. He closed his eyes, overwhelmed by emotions, terrified by how close he came to losing her.

The afternoon became cloudy, making the room dim. He watched the shadows of the trees dancing on the far wall. Cassie stirred. "I need to change," she mumbled. She stood by the side of the bed and unbuttoned the pale-blue blouse she wore, looking at him without emotion as she did so. She removed her bra, letting it drop with the blouse on the floor. He remained absolutely still, although inside, he was humming. She was just so incredibly beautiful. So soft, so supple, but somehow he knew she was not ready for him to touch her yet, to make love to her, although he longed to with every fiber of his being.

She reached for a T-shirt he had accidentally left on one of the bedposts and slipped it over her head, further ruffling her hair. She unsnapped and unzipped her jeans, her bare legs stepping out of them as they, too, fell to the floor. Hands-first, she slid across the bed, and curled up next to him. His hands almost quaked as they grazed across her skin, bringing them around in front to link just below her breasts. He closed his eyes, hardening himself against the urge to stroke her further, to draw her to him intimately, to make love to her. He dozed on and off as she slept, watching the glowing red numbers of the alarm clock. At three o'clock he separated from her, getting up to call a cab. This time, it was he with the rose-colored paper, leaving a note on the bedside table, on top of the alarm clock and braced by the lamp. It read:

I love you, Cass. I went to the stadium, but
I'll be back as soon as the concert's over.
I'm sorry for hurting you, but
I'll fix it, I promise. —Josh

He watched her sleep a few minutes longer, but the lights of the taxi shone through the soft rain which began to fall an hour earlier. He kissed her on the cheek, and left.

CASSIE AWOKE IN THE darkness. She squinted at the clock, 11:30. She heard footsteps downstairs. Josh must be home. Sleepily, she went down to greet him; they needed to talk things through. She flicked a light switch but remained in the dark. *The storm must have taken out the electricity.* Although the thunder she heard was soft and distant. She fumed as it seemed every time someone yawned, the electricity went out.

"Josh?"

He didn't reply. Maybe realizing the power was out, he had gone down to the basement to check the circuit breaker. She reached the hardwood on the first floor and turned.

In the hallway, a black figure stood silhouetted by the outdoor light that filtered in. She knew immediately it was not Josh, as the intruder was much shorter. Gasping, she turned to run back upstairs, but strong arms wrapped around her legs, sending her crashing down. Her head hit the wooden arm of the couch hard as she fell and sparks of light flittered across her vision, even in the darkness. Her assailant had one leg straddling her back, one grinding a knee into the middle of it. She struggled for the breath which left her when she fell and heard the sharp noise of adhesive pulling and the rip of tape. She struggled to dislodge the man, but he had managed to pinion her arms, too. Warm blood oozed from her head and through the haze of its throbbing she thought, oddly, about looking like a fish flopping helplessly around on the floor.

The attacker grabbed the front of her hair and yanked her head back hard, slapping the tape across her mouth. She nearly became hysterical, having not caught her breath yet and alarmed it was now cut off to her. *I can't die here!* She thought about having left things poorly with Sarah and Josh. *Whatever else happens, I can't let this man kill me tonight.*

As if hearing her silent prayer, the man shifted, lifting some of the weight from her back and arms. She felt the blood rushing back, creating a warm sensation. She tried to squirm away from him, but he was unnaturally strong. He flipped her to her back like he was flipping flapjacks, and she grabbed at his crotch, squeezing with all her might and trying to dig her fingernails through his jeans. In the streetlight shining through the porch window, she could see he wore a dark, solid-colored ski mask. The man grunted, feeling the pain, and then, to her horror, began laughing.

He took one of her wrists and swung it over her head and onto the floor. Her wrist hit the wood with a sharp sound, sending a shock wave down her arm. The way it was contorted caused additional pain. A cry tried to escape but was blocked by the tape. Seconds later, the second wrist was trapped with the first and her assailant produced some rough rope, which he looped several times around her wrists, and then took up through the middle of her hands, to loop those coils together. With a grunt of satisfaction, he pulled the rope taut, and the fibers cut into her skin. She realized, with a flash of sheer terror, he had been waiting for her, prepared with rope and tape to subdue her; this wasn't just a prowler.

He released his grip. Frantically, she tried to swing her arms down to hit him in the stomach or crotch again, but before she could make contact, he punched her across the jaw. Her head turned with the blow and knocked against the wood on the other side, balancing out the injury by adding pain to that side of her face as well. Her eyes were open wide with injury and fear, but her head was clear enough to know to bring her hands up to block the next blows. When she blocked her face, he hit her stomach, and she became afraid she would throw up and choke on her own vomit. Pain receptors fired rapidly, their signals colliding in her brain, and she felt a sinking sensation, as if slowly going under the surface of a pond. Somewhere, the sound of the key in the door registered.

The attacker's head snapped around, and then he bolted across the room. She curled the pain around her like a blanket, trying to gather it to her in order to conquer it.

CHAPTER TWENTY-THREE

Ryan swung the car into the driveway. Seeing no lights on, Josh surmised Cassie was still sleeping.

"Why don't you come in and have a beer with me?" he suggested. "I'm too wound up to sleep just yet."

"I don't know..." He hesitated, looking up at the dark windows.

"Come on, she's asleep. If she wakes up, you make your excuses and leave. Just one."

"Okay." He shut off the engine.

"Here's the key," Josh offered. "I'll get my bag out of the back. Pop the trunk."

Ryan rushed up the sidewalk, pulling his coat over his head to ward off the rain. He unlocked the door and opened it, but as he turned back to check on Josh's progress, he heard a groan from inside. He let the door fall all the way open and the light fell on Cassie's figure on the floor curled up on her side.

"Shit!" He took a halting step forward. "Josh! Josh!"

Josh heard the panic in his voice and dropped the leather duffle bag on the driveway, leaving the trunk open as he rushed to the door.

Ryan stepped into the house and crossed to crouch next to Cassie. He thought she was crying, as her back was shaking, but no noise was coming out of her mouth. He was just reaching out to her when Josh bolted into the room.

"Oh, my God," he said, his voice hollow. He came toward her and caught a movement in the shadows from the corner of his eye.

"Josh! Someone's over there!" Ryan sprung toward the figure and raced after him as he dodged furniture, heading for the back door. The intruder knocked a chair across the threshold of the family room, slowing him down, and escaped out the back door.

Josh knelt. "Cass?" His fingertips brushed her, and she flinched. "Oh, God, baby. Who did this to you?"

She rolled over to her back. He registered her wide, terrorized eyes, and then she went limp.

"Josh. He got away. Is she okay?" Ryan came back and fumbled for the light switch. The ineffective click sounded loud in the still room.

Josh gingerly shook Cassie by the shoulders, intending to awaken her, when his hands came across the rope on her wrists. "He tied her up. The son-of-a-bitch tied her up!"

Ryan fell to his knees beside him, taking over even through his own shock. "Do you remember where the phone is? Do you think you could find it in the dark?"

"I have my cell," he mumbled.

"Good. Call 9-1-1."

He sat back on his haunches as he dialed, and Ryan's eyes strained in the dark. "She's got tape over her mouth." He hesitated a moment then ripped it off quickly in one motion. Her body seemed to automatically take a deep breath. "She's breathing."

Josh was talking to the dispatcher now and felt like he had gotten a grip a little. "Shit! She's bleeding, man!"

He set the phone down, despite the loud protests of the dispatcher who continued to tell him to stay on the line. His hands again found hers, and discovered they were cold. He struggled with the rope. When it came free, her arms fell to her sides.

Now Ryan seemed to be in a daze.

"Get her a blanket. The bedrooms are upstairs."

Without saying anything, Ryan got up and took the stairs two at a time. He was relieved to hear the blare of sirens and see the reflection of the red lights chasing themselves around the room.

Josh heard them, too. He bent over her body, whispering to her, "It's okay, baby. They're here now. They're going to help you."

The next minute, the room was full of shouted orders and people rushing around. He hated to leave her side, but he knew he had to in order for her to get the help she needed. He raised his hands. "In here! My girlfriend's hurt! Hurry!" Even as two burly policemen slammed him against the wall, he called out, "It's okay, Cass. Everything is going to be okay, now."

A policeman quickly found the circuit box in the basement and light burst forth throughout the house. Josh strained to look over his shoulder with the police officer's forearm across his upper back, as the man leaned in, giving it his full weight. Cassie lay in a pool of blood, so much blood, dressed only in underwear and his T-shirt, the blanket pulled back so the emergency technicians could assess her wounds. His blood-splattered shirt, ripped a little by the attacker, seemed to mock him, emphasizing he hadn't protected her from this. The piece of rope he removed from her wrists was steeped in blood, as was her matted hair. Bruises had already begun to form on her arms and face. Her wrists were scraped raw and swollen. Who would have done this to her?

Ryan was pressed up against the wall as well. He, too, struggled against the officers so he could turn his head to see her. His eyes were wide and then he looked at Josh.

"She's going to be okay, buddy. They're going to take care of her."

He nodded numbly, but he didn't believe it.

THE HOSPITAL FELT LIKE a cage. Josh alternated between pacing around like a panther who has caught the scent of a seeing-eye dog at the zoo and remaining absolutely motionless. At the moment, he was doing the latter, leaning forward, his hands laced behind his head, eyes closed. He was imagining what Cassie must have gone through, alone and besieged in her own house, not knowing if anyone was coming to help her, not knowing what the man was going to do to her. He flashed back through the entire scenario, hearing Ryan's panicked shout, seeing her in the streetlight, bound, bloody, tape over her mouth, and those beautiful blue eyes wild with terror and pain. Then, when the lights came up, seeing the bruises and swelling and her body, crumpled and discarded like yesterday's newspaper. He sprang up and tried to pace the anger and fear and guilt away. He should have been there to stop it. He should have protected her. God, how he wished he could have taken her place, taken each blow, and dealt a few of his own.

Josh looked up and saw Sarah coming. Her face was furious and agonized, and her feet clipped away the miles of carpeting like a marathoner. Those eyes, Cassie's eyes, mirrored his own suffering and he wanted to look away, but couldn't.

"Why?" she screamed, still feet away from him. "Why?" And then she was on him, beating on him. He held his hands up and out to his sides and let her have free rein, whaling and whaling, fist over fist until she was exhausted. "Why?" she said, weakly now, and covered her face with her hands. He hesitated, then dropped his arms clumsily around her, giving her a refuge for the storm of tears that came next.

"I'm sorry," he choked out. "I should have been there. I should have stopped him."

She collected herself. "No. It's not your fault. It's not your fault." She slipped her arms around his body and melted against him.

Her husband, Brad, jogged up the hall now, slowing as he neared them, his jaw hanging open, probably wondering why his wife was hugging the man she had undoubtedly been cursing the entire ride over.

A uniformed policeman approached from the opposite side of the hall. He was in his early twenties, stocky, with short, brown hair. "Mr. Dunningham?"

"Yes?"

"I'm Officer Reeves. I've been working with Ms. McCallister, because of the letters she received."

"I'm sorry, what letters are you talking about?"

His mouth dropped open and he seemed to struggle with figuring out a way to backpedal.

Sarah stepped forward. "Officer. What letters are you talking about?"

"And you are?"

"Sarah Brooks, Cassie's sister."

"And..." he said slowly, looking baffled, "she didn't tell you about the threatening letters she has been receiving?"

"What threatening letters?" Josh and Sarah asked at the same time.

The officer flipped open a notebook. He exhaled and began reading, "On Monday of this week, Ms. McCallister received her first letter at her place of business, Ornstein and Cruthers, on 57th Street. Message was on red embossing tape and said, 'Stay away from Josh...or else!'" He glanced up. "Ms. McCallister got description of delivery person...straight, blond hair, freckled, big chested, about 23 or 24 years of age. Envelope also contained a razor blade, which Ms. McCallister sliced her finger on." He flipped a page. "The second letter came the same day, under the windshield wiper of her 2013 black Chevy Cavalier, in the building's parking garage. Came complete with dead bug and was a little more succinct. Read, 'Die bitch!' in capital letters, same red tape. The third came two days later in Meijer's store parking lot on 5th and Main. 'The only good whore's a dead whore.' The fourth letter upset her enough to call me, as it was found on the door of her residence." He skimmed for the pertinent details, 'I'll kill you if I see you near him again.' Victim also reported a license plate number on a vehicle she had seen frequently. We ran it, but it was a dead end." He flipped the book shut. "Those letters."

"Angela," Josh breathed.

"The girl from San Diego?"

"Yeah. She's a nut. I mean, a real case," he added.

"Wait. Wait!" the police officer said excitedly, thumbing through his notes again. "Yes. The license plate number we ran was registered to one Angela Sabolti. We dismissed it because the vic, uh...Ms. McCallister, wasn't confident enough she had gotten the numbers straight, and she didn't know any Angela Sabolti. And besides, she came up as the daughter of the local police chief in some podunk town in Nebraska. Does this Angela you know fit the description Ms. McCallister gave us?"

"To a tee."

Ryan nodded.

Just then, a doctor came out of Cassie's room, and they all circled him. "I take it you're the family of Cassandra McCallister?" Josh, Sarah and Brad nodded their heads. "Well, she's a very lucky girl. X-rays show no broken bones, and we don't believe she has any serious internal injuries. She has suffered a concussion, bruised ribs, lacerations on her wrists, and, in general, is pretty beat up. We stitched up a cut near her temple and are watching swelling there. She has a couple of loose teeth, but those might tighten up on their own, or she may have to see a dentist. All in all, it was good you, Mr. Dunningham, and Mr. Sandoval, interrupted the attack. Because what he started here would have been a whole lot worse. With this level of violence, he may not have stopped...but, that's neither here nor there. She is awake, but on a lot of pain meds, so I don't know how coherent she will be. Two family members may go in." Sarah and Brad moved forward. "She's been asking for you, Mr. Dunningham since she came to. Won't take our word for it that you're okay."

Josh, Sarah, and Brad exchanged glances. Brad cleared his throat. "I'll stay here."

Immediately Sarah stepped forward, with Josh on her heels, but they stopped when the police officer addressed them. "I'll put out an A.P.B. on this Angela Sabolti, but then I'm going to need to talk to Ms. McCallister." The two nodded and continued through the doorway.

When Sarah saw Cassie on the bed, she drew her breath in sharply. "Oh, Cass, baby girl." She sobbed. The hospital lights made clear every bruise. Add to this the fact she looked small and pale on the bed, and Josh almost had to look away.

"Sarah," she said weakly. She lifted a bandaged wrist and Sarah sat in a chair pulled to the bed and laid her head on Cassie's chest. "Hey...you're the big sister. You're supposed to be the strong one."

Sarah sniffled. "I know. You're right."

"Josh, come here. You're okay?" He shuffled over to the other side of the bed.

"Yeah, baby. I'm fine." He raised her hand and kissed it.

"Thank God!" She closed her eyes and let out a breath. "I knew you were coming home..." She trembled.

Josh laid his hand on her shoulder. "It's okay. I'm right here. Everything is fine."

After a sharp rap on the door, Officer Reeves stuck his head into the room. "Ms. McCallister? If you're feeling up to it, I'd like to take your statement."

"She's tired," Josh stated. "Can't this wait 'til later?"

"I'm afraid not. Her attacker is still at large. The more information we get now—"

"It's okay. I just want to get it over with."

"I understand this is difficult, Ms. McCallister. So please, take your time." He opened his notebook again and drew a pen from his pocket.

"Okay." She frowned. "I don't know how much help I can be. He wore a mask."

"That's okay, ma'am. Anything you remember would be helpful."

"All right. I was sleeping. It had been a..." she glanced over at Josh, "...difficult day. I heard a noise. I thought Josh was home. But... he was in my foyer." She became agitated, her voice tight, and Josh reached over to hold her hand. She took a deep breath. "I tried to run, but he grabbed me. I hit my head on the arm of the couch as I fell, and the rest is a little unclear." She paused. "He had one knee in my back and my arms pinned by my sides with his body as he sort of half-straddled me. He yanked my head up by my hair and put tape over my mouth. I was having trouble breathing. Then he tied my hands...and flipped me over...he was incredibly strong. No, wait. My hands were free when he flipped me because I grabbed—" She looked at Josh uneasily.

"Go on," the officer urged.

"I grabbed..." she rushed the rest out, "his crotch. It was the only thing I could reach."

"Cassie, you don't have to be embarrassed by that. You were defending yourself."

"Embarrassed? Hell, Cass. You should be proud. I hope you got him good," Sarah said, lightening the mood.

She continued. "After he tied my hands up, he let them go for a second and I swung at him...but I never connected. He started hitting me, over and over, and over again. I tried to block his punches..." Her eyes were wide, and her gaze jerked from one person to the next.

"Isn't that enough?" Josh asked testily.

Before Officer Reeves could answer, Cassie spoke again. "That's all I really remember. I thought I was going to pass out...and then Josh and Ryan were there."

"Not much more, Ms. McCallister. Did the attacker say anything?"

"No, not a word. He just kept hitting me." Tears spilled onto her cheeks. "But...he laughed."

"He laughed?"

Josh's stomach pitched. What kind of sick bastard got off on hurting a woman like this?

She nodded. "When I grabbed him and tried to hurt him, he laughed...like he was throwing it in my face how useless I was against him." Pain was etched on her face and she closed her eyes, squeezing more tears out. "I'm sorry, that's all I remember."

"No, Ms. McCallister." The officer rose, shutting his book and patting her leg. "You did great. I'm sorry this happened, but we'll do everything we can to catch this man. There's a chance he was just a hired thug working for this Angela Sabolti."

"Angela who?"

"Remember the license plate number you gave me? Mr. Dunningham appears to know the woman who owns that car."

Cassie turned to Josh. He was looking down at his hand as he rubbed it over hers on the sheet. "She was the one from San Diego," he said quietly.

She closed her eyes as if she received another blow but said nothing.

"She's the one doing this?" Sarah cried out angrily. "The slut you were lip-locked with when Cassie came out to see you? It's her?"

"Sarah!" Cassie scolded.

"No, Cass. Your sister has every right to be angry with me. But why didn't you tell me you were being threatened by her?"

"I didn't want you to worry. It might affect the way you performed."

"That's bullshit! You should have told me. Did you think I'd give a damn about a crappy performance when someone was out to hurt you? I could have hired someone to protect you. I could have—"

"I didn't think it was serious. And I was going to tell you Friday night when I saw you."

Friday night... "But then I acted like a jackass. I get it now." The thought sobered him. She would have told him that night if Lanny hadn't drugged him, and he hadn't gone off on her. She would have told him, and he would never have left her and this wouldn't have happened.

The young police officer cleared his throat. "In any case, Ms. McCallister, I'll keep you apprised of my progress on the case."

"Thank you." She closed her eyes again.

The doctor came in as the officer exited. "I think it's high time my patient got some rest."

"Okay." Sarah turned to smile down at her sister. "I'll be right outside, Termite, if you need anything." She patted her hand, then left.

Josh bent over her. "I love you, Cass." He brushed his lips over the corner of her mouth which showed less bruising. She didn't stir. He didn't want to leave her, but the doctor was making impatient noises behind him, so he scooted out to let her sleep.

In the hallway, Sarah was going off on the policeman. "Why didn't you inform us my sister was being threatened?"

"Ms. McCallister requested I not contact either of you until she got a chance to tell you first. I encouraged her to do that as soon as possible, because it would be difficult for me to find out who wanted her to stay away from Mr. Dunningham, without talking to Mr. Dunningham. She assured me she would, and I gave her a couple of days. Of course, now I regret that decision. What has happened here is awful, and I'm partially to blame." He spoke with deep regret then removed a card from his pocket and handed it to her. "If you would like to contact my commanding officer, his name is on there, along with mine." He turned to leave.

Sarah put a hand on his arm, detaining him. "I'm sorry. I had no right to question you. You couldn't have foreseen what happened. None of us could."

"Thank you, ma'am. If you should have any questions or concerns, use the number on the card to contact me."

Josh listened to the conversation with one ear as he leaned a hand against the glass in a bank of windows across the hall from Cassie's room. Dawn was still a ways off as he stared blindly out across the hospital parking lot.

Ryan came up behind him. "Josh...you okay?"

"No, man," he said, shaking his head. "This is all my fault."

"Don't be ridiculous. You didn't do this to her."

He turned around. "The hell I didn't! I did it to her just as much as the bastard who put those bruises on her face. Stinkin,' messed-up Angela." He spun back toward the window. "I should just distance myself from Cassie. Get as far away from her as possible. Keep her safe."

"No, Josh," Sarah said, stepping forward. "That would kill her."

He turned around to look at her in surprise, then dropped his head, saying quietly, "Well, knowing me isn't doing her a hell of a lot of good either."

"I think Sarah's right," Ryan added. "You can't just lie down and give these assholes what they want."

"Easy for you to say, Ry. You didn't just walk in to find your girlfriend tied up and beaten, lying in the fetal position. Oh, damn!" He scoured his face with his hand. "I've got to get out of here for a while. You'll stay?" he asked Sarah. She nodded. He put his hands on her shoulders, telling her earnestly. "I'm going to get a private bodyguard for her until this thing is over. Nobody will get near her again."

She patted his hand. "Okay."

CHAPTER TWENTY-FOUR

A few days later, Ryan, Josh and Cassie were hanging out in a dressing room before a concert playing a none-too-friendly hand or two of Spades.

"Let's see...brings it to...negative 33 for Josh, 52 for Ryan, and...173 for little ol' me."

"Stop gloating, McCallister," Josh growled. "It doesn't become you."

Cassie was feeling and looking much better. Makeup went a long way to cover up the bruises on her face, though her gash was still bandaged. And she was loosening up a little bit. Though Josh teased her, it did his heart good to see her smile again.

"You're like the Attila the Hun of Spades," Josh complained.

Ryan frowned. "Yeah."

"Ohh. Spoiled sports. Even Eduardo here could do a better job than you two."

The big, hulking, Hispanic bodyguard looked up from the magazine he was paging through. "I told you, ma'am. I don't play no Spades."

"Exactly!" Cassie said, smiling sunnily at Josh and Ryan.

Someone rapped on the door.

Eduardo bolted out of his seat, slamming the magazine on top of the bar he was sitting at, suddenly professional. "You were expecting somebody?"

"No," Josh responded, eyeing the door.

"Okay. Miss?" He motioned for Cassie to get behind the bar and pulled out his revolver. He went to the inside of the door and motioned for Josh to open it.

Ryan barely got a glimpse of Angela before Josh was pushing her up against the far wall of the hallway. His hands were around her throat. "Just who the hell do you think you are?"

"Josh. Hey, if you like it rough, I'd be happy to oblige." Even with his hands around her neck, she was able to smile at him suggestively.

"Rough? Rough? Like the guy you hired was, with Cassie? I'll show you rough, Angela!"

"Josh!" Ryan warned, though he was glaring at the girl, too.

"I don't know what you're talking about," she said, although she paled some at the mention of Cassie's name. Eduardo watched but made no move to interfere.

"Oh, and I guess you don't know about the threatening letters she's been getting, and you haven't been following her around. Careful now, Angela, because Cassie gave the cops your license plate numbers, so this is no time to lie."

"Okay."

Josh loosened his hold a fraction.

"So I sent her some notes." Her hands moved up to Josh's shoulders, trying to soothe him. "She needed to get the message, Joshie. She needed to know she was interfering with our relationship."

"Our relationship? Our relationship? WE HAVE NO RELATIONSHIP!"

The first flicker of anger sparked in her eyes. She shifted, looking around at the unfriendly faces in front of her. "Oh. So you're just gonna deny we have a thing going, in front of your buddies? You're going to deny you didn't just do me last night?" She stuck her chin out.

Cassie walked up from behind Josh, laying a hand on his shoulder. "Funny thing is, *Angela*, even though our hotel bed was big, I'm pretty sure Josh and I would have seen you in it last night."

Angela lunged for Cassie, but didn't even get within feet of her before Josh and Ryan had her pinned again to the wall. "So you think you're going to do the dirty work yourself this time instead of hiring a man to beat up a defenseless woman for you? To jump her in her own house, tie her up, and beat the living crap out of her?"

As Josh got in her face, the anger which was in her eyes the second before evaporated, replaced by fear. "What are you talking about? I didn't do that!"

"Oh, yeah? So, what's this then?" Ryan grabbed Cassie's arm to hold it up. "Those are rope burns from where your dickless friend tied her up, and the bandage on her head is not for show. She needed twenty-two stitches to fix what he did to her!"

Angela's horror-stricken eyes shifted from Cassie to Josh. "I didn't do that, Josh. I swear! Sure, I sent her a few notes, but I didn't hire no one to hurt her. I wouldn't do that."

Just then, two of the stadium security guards rushed up. Josh and Ryan handed her over to them. "Take her up to your office and call Detective Reeves. We'll be right up in a minute."

Angela was hauled off, somewhat subdued now and those who gathered started to disperse. Josh, Ryan, Eduardo and Cassie returned to the dressing room. Josh took her into his arms. "Are you all right?"

"I'm fine." Her forehead was furrowed. "But you know...I don't think she did it."

"What? You saw her. She's like sixty-three crayons short of a box of sixty-four."

Cassie smiled. "She looked like she was telling the truth."

"She probably believes it is the truth. Her grasp of reality is tenuous, at best. We're going to go up there. We'll get to the bottom of this, trust me."

"Maybe I should go, too?" Eduardo offered. "It might help if someone a little less...passionate, was available."

"Are you calling us hotheads, Eduardo?" Ryan asked with a grin as the three turned to go.

"Si. I am." The trio laughed as Cassie followed them to the door.

"I'm locking this door, Cass, just in case. Don't open it for anyone but me." He bent to softly kiss her on the lips. "This will all be over soon."

The door closed behind them and the room that was embroiled in turmoil minutes before became quiet. She went back to the couch and sat. She shuffled cards for a while then pushed them aside. She decided to lie down. Sleeping had been difficult because of her soreness and flashbacks, so she shut her eyes and curled up on her side on the couch. *Maybe Josh is right.* She yawned. *Maybe this will all be over soon.*

She woke in the dark. Was that a woman's scream? Bolting up, heart pounding in her chest, she listened, but didn't hear anything other than the lazy ceiling fan above her head. She was about to chalk it up to another bad dream, when she heard it again. It came from the adjacent dressing room,

Lanny's dressing room. Alarmed, she left the safety of her room to look for one of the security guards. No one was around. *They all must be wrapped up with Angela.* She decided to go back and call Josh's cell phone. Just as she passed in front of Lanny's door, it swung open.

"Oh. Lanny!" she said, her hand over her heart. "Is everything okay? I thought I heard a woman screaming."

"Oh, well now. I had one of those horror flicks on. There's a lot of screamin' in those. Say, where is everybody?"

"They all went to the security office. Angela showed up, so they have her up there and are questioning her, I guess."

"Is that so?" he asked, narrowing his eyes. "Well, do you want to wait with me until Josh and them get back? I could find somethin' other than a horror show to watch. There's got to be some romance on or somethin'."

She narrowed her eyes at him. "No, thanks. I think I'll just go back and—"

He grabbed her arm, pulling her toward his room. "I don't think so."

"Get your hands off me!" She struggled but was surprised by how strong the wiry man was. "Let go!"

With one final shove he pushed her through the door. She managed not to fall, but when she turned to face him her attention was diverted to the right where a young girl dressed in only black jeans and a bra, knelt on the floor. She was bent over double, her hands tied behind her back with a familiar-looking brown rope, and equally familiar-looking silver duct tape pressed over her mouth. Her curly black hair was swept up in a high ponytail and tears were rolling down her face. She looked terrified. Across her back, Cassie spotted huge welts.

She turned to notice for the first time, Lanny held a coiled belt in one hand. "Wh-what's going on here?" She backed toward the girl.

"Oh, I think you know." He locked the door and took a couple of slow steps toward her. "She," he said, gesturing to the girl, "...what's your name again, hon? Oh, yeah. I forgot, you can't talk right now. Anyway, this little bitch came in here early to see if she could beat the crowds and get a good screw, didn't ya darlin'? You see, not everybody is in to ol' Joshie. Somes want a little piece of the Lanster."

Cassie sprung for the door, but anticipating her move, Lanny caught her and swung her up against a wall. He grabbed her face hard, pressing against her with his body. "Maybe you'd be interested in getting' a lil' bit of ol' Lanny, too? Huh? You're shakin,' Cassie. You have no idea what a turn-on that is." He shifted so he could run his hand up her inner thigh.

Just then, she heard voices in the hall. Josh and Ryan had returned. "JOSH!"

Hearing her, Josh broke into a run, Ryan on his heels, and yanked open the door to his dressing room. He flipped on the light, and his eyes scanned the empty room.

"JOSH!" Her voice sounded even more frightened this time.

Reversing direction, they ran to Lanny's room. Ryan reached it first and tried the door. "It's locked."

"Hey, Joshie," Lanny called out. "Come on in, I'm having myself some fun with your girlfriend."

Behind the door, there came the sound of movement and a short, sharp scream. "Lanny. If you touch her, I'll—"

"Oh, it'll go way beyond touchin,' Joshie. You can bet on that!" More movement. "Hey, you. Get back, you little bitch!"

A muffled scream was followed by Cassie's, "No! Don't hurt her!"

"*Getoffme*!" With a loud thud, the wall shook. They heard a moan and a crack, and another muffled cry.

A wave of panic gripped Josh. He threw his shoulder into the door, but it wouldn't budge. He and Ryan backed up.

"On three," Ryan said. "ONE, TWO..." They rushed the door, slammed their bodies into it. It cracked but held firm. "Again, ONE, TWO..." This time the jam broke and the pair went flying into the room. It took several seconds to decipher the strange scene before them. A few feet away, a half-naked girl, bound and gagged, knelt on the floor. Behind a couch, Cassie stood with Lanny behind her, one of his hands fisted in her hair, yanking, the other arm wrapped around her chest with a syringe to her throat. They froze. The girl crawled slowly to the safety of the door. Ryan helped her to her feet and she ran down the hall.

"That's right, you little whore. Crawl your scrawny ass on out of here. I've got something better now," Lanny sneered, scraping his cheek against Cassie's but looking straight into Josh's eyes.

He took a step forward but felt Ryan's restraining hand on his arm. Josh swallowed. He saw the fear in Cassie's eyes and once again, felt useless to do anything about it.

"What's going on here, Lanny?" he asked evenly.

"Oh, come on now, Josh, you're a bright boy. You can guess what's goin' on here, can't ya? I'm just having a little fun with your hot, little thing here." He let go of her hair and slid his hand slowly down her arm and across her stomach, then yanked her closer to him. His eyes were red, his hair was greasy, and the veins bulged in his arms. "Yeah, we're just havin' a little fun here, aren't we, baby?" His teeth were at the edge of her ear, and the pinprick of the needle below her chin. "Just havin' fun, just like we did the other night at your house, huh, sugar?" She didn't respond. "Huh?" He slapped her on the cheek. "Huh?" He slapped her harder. Josh surged toward him, but Ryan managed to pull him back.

"Josh! He'll kill her."

"That's right," Lanny barked. "Listen to your partner there. Ryan always was the smarter one. Although that's not saying much," he chuckled coarsely. "I still can't believe you stupid bastards thought I was your *friend* all these years." He spat the word out with contempt. "I was just along for the ride. And now the ride's over, I might as well take a little something with me." His hand lowered to Cassie's breast, and something snapped inside of Josh. Like a wild animal, he ran up the couch and launched himself onto Lanny, knocking him away from Cassie and to the floor.

Josh rode Lanny down to the floor and Ryan leaped after him to catch Cassie. Her eyes rolled back in her head and she went limp, the syringe stuck in her neck. He pulled the needle out as he lowered her to the floor, but Lanny knew what he was doing. He probably hit the jugular, and poison was pumping through her body.

Meanwhile, Josh slammed his fist into Lanny's head. His face was covered with blood, but he still managed to reach up and grab Josh's head and drive his own into Josh's face. Blood spurted from Josh's nose. The drugs he had taken seemed to course through Lanny's system, giving him inhuman strength. He threw Josh off and stumbled to his feet. Lanny took a swing and Josh ducked just in time, coming up under the shorter man's armpit and lifting him off his feet with his head. The pair tumbled over the back of the couch and crashed through a coffee table and onto the floor in a savage embrace. Josh was barely able to come out on top, but he eventually pummeled Lanny until he at last, mercifully, lay still.

Ryan had tuned out the carnage, grabbing a bottle of gin from the bar and using it to chafe Cassie's wrists and dampen her face in a futile effort to arouse her. "Come on, Cass baby. Stay with us."

Josh staggered around the end of the couch, blood dripping from his nose and smeared across his knuckles, and saw Cassie draped across Ryan's lap, lifeless. As he listened to Ryan's desperate pleas, it dawned on him finally what happened. "Oh, my God!" He fell to his knees. "What did I do?"

At the same time, a half-dozen men came bursting through the door, sent there by the girl who escaped. They looked around at the bloodshed, trying to determine what needed to be done.

Ryan shouted, "We need medical attention. Quick!" Cell phones snapped open and two men grabbed Lanny's body and dragged it away from the wreckage of the coffee-table. Ryan looked into his friend's grief-stricken eyes and then back at Cassie. He saw the syringe lying on the floor a few inches away. "Look. He only got half of it in. Maybe it will be okay. And we can take this in, and they'll know what's in her system. Ambulances will be here any second now to take her to the hospital. It'll be okay."

More than anything else, Josh wanted to believe him. He sunk to the floor and buried his head in his hands.

CHAPTER TWENTY-FIVE

Stagehands took the huge "Money Back Guaranteed" sign down and hauled it off to the truck. The sound board was loaded, the amplifiers were gone, but a bunch of cords still snaked their way across the stage, along with some mike stands and empty water bottles. Josh stood in the middle of the stage, his hands on his hips, watching as the lights came down, remembering the first time they had gone up.

Cassie moved over to him and slid her hands around his waist. Neither spoke for a while. "Are you sad?" She looked up, wrinkling her nose in a thoughtful expression which made him want to kiss her.

He turned to face her, putting his arms around her. "No way."

"Oh, come on. You've got to be a little sad."

He looked around the auditorium some more. "Okay, maybe a little. It was a good ride. But I'm ready to move on with my life."

Ryan walked up behind them, looping a cord through his hands and around his elbow.

"How 'bout you, Ry?" She hooked her other arm around his waist. "Any regrets over leaving all this behind?"

He looked down into her eyes with almost as much affection as Josh would. "None." Then he looked up at him with a big grin. "Sure had some good times, though."

"We sure did."

"But here comes my future, right here."

The trio looked up as Paige's sweet southern voice called out. "Hey, y'all. I don't know if you realize this, but there's a bunch of people having a party for you."

Ryan collected the brunette into his arms, throwing the cord onto the floor. "All she wants to do is party, party, party."

"You, stop." She giggled as he nuzzled her neck.

Josh said softly to Cassie, "I think there's some champagne waiting for us somewhere. Let's go toast the future."

The four headed to an inner room where most of the crew and their families were already imbibing. When they walked in, people started to clap. Josh looked around at all the people he worked with for the past five or six years. "I wasn't expecting this," he said, a little choked up. He milled around, thanking all the people for their loyalty and wishing them luck on their next endeavors.

Later, he asked Cassie to sneak off with him again. Closing the door on the sounds of loud partying, they headed toward the auditorium. "Wait," Cassie said, turning around, "I need to grab my sweater from your dressing room. It's cold."

"No!" Josh said, grabbing her arm. "I mean...let me keep you warm." He ran his hands up and down her arms.

"Okay," she agreed, giving him a curious look.

They walked, arm in arm, to the stage area, where the lights were on.

"Why are these on?"

"I wanted one last time to be in the spotlight." He slid his arms around her waist.

"You really are going to miss it, huh?"

"Cassie, I have something to ask you," he announced, changing the subject.

"Okay."

He cleared his throat nervously and looked out into the blackness where an audience would usually be sitting. "We've known each other for about a month. And in that time I've...picked you up at a bar...you caught me cheating on you...I cussed you out...you've been beaten up, had your face stitched up and been shot with an almost lethal injection...have I left anything out?"

She smiled. "No, I think that about covers it."

"In short, you've had more bad things happen to you in one month than most soap opera characters have happen to them in one year. So, would you marry me?"

She laughed. "Well, with that kind of proposal, who could resist?"

"No, Cass," he said seriously. He dropped to one knee. "I know you've been down this road before, and the thought of becoming engaged scares you, but I promise this won't be a long engagement. I want to spend the rest of my life loving you, laughing with you, weeding with you, singing karaoke and shooting hoops with those two crazy boys from down the block, and just being with you. So, what do you say, Cassie McCallister? Would you consider becoming Cassie Dunningham?" He tried to pull something out of his pocket. "Wait a minute, it's in here somewhere...ah."

He pulled out the most gorgeous diamond and sapphire engagement ring Cassie ever laid eyes on. When Josh first knelt and she realized what his intentions were, her stomach dropped like she took a dip in the road too fast. At first she thought it was panic, as she couldn't help but flashback to Troy's proposal. But the more Josh talked about the two of them, the more she realized what happened between her and Troy was in the past, and her future lay at her feet. The excitement began to bubble up inside her. As he held the ring near her finger, waiting for her reply, she could find no words. All she could do was nod her head vigorously, laughing for joy. He slipped the ring on her finger and stood, and she jumped into his arms.

He embraced her tightly, then held her at arm's length for a minute. "You mean it? You're sure?"

"I've never been surer of anything in my life."

"So, you're saying, if we could, you'd get married right now, without a doubt."

"Without a doubt."

"I want you to know, you can back out anytime you want, anytime you feel a flicker of a doubt. I will warn you though, if you do, I'm liable to chase after you."

"You don't have to chase anymore, I'm yours."

"Good. Just to be clear, you're saying, if a priest was here right now, and a dress and a tux and all that, you'd marry me?"

"Josh, I don't know what to say to make you understand. This is what I want. Yes, if a priest was here right now, I would be ready to take those vows."

He breathed a sigh of relief. "Good." He turned and looked out into the blackness. "Is there a priest out there?"

A man dressed in black with the familiar white collar stepped into the lights, holding a Bible and smiling.

"Oh, my gosh! Are we getting married right now?" She beamed at him.

He held her hands as the priest climbed some steps up to the stage. He stood in front of them and opened his Bible.

"Oh, wait," Josh said. "We need a matron of honor." Again, he looked offstage. "Is there a matron of honor out there anywhere?"

Sarah came running up, giggling. Cassie's hand went to her heart and then she threw her arms around her sister. "Boy, you weren't kidding about a short engagement."

He winked. "I'm a man of my word. But still...I need a best man to keep me straight..."

Ryan strode into the light, sharply dressed in a tuxedo. "Oh, my!" she exclaimed as he walked up and kissed her hand.

"Now, Cass," Josh said quietly to her, "this is your last chance. If you'd rather do this some other time, some other way, I'm fine with it. I just didn't want a long engagement where you may begin to have doubts and wonder if I'd pull a Troy on you. We can wait as long as you want."

Cassie grabbed Sarah's hand and Ryan's hand. "No, Josh. I want to marry you, right here, right now."

"Okay, then." Josh dramatically put his hand over his eyes as if searching the inkiness in front of him. "I wonder if there's anyone else out there. Hey, Chuck?"

"Yeah, Josh," came a voice from behind the curtains.

"Do you think you could bring up the house lights?"

"Sure."

The house lights came up and to her surprise, many of the seats were occupied. She saw her neighbor, Roger Frey, and Joe and Matt...Heather was right next to them...the entire crew was assembled, as well as Paige...people from work, Colin the Perv included...all dressed in their Sunday best.

Cassie kissed him. "I can't believe you."

Josh turned to the priest, holding both her hands. "I think we're ready now."

The priest opened the book and began speaking. As he did, Josh kept looking out into the audience, then back at the priest, then out to the audience again.

"Dearly Beloved..."

"Just a minute, Father. Sorry to interrupt." She stared at him. He leaned in, as if to whisper to her, but said loud enough for everyone to hear. "I think we're a little underdressed, Cass, don't you? I mean look, Joe Frey's wearing a tie, and Ryan here got all decked out..." He raised his voice. "Ladies and gentlemen, I'd like to beg your patience for a minute. Cassie and I are going to go get changed. We'll be right back. Help yourself to champagne while you wait, except for you, Joe and Matt, there's sparkling cider somewhere for you." As he spoke, four uniformed waiters with laden trays entered from the back of the auditorium and came sweeping up the long aisles, which Cassie noticed now, were decorated with bows and flowers. He turned back to Cassie, her mouth hanging open. "You need to go with your sister now. Bad luck and all that."

"Come on, Cass." Sarah grabbed her arm and began leading her backstage.

"B-but all the people..." She looked back, but all of the guests seemed to be enjoying themselves. Josh had disappeared somewhere. "Okay," she said slowly. "He had this all planned...all of it..."

"That's right. That man is incredible when he has a goal in mind. That last day you were in the hospital...he practically put the whole thing together then."

"You're kidding."

"Nope," Sarah replied, opening Josh's dressing room door wide. Cassie started inside but stopped. It no longer looked like a dressing room. It looked like a floral shop. Dozens of pink, yellow and white roses lined the walls, and on the middle of the table was a beautiful bouquet of red orchids and white calla lilies. Hanging from the top of the mirror of the dressing table was the most stunning wedding dress she had ever seen. It had wide, sheer straps down to a heart-shaped bodice. The waist cinched in with soft pleats and the most exquisite beadwork below. The skirt was satiny smooth except for another arrangement of beads above the hem.

Cassie walked toward it as if in a trance.

"I hope you like it. Josh said the sky was the limit, and I took him at his word. By the way, Cass," Sarah said seriously, "I was wrong about him. He's a great guy. And together, the two of you are magical. It's obvious he adores you. He's light and breezy and you guys have fun together, and you need that. He apologizes when he's wrong, and believe me, that's a rare feature in a man. And he's not hard on the eyes, is he, sis?" She gave Cassie a squeeze. "Well, come on. Hurry up. You've got people waiting. I've got five veils you can choose from, there's a seamstress and a hairdresser outside, if you need them, and the most magnificent diamond necklace in that black velvet box over there. Josh picked that out himself. And I need to get into my equally striking bridesmaid's dress."

Her sister disappeared into the bathroom, and Cassie stood, still a little dazed, gazing around the room again at the flowers, and the dress... She wanted to run out and squeeze Josh and thank him for making her every dream come true. *But I guess I'll have time for that later.*

The wedding went off flawlessly, with Roger walking Cassie down the aisle, and Heather, Sarah, Ryan and David Sandoval standing up for the couple. Josh had rented out a restaurant for the night and a limo awaited them after the ceremony. Cassie lingered, thanking Ryan and Paige for all their help with the arrangements.

"Dunningham!"

Cassie continued talking.

"Dunningham, shake a leg."

"Um..." Ryan prompted. "I think your husband is calling you."

The sound of the word "husband" made her heart soar. "Oh. I guess that is me he's calling. I forgot I had a new name." She laughed, gave the couple each a kiss, and joined Josh, where he stood, holding the door to the limo open wide. As she kissed him, she couldn't help but think of it as the doorway to their wonderful future.

Note from author

Thank you for reading ROCK ME, GENTLY, part of my ROCKING ROMANCE COLLECTION. I hope you enjoyed it! Now that you've read the book, won't you please consider writing a review? Reviews are one of the best ways readers discover great new books. They don't need to be fancy or long, just a sentence or two honestly describing your opinion of/experience with the book. I would sincerely appreciate it.

Want more from M.J. Schiller?
Page forward for
an excerpt from
THE HEART TEACHES BEST
Real Romance Collection

Prologue

The call had come in the night before—murder at Phat Jack's, the newest club in downtown L.A. When Cooper got there, several squad cars already occupied the parking lot, slanted haphazardly across the entrance. Their lights cast blasts of colors onto the surrounding buildings, reminding him of the laser lights bouncing around the dance floor inside. He scooted under the yellow tape, flashing his badge at the uniforms who were trying to keep the curious onlookers back. The body of Sydney Essex, the famous author, had been found on the pavement next to her car, her deep blue eyes wide and unseeing, ligature marks prominent on her slender neck, head tipped at an odd angle.

Cooper was getting the details from the first to arrive on the scene when the blonde broke through the crowd, ducking under the tape and running, screaming, toward the car. Two uniforms caught her up by the waist, though she struggled against them, hysterically calling out, "Syd! Syd! Oh, my God! No! *No!*" She collapsed in their arms, a puddle of tears melting onto them as they stood, emotionless, not allowing themselves to be affected by her pain as they had been trained to do.

"Who's that?" he asked.

"Must be the sister," the officer he was talking to responded, shrugging. "Looks like the vic."

Cooper tuned out the rest of the conversation as he looked at the crumpled form of the crying girl on the sidewalk. They hadn't reached the next of kin yet, so how did she know to come to Phat Jack's? Then it dawned on him, she must have been meeting her sister here. So, she was looking forward to drinks with her sister one minute, viewing her broken body the next. He knew they were supposed to distance themselves from the victims, but during times like these, it was nearly impossible.

CHAPTER ONE

Cooper Sullivan nursed his scotch, letting his eyes roam over the crowded bar. He didn't know what he was doing there, but he always found himself returning to the scene of the crime.

He found it helpful to immerse himself in the environment. He wanted to figure out the players and the playing field. From what he could tell so far, the new club was about the most pretentious place he'd ever been in. Definite haven for the young and rich. He stuck out like a sore thumb; his suit was not as pressed, his shoes not as expensive or polished, even his posture was too loose. He felt completely out of place, and glad of it.

He swiveled on his stool and admired the bar set up. At least that was interesting. Multicolored bottles of every alcohol known to man were sitting on a glowing, translucent polymer shelving, backlit against the mirrored wall which ran the length of the deep, dark mahogany bar, giving the place a sort of sci-fi feel. A black leather bumper covered the edges of the bar, complimented by a white tube of lighting, adding another futuristic touch. The bartenders wore black tuxedo vests, males with tight, short-sleeved shirts, females with no shirts at all, red bow ties around their necks, giving them an elegance that allowed them free reign to overcharge their customers.

As he soaked everything in, Cooper's eyes landed on the reflection of a young woman in the mirror. Her long, straight, blond hair was twisted up in a clip, and she wore an elegant, short black dress which v-ed down temptingly across her chest. On her right shoulder hung a black evening bag from its long, rhinestone strap, sparkling boldly against the black, silky fabric of her dress. He studied her face. It looked so familiar, somehow. She had a long, graceful neck rising to a sculpted chin, and big, blue, doe eyes with long lashes. He turned his head so he could get a look at her straight on. She tapped her foot up and down as she sat with legs crossed, the fabric of her dress pulled beguilingly above the knee. Her elbow was on the bar, chin on her fist. Was she waiting for someone?

As Cooper watched, she looked up and caught his eye. He smiled, and she gave a nervous half-smile before dropping her eyes and looking away. He was not the only one who felt out of place in this environment; he was sure of it. He found the woman's reaction to him so charming he began to wonder why someone like her was there in the first place. A large, African-American man approached her, blocking his view, and he turned away.

He took another drink of the scotch, letting it roll around on his tongue before swallowing it. A loud trill of feminine laughter, accompanied with the low hum of male posturing, drew his attention in the other direction. Three beefy-looking guys in shirts and ties were entertaining a black-haired siren in a red dress to his right. She was the opposite of the girl to his left, totally at home in the bar scene. Her dress was short and tight, with fringes at the bottom like a 1920's flapper. It sparkled all over, and her breasts all but flowed out of the top, pressed up as if someone took a rolling pin to her midsection to form the mounds above it. She reached up now and ran a long, painted fingernail under one of her male entourage's chin, making all three take in a breath and adjust their stances, hopeful. He wondered if they had any idea how foolish they looked as she played them like an orchestra's well-tuned string section. He chuckled to himself and shook his head. Poor slobs. More than likely none of them even stood a chance. His bet was on the bartender the girl kept flitting her eyes toward.

He leaned back against the bar, and caught sight of the blonde again, this time as she was being led out onto the dance floor. The large man with her, his skin a dark-chocolate brown, moved his hand from her elbow to the skin of the small of her back, where the dress gave way to silky flesh. Cooper saw the girl flinch at the man's touch, and instinctively sat up straighter, his body on the alert. He didn't know why his jaw became tight and his stomach knotted; he just knew he didn't like the way the man was touching her.

The two began to slow dance to a sultry song, swaying on the floor amidst the others. When another couple blocked his view, he shifted over a seat so he could still see her. The man now put his colossal paw under the girl's chin and lifted her face. She was shaking her head and not looking him in the eye, her face flushed but, he guessed, not from the dancing. The man pulled her closer, but body language was clear, as she leaned her upper body as far away from him as possible. His hand slid down from where it was holding hers to grip her wrist. She seemed to be struggling with him now as he leaned in, as if to kiss her. Cooper sat up and took a step forward, but she abruptly pulled out of her partner's grip and began rushing toward the bar, her jaw set. The big man trailed after her.

"Come on, baby. Don't be like that, now." He grabbed the blonde around the waist and spun her toward him.

"Get your hands off me!" she hissed, passion, and perhaps fear, heating her words as she pushed him.

Maybe seeing the fire in her eyes, he released his hold, backing away. "All right. All right." He chuckled at her reaction, watching her butt like she was a piece of meat and he was the world's hungriest carnivore. "I'll take it slow."

"Just 'take it' someplace else," she said with finality, but he didn't appear to get the message.

Cooper tried to act preoccupied as the girl returned to the stool one seat over, tilting his glass back as she raised her hand to order another drink. The man stepped, again, between them. When he spoke, she jumped, seeming surprised to hear his voice so close. He slipped his arms around her waist. "Come on, baby," he begged, his voice velvety smooth. "You know you want to."

"Stop! *Please!* I'm *not* interested!" The desperateness in her voice had Cooper setting his drink down. As he turned, he saw the man's hands come up from her waist. He couldn't tell for sure, but he thought the man had touched her breasts. His suspicion was confirmed a few seconds later when he felt a few drops hit him as the girl whooshed the man with her drink and turned to leave.

"Listen, bitch! Nobody throws a drink in my face." The man grabbed the girl roughly by the arms.

"Let her go." Cooper's voice was a low growl.

He saw the big man's back stiffen. With as little effort as it took to pop a beer cap, the man tossed the girl aside. She crashed into the bar and fell against the stool, sliding down even as she attempted to right herself. Her attacker turned around slowly, and Cooper stepped up until they were chest-to-chest. The dark-skinned man stared down his somewhat flattened nose at him. He was a good deal taller than Cooper's six-three and weighed maybe seventy-five pounds more. He noticed now how truly massive the man's arms were, but it only made him madder. Why the hell did a guy like that need to push a woman around?

"You gonna do something about it?" his opponent snarled.

"Yeah. I'm going to do something about it." He shook his blond hair out of his eyes, ready to get a couple of shots in before the brute pummeled him. The bartender reached across the bar just as a couple of bouncers made their way over to the fray.

"No one's pushing a woman around in here," the bartender snapped. The distraction allowed the bouncers time to reach them. They clasped their hands on the big man's shoulders and grabbed a hold of the back of his pants. "Get out of here, and don't show your face in here ever again," the bartender added, brave from his position behind the bar. The troublemaker shook off the bouncers and took a swing at Cooper. He ducked and came up, landing a punch in the man's ribs. The bouncers seized the man once more and started pulling him away.

"Okay, okay! Damn!" He shrugged them off again, but seeming to measure the aggressive stares he was getting from every man in the room now, he seemed to decide to cut his losses. Straightening his suit coat, he turned and strode out of the room, the bouncers following in his wake.

Cooper bent down and offered the girl his hand. She had been watching, wide-eyed and stunned, from her position on the floor. "Are you okay?" he asked, concerned by the way her hand was shaking in his.

She found her voice. "Y-yes. Yes. Thank you." She looked confused and he wondered for a moment if she hit her head. "I...I...this was all wrong. I shouldn't have come here. I'm sorry." She looked at him, tears in her eyes, and then turned and rushed away.

"Wait. Wait!" He hurriedly pulled out his wallet and plopped some bills down on the bar. He had just recognized her. She was the sister of the victim.

TO FIND OUT WHAT HAPPENS NEXT, PURCHASE THE HEART TEACHES BEST!

ALSO FROM M.J. SCHILLER

ROMANTIC REALMS COLLECTION:

TAKEN BY STORM
AN UNCOMMON LOVE
LEAP INTO THE KNIGHT
LADY OF THE KNIGHT
A KNIGHT TO REMEMBER

ROCKING ROMANCE COLLECTION:

TRAPPED UNDER ICE
ABANDON ALL HOPE
BETWEEN ROCK AND A HARD PLACE
ROCK ME, GENTLY
MIDNIGHT MELODY

LOVE AND CHAOS SERIES:

ROCKED BY GRACE
ROCKED BY LOVE
ROCK IT TO THE MOON
ROCK OF SALVATION

REAL ROMANCE COLLECTION:

UPON A MIDNIGHT CLEAR
THE HEART TEACHES BEST
DAMAGE DONE
BLACKOUT
HOMETOWN HEARTACHE
TAKE A CHANCE ON ME

DEVILISH DESIRES SERIES:

TO HELL IN A COACH BAG
DAMNED IF I DO
THE DEVIL YOU KNOW
SATAN, LINE ONE
PITCHFORK IN THE ROAD
SIN WORTH THE PENANCE
HELL HATH NO FURY
TEN MINUTES IN THE SIN BIN
DEVIL'S IN THE DETAILS
DEVIL'S ADVOCATE
HADE'S NIGHT

INSATIABLE FIRE SERIES:

BEATING IN TIME
LEAD ME ON
ROCK WITH THE RHYTHM
BASSIST'S INSTINCTS

OTHER:

HEARTS FLUSH

ABOUT THE AUTHOR

Bestselling author M.J. Schiller is a retired lunch lady/romance-romantic suspense writer. She enjoys writing novels whose characters include rock stars, desert princes, teachers, futuristic Knights, construction workers, cops, and a wide variety of others. In her mind everybody has a romance. She is the mother of a twenty-seven-year-old and three twenty-five-year-olds. That's right, triplets! So having recently taught four children to drive, she likes to escape from life on occasion by pretending to be a rock star at karaoke. However...you won't be seeing her name on any record labels soon.

www.ingramcontent.com/pod-product-compliance
Lightning Source LLC
Chambersburg PA
CBHW061221170626
46809CB00007B/2548